BLOODLUST SHADOWS

BOOKS BY LUANNE BENNETT

The Charley Underwood series

Bloodlust Blues

Bloodlust Bites

Bloodlust Curse

The Fitheach Trilogy

The Amulet Thief

The Blood Thief

The Destiny Thief

The Katie Bishop Series

Crossroads of Bones

Blackthorn Grove

Shifter's Moon

Dark Nightingale

Bayou Kings

Conjure Queen

Dirt Witch

Daddy Darkest

House of Winterborne Series

Dark Legacy

Savage Sons

King's Reckoning

BLOODLUST SHADOWS

LUANNE BENNETT

SECOND SKY

Published by Second Sky in 2025

An imprint of Storyfire Ltd.
Carmelite House
50 Victoria Embankment
London EC4Y 0DZ

www.secondskybooks.com

The authorised representative in the EEA is Hachette Ireland
8 Castlecourt Centre
Dublin 15 D15 XTP3
Ireland
(email: info@hbgi.ie)

ISBN: 978-1-83618-631-1
eBook ISBN: 978-1-83618-630-4

For all the hunters out there who never stop searching.
Ever.

ONE
SAMUEL

Boston, 1887

Watching the door from a distance, I leaned against the side of the building and debated whether to walk up to it and knock. What if someone recognized me? Someone with connections to my family.

"The hell with it," I muttered, taking a deep breath before pushing away from the wall. I straightened my jacket and headed down the alley, looking over my shoulder as I approached the entrance. With my luck I'd be jumped and robbed before my knuckles hit the door. But I'd been given the address on good authority, so there was that. And though completely out of character, I was thrilled to explore the dark side for a change and make the most of the night.

I knocked twice, reciting the required phrase as a rectangular slot slid open at eye level. "I'm here to see Chester Knocks." After the ridiculous words left my mouth, the door opened just enough for me to slip inside, second thoughts running through my head the moment it slammed shut behind me and the sounds of savagery filled my ears.

The man working the door stared at me with bloodshot eyes and held out his hand. "That'll be three."

"Dollars?" And that was just to walk inside.

After paying the fee, he motioned to another door at the end of a hallway, his grin revealing a mouthful of derelict teeth. "Enjoy."

"Yes." A nervous laugh escaped me. "I'll do that."

While walking down the dim hallway, the sounds beyond the second door grew louder. There was no turning back now, although I certainly could have. But I was eager to explore the depths of human degradation. Only as a spectator.

But what did that make me?

As I reached for the handle, the door flew open. A gentleman who dwarfed me—and I was sizable—muscled someone past me toward the exit. He tossed the man into the alley and slammed the door shut with a growl.

This was a bad idea, and I wondered if leaving was an option at this point.

The man stomped back down the hallway and stopped in front of me, his scruffy ginger beard spattered with blood. "Well? Are you coming in?" His eyes bulged with impatience as he flicked his head toward the doorway, the smell of whiskey lingering on his breath.

Adrenaline crept up my throat, but I considered myself bright enough not to argue with the man and followed him in. The warehouse was packed, the dense crowd obstructing my view of the events taking place in the center of the room.

"Place your bet," a man to my right said as I walked inside. There was a rather large revolver strapped to his hip, and his pockets were overflowing with cash that I doubted anyone would dare attempt to pilfer.

I glanced back at the crowd. "I can't even see what's happening, let alone who it's happening to." If I was about to lose my money, I intended to at least see who I was wagering on.

Make an educated guess based on the least battered man in the ring.

The bookie fondled the grip of his gun as a smile slid up his face, but before I found myself being forced toward the exit like the unfortunate gentleman on my way in, a man with blond hair and piercing hazel eyes appeared to my right and draped his arm over my shoulders.

"Take it easy, Mikey." He smiled at the bookie. "Why don't you let my friend here get his feet wet first."

The man's grin faded as his hand slipped away from the gun. "It's too late to bet on this round anyway."

The blond man stared at the bookie for a few more seconds. "That's right, so why don't you run along."

The bookie quickly walked away, so it appeared my new friend pulled some weight in the place.

The crowd parted for us as he steered me toward the ring, giving me my first look at the spectacle taking place in the center of the room. Both fighters looked like they'd already gone several rounds, their hands gloveless, knuckles shredded. Blood smeared their faces, arms, and chests, and one of them had an eye the size of a goose egg.

"Christ." I glanced away. What did I expect? It was an underground fight, for fuck's sake.

His lips quirked into a smile. "This really is your first time."

"And probably my last," I said with a chuckle.

My eyes snapped back to the ring as an uppercut blow made contact with the underside of a chin, blood flying from the recipient's mouth. This time I couldn't look away. After thirty-four years of upstanding citizenship, I found the sight of two men beating each other senseless inexplicably fascinating.

"You get a taste for it," my new friend said, holding out his hand. "Shane Ronan."

I shook it. "Samuel Cain."

There was a flicker in his eyes, and for a moment I thought

he was going to ask me if I was one of *the* Cains as in Cain Industries, which I was. But he just stared at me as if he recognized my face.

I pulled my eyes away from his and looked back at the makeshift ring when the man with the egg-sized eye got hit so hard his head snapped back. Blood sprayed the crowd. Then his head dropped forward, his blank gaze fixed at nothing as he teetered. I did a double take when Ronan's tongue darted to the corner of his mouth, lapping at a drop of blood that had hit his face.

Catching me staring at him, Ronan smiled. "Like I said, you get a taste for it." His grin went flat as the man stumbled sideways and started to go down, eventually crumpling to the cement floor. "Damn it!"

"I guess you bet on the wrong man?"

He nodded to the fighter who was still standing. "I bet on the winner, but I expected to get my money's worth before he went in for the kill."

By the way the loser was sprawled motionless on the floor with his eyes barely cracked open, the word *kill* might have been accurate.

Shane Ronan surveyed the crowd. "The good stuff's over now. Nothing but a bunch of pussies lined up for the rest of the night." He brought his eyes back around to mine. "I'm thirsty. You want to get out of here and get a drink?"

The question caught me off guard. I felt awkward, my gut telling me to leave.

Seeing my hesitation, he took a step back and threw his hands up. "I ain't no fairy, if that's what you're thinking."

I'd only met the man minutes earlier, and I wasn't sure I wanted to get to know him. "No, I was— I was just thinking about how early I have to get up in the morning. I should probably call it a night." And there was the abundance of reasons I shouldn't have come here in the first place, like the rough section of town and the undesirable crowd. This wasn't my world, but my curiosity had gotten the best of me. I wanted to see this place for myself. Experience something different for a change. Something to stir the boredom that had settled like sediment at the bottom of my stomach.

His harsh stare softened. "Then you better run home and tuck yourself in." He patted me on the shoulder, gazing at me with an unsettling smile. "Pleasure to meet you, Samuel Cain. See you next time."

There won't be a next time, I wanted to say as he walked away. The desire to visit this place was out of my system now, my appetite for savagery not so ravenous after all.

On my way out, I began to think maybe I'd been too quick to brush the man off. I was starting to crave a drink myself, but when I looked back Ronan was gone. He'd disappeared into the crowd. It was probably for the best.

There wasn't a soul in sight when I stepped through the door into the alley. The perfect setting for a crime in this part of town. "Well, you wanted excitement," I muttered as I headed toward the street, hoping to minimize my chances of making the front page of the *Herald* by morning.

Four blocks later I realized I'd gotten myself turned around. I'd strayed too far south. Based on my surroundings, that wasn't a good thing. And there were no carriages in this part of town to take me home safely.

I stopped to get my bearings before I ended up in the harbor, then turned around and continued north. But as luck would have it, I picked the wrong street and interrupted a couple of gentlemen conducting business in the shadows of a building. One of them stepped out from the darkness as I tried to slip past.

He cut me off. "What's your hurry?"

A knot tightened in my stomach as I followed his gaze down to the expensive watch around my wrist. "Well, fuck."

TWO

Samuel stormed into his house five paces ahead of me, a darkness in his eyes I'd seen only once before—when he killed his maker. We'd just come from the Stag where I'd received a message from the man he claimed destroyed his life. Now he was giving me the silent treatment. On the drive over, he barely acknowledged me sitting next to him.

"Talk to me, Samuel!" A ball of light slipped through my fingers and slammed into the wall to his right. I didn't mean to do it. It was an involuntary reaction to being shut out. To him refusing to stop and even look at me. A new customer had shown up at my bar a week ago. Shane Ronan, Samuel's century-old nemesis. He revealed himself tonight with a gift for Samuel—the ace of spades along with a message that an old friend had stopped by to see him. When I delivered it to Samuel, he knew instantly who it was from. So one could argue that I had a right to know everything about this Ronan guy now that he'd insinuated himself into my life.

Samuel came to a halt when the magic singed the wall and

sent a picture crashing to the floor. He turned and focused his intense gaze on me. "You need to leave. Go home, Charley." His pupils expanded, turning his eyes completely black. Into tunnels of rage.

I stopped a few feet away from him as my stomach sank, like a weight had been placed on my vital organs. "What? Why are you talking to me like this?"

"This isn't the place for you right now." A scowl came over his face as his chin lowered. "Unless you want to see what it feels like to have a set of fangs at your throat." His face relaxed. "But you like that feeling, don't you?"

"Keep talking to me like that and it'll be the last time you ever touch me." He could have slapped me in the face and done less damage to my heart.

"Are we done here?" He held my gaze for a moment and then continued into the living room.

Fighting the urge to walk out the door, I followed him. I barely recognized the man walking away from me, but I intended to find out which of his personas was authentic. If it was the callous vampire I was seeing at that moment, it was better to find out now.

But I didn't believe that. Not for a second.

"Look at me," I demanded when he stood near the fireplace with his back to me.

He turned, his eyes more troubled than cruel. "You don't understand."

"You mean that you're really just an asshole and I've been a fool all this time? Because that's what I'm understanding right now. Tell me, Samuel. I can handle it." I was barely holding it together, but I damn sure wasn't going to let him see me fall apart. But if he didn't start talking, it would break me.

As the silence between us grew, I spoke. "What did Shane Ronan do to you?"

His tense shoulders relaxed. "I'm sorry. I had no right to talk to you like that."

"No, you didn't." I steadied my gaze on his, watching his eyes flash with emotions. It took everything I had not to cross the room and throw myself at him. Shake the truth out of him. "We're partners, Samuel. I deserve to know what's happening."

He combed his fingers over the top of his head and nodded. "You're right. You're in the middle of it now."

The spider inside me stirred.

"In the middle of what?"

"Ronan didn't come here to pay an old friend a visit." Samuel paused and studied me for a moment. "He's here to play a game. To kill me."

I didn't see that coming. How could an annoying stranger with a knack for card tricks possibly stand up to a vampire like Samuel?

He went to the window and looked out, his eyes scanning the yard as if Ronan might have been out there somewhere. "He'll take his time before making a move. Play a cat and mouse game." Then he looked back at me. "And he'll use anything or anyone important to me to do it. That means you, Charley."

"So that's why you were talking to me like that. You're trying to drive me away to protect me, and you thought an insult would work?" I shook my head and huffed. "You know me better than that."

"This isn't a joke."

"I've met the guy, Samuel. He gives me a bad case of the creeps, but he doesn't seem that dangerous."

Samuel came closer and locked eyes with me. "You have no idea what that vampire is capable of."

Vampire?

It shouldn't have surprised me. If Ronan was around over a century ago, he had to be something other than human. But he didn't give off vampire vibes. More like a mage or a magician, with those sneaky card tricks.

Samuel kept piling on more surprises. "Ronan isn't just any vampire. He's the vampire who delivered me to Victor Steele."

I looked at him blankly, trying to make sense of it all. "You mean the night Steele tried to kill you and accidentally turned you instead?" The guy who'd sat at my bar for the past week was a mouse compared to Samuel. In every way. It didn't make sense. "How?"

"It's a long story."

"I have all night."

"Victor Steele was Shane Ronan's maker."

"Wait... Victor Steele was your maker so..."

Samuel just stared back at me while it sank in. Christ, I couldn't even reconcile what he'd just said. What did that make the two of them? Vampire siblings?

"I don't know what to say." I got such a used car salesman vibe from the vampire formally known as *Decker* that the idea of him and Samuel being family was disturbing.

"There is nothing to say. It's just the facts."

I sat down on the sofa because my legs suddenly felt weak. "So... why would he want to kill you?"

"A vampire knows when his maker is in danger. He must have felt it the moment Steele met his ultimate death and came running." Samuel's face hardened again. "When I sent that bastard straight to hell. Few vampires could have pulled that off, and finding me here at the scene of the crime makes me the number one suspect."

"Well, you did kill Steele." And thank God for that. "So you're saying he's here to get revenge?"

Samuel nodded. "There's nothing more dangerous than a vampire out to avenge his maker's death. He'll stop at nothing, and he'll probably take a shot at you. To manipulate me."

"If you haven't noticed, I'm not afraid of vampires." I

snorted. "And I'm certainly not afraid of that little pissant." My magic was no joke. I'd killed my own father with it. Even Ian Masterson treaded lightly around me these days, and he was a whole lot scarier than this Shane Ronan character. I was kind of surprised that Samuel was so concerned about him showing up here.

"I realize you're not exactly helpless." Samuel sat down next to me and took my hands, glancing through the doorway at the burned spot on the wall. "There's fire in these. But Ronan is very sly. He's not a vampire to be underestimated. He's a snake, Charley, and he will go after you if it suits his game."

I pulled my hands away from his. "Good luck to the bastard."

"Don't be fooled by his appearance. You see what he wants you to see."

"Why does it sound like you mean that literally?"

"Because I do. Ronan isn't just a vampire. He's a mimic."

The word didn't register immediately, although the image of a Vegas impersonator came to mind. "Can you be more specific?"

"He has the ability to disguise himself. To shapeshift into someone else. The man you were talking to at the Stag was Shane Ronan, but the face and body belonged to someone else."

I stared at Samuel for a moment, incredulous. "That son of a bitch." Then a frightening thought occurred to me. "What if he shows up at the bar again as someone else? Or himself? I don't even know what he looks like. Do you have a picture of him?"

"Take it easy," he said when he saw the fear on my face. "He's delivered his message. Now he'll wait for me to make a move. In the meantime, if any more strangers walk into the bar, pick up the phone."

He'd be getting a call if a tourist popped in for directions.

I took a deep breath and let my nerves settle. "Tell me more about this vampire."

Samuel stood up and started to pace the room. "After I was turned, I went to Chicago. Years later, I ended up in New Orleans and ran into Ronan down there." He chuckled. "Should have seen the look on his face when he saw me."

Since Victor Steele had attacked Samuel and left him to die, I bet Ronan was surprised. I'm sure they both assumed he was dead.

"Ronan was quite the hustler. He ran a scam with card tricks in the bars around the French Quarter. Used to dupe tourists out of their hard-earned money with that one-of-a-kind deck of his." Samuel looked back at me. "Those cards are laced with magic. He was working with a witch to pull off those tricks."

It made sense now, how that ace of spades always made its way back to him.

"That's how I knew he was here," Samuel continued. "When you handed me that card, along with his message. No one else has a deck like that. That ace is his signature card. The one that always guarantees the house will win."

Sorry. House wins. That's what Decker... or Shane Ronan... had said to Candy tonight when he pulled the ace of spades on her back at the bar.

But I didn't care who or what Ronan pretended to be. He was a fraction of the vampire Samuel was. At least that's what I wanted to believe. "How do we get rid of him?" The look on Samuel's face did nothing to assure me that we could. "Oh, come on, Samuel. You don't seriously think that vampire stands a chance in hell against you?"

"Again, you underestimate him."

"Maybe. But in a fight, my money is on you."

He laughed quietly. "It's funny you should say that because

that's how Ronan and I met. At a fight. An illegal bareknuckle boxing club."

"You're into illegal fighting?" Something else I didn't know about him and wasn't sure I wanted to.

"Don't worry. It was my first and last venture into that seedy world." Samuel sat back down next to me and ran his hand through his hair. "It was all a setup that night. Ronan followed me there and managed to strike up a conversation. It was all part of a game. The short of it is, I was mugged after I left." Darkness rolled over his face again, a quiet rage seeming to simmer just below the surface. "Then that vampire fucking shattered my life."

Samuel had me on the edge of my seat, and then he shut down on me again. It was beyond frustrating, but his mood had turned so dark I didn't dare push him to continue. I'd give him some space. Maybe a day. But the conversation wasn't over because I'd just been thrown into the middle of this game. Shane Ronan was now my enemy too, and I intended to find out exactly who I was dealing with.

THREE

After leaving Samuel's house that morning, I stayed on edge all afternoon. But Ronan was a vampire, so if he did decide to come after me like Samuel suggested he might, he'd have to wait until sundown to make a move. Let him. I'd give that vampire a run for his money. Make him think twice about bringing his war to my door.

A good part of the afternoon had been spent obsessing over that spider inside me. Not mine, the one I took from my father. His birthright. The one I'd inhaled when he tried to use it up at the lake to control me. I still couldn't feel it. Not like I felt my own spider crawling around in there, more often than I liked. And I still didn't know which one had saved me the night my father tried to force me over a cliff. My body and mind had submitted to it. Become the spider that saved me from crashing into the river below.

Maybe they both saved me.

Anyway, I was glad when it was time to leave for the bar so I could focus on running my business instead of Ronan and that eight-legged birthright hiding somewhere inside me.

Dog's truck was parked out front when I pulled up to the

Stag. It wasn't a delivery day, so I couldn't think of a reason for him to show up this early. Unless he was in one of his cleaning moods and decided to give the kitchen a thorough scrubbing before we opened. It definitely needed one, and being rainy and overcast, he probably had nothing better to do. The whole bar was due for a good cleaning.

The moment I walked through the front door, I heard a loud bang come from the kitchen followed by a few choice words.

"Damn it!" Dog yelled.

I went into the kitchen to see what all the noise was about and found him gripping his hand. There was blood all over his palm. "Jesus, Dog. What did you do?"

He scowled. "What does it look like? I nicked myself with the knife."

It was more than a nick. He was bleeding like a stuck pig, and I could see the wound from several feet away. "You might need a few stitches."

"Fuck stitches," he growled, dropping down on all fours as the wolf emerged. He lifted his massive paw and started licking the cut. When the wound was healed, the wolf faded and Dog reappeared.

"Feel better?" I said as he grabbed his clothes and started to dress. He was definitely in a mood.

"Humph," he grunted. "It was barely a scratch."

I picked up on a strange scent in the air. "What's that smell?" It was musky, mixed with something I couldn't identify. Like bad cologne. I leaned closer and took a whiff. "Is it coming from your wolf?" I'd been around Dog's wolf for most of my life, but I'd never noticed it before. He usually smelled distinctly... canine.

He pushed his long black hair out of his face and grumbled, revealing a heavily creased forehead from the way his brow was knitted together. "I don't smell anything. It's probably that new cleaner I've been using."

Didn't smell like cleaner to me, and it was just a question.

I grabbed his hand to inspect it. There was barely a pink line where the wound had been. "Wish I healed that fast."

Dog had working hands. They were big and callused from years of manual labor, not from working in a kitchen. Rough patches from building the pack's compound out in the woods. An ongoing project that never seemed to end because there was always something that needed to be built or repaired. But the wolves would sooner retire to Florida than let outsiders in to help with the upkeep. The compound was invitation only, and those invites were rare. I couldn't remember the last time I'd been out there.

He pulled his hand away. "Quit fussing. I'm fine."

"And you're in a shitty mood today too," I said on my way to the kitchen door. "Have you heard from Lucy?" She was supposed to open and should have been in by now.

Dog glanced through the order window. "She just walked in."

I went back out to help her set up for the night since Beau wasn't coming in for another half hour. "You're late," I said when she grabbed her bar apron and brushed past me without so much as a hello. I was probably reciting those words in my sleep considering how my bartenders regarded their schedules as mere suggestions these days.

"Quit being so bossy," she snapped on her way to the kitchen. "I'm here, ain't I?" She came back out a minute later carrying a bin full of fresh glasses, her nose scrunched up. "Smells like a cat's ass in there."

"Oh yeah? How do you know what a cat's ass smells like?"

She dumped the bin on top of the bar so hard I was surprised some of the glasses didn't break. "Don't start with me, Charley. I'm not in the mood."

Was she ever? The woman had no shame. "What's your problem?"

Dog came out of the kitchen before she could stick her foot in her mouth any farther. Still giving off that jumpy vibe, he pointed his thumb at her. "I need to teach Lucy Lu here how to cook."

She put her hands on her hips and glared at him. "What did you just call me?"

"Well, that was out of left field," I said, waiting for him to elaborate.

"Sure as hell was." Lucy stretched her neck out toward him. "And I don't cook." She turned around and got busy unloading the glasses from the bin. "Good thing I don't have kids, 'cuz they would have starved to death by now."

He stared at her for a moment like she was half-baked before bringing his eyes back to mine. "I need backup in the kitchen."

Dog was downright territorial about that kitchen. No one dared to touch anything in there without his supervision, so that statement needed some clarification. "You mean I need to replace Mutt?"

Walter "Mutt" Kramer had been Dog's "sous-chef." The man did everything from prepping garnish to washing dishes, until he got possessed and went on a murder spree. After Mutt attacked me in the back alley and Samuel killed him, I'd hired Tucker to pick up the slack wherever needed. But a good bartender is hard to come by in this town, and with her experience working clubs down in Atlanta, slinging drinks behind the bar was a better use of her skills.

"I don't need someone to wash dishes," Dog said. "I need someone who can cook a decent burger and work the fryer."

My heart skipped a beat. "You're not planning to quit on me, are you?" Maybe that's why he was acting so strange. He was trying to get up the nerve to tell me.

Seeing my horrified face, he let out a deep groan and rubbed his forehead. "No, Charley. I'm not quitting. But sometimes I need to take a night off."

It suddenly occurred to me that Dog had been working seven days a week since Mutt... left. For the most part, so had I. But this was my bar. I could work myself to death here if I chose to, but it was selfish of me to expect the same from Dog or any of my other employees.

"You're absolutely right." I felt about three inches tall.

"Now, wait a minute." Lucy pulled her apron off and tossed it on the bar. "If you think I'm frying up burgers, I'll give you *my* notice right now."

There were days when I would have taken her up on her threat but today wasn't one of them. "Calm down, Lucy. No one's asking you to cook." I looked back at Dog. "I'll put a sign in the window right now, and I'll help in the kitchen until we can find someone part-time." I wasn't a great cook, but I could make a burger. And it was just temporary. I hooked my thumb toward the front door. "You need tonight off? I can handle the kitchen for one night."

Dog stared at me blankly like I'd said something exceptionally stupid. Then he shook his head and walked away. "I'll be in the kitchen cutting potatoes."

"I guess that's a *no*?"

He just kept walking.

I glanced at Lucy. "Did I say something wrong?"

She tied her apron back on. "He's just pointing out that he has a life. We don't all eat, sleep, and breathe this place, you know." The woman was in rare form today, and that was saying a lot for Lucy Wyatt, queen of the loud mouths.

"All right. You've made your point," I said when she kept going on and on about how insensitive I was to the needs of my employees. "Are you going to ask for the night off next?"

She set a glass down on the bar and squinted at me. "Sure, why not. Health insurance would be nice too."

I'd had about enough of her, and we weren't even open yet. "If you don't shut your mouth..." I muttered as I started to walk away.

Her eyes got even thinner. "What did you say?"

I usually tried to ignore her attitude, and I had real problems to deal with at that moment. But today she struck a nerve.

My eyes snapped to hers as a rush of angry adrenaline hit me hard. "I said, if you don't shut your mouth I'll shut it for you."

She opened that offensive mouth to reply, but before she could finish spewing the first word, she went silent. Just zipped it, her jaw dropping as she gripped her throat like she was choking on a chicken bone.

"Lucy?" I approached her, praying I wouldn't have to administer the Heimlich maneuver because that first aid course I'd taken years ago was a distant memory at best. "Are you okay?"

She threw a hand up to stop me from coming any closer, clamping her other hand over her mouth as her eyes grew wider. When I took another step, she shook her head and backed up, hitting the wall.

I cocked my head and stared at her, recognizing the look in her eyes as fear, and that woman feared nothing. She was a five-foot-tall spitfire who vomited her opinions regardless of the consequences, but at that moment she had nothing to say—or couldn't.

My lungs filled sharply as I turned away from her and looked down at my hands. Had I used my magic on her without even knowing it? But there wasn't even the tiniest glow coming from them.

Dog came out of the kitchen, grumbling on his way to the front door. "I left my phone in the truck." He glanced at Lucy when she slid along the wall past me and took off toward the ladies' room. "What's wrong with her now?"

I stared at the bathroom door as she ran inside and slammed it shut. "Uh... I have no idea." A nervous laugh escaped me. "It's Lucy, so there's no telling."

Ignorance was bliss at the moment.

He continued toward the door. "I changed my mind. I don't want that woman anywhere near my kitchen."

"Don't worry. I have no intention of giving her access to knives."

While Dog went out to his truck to find his phone, I went to the back room to look for that help wanted sign. I also needed to call Patrick because we had deliveries this weekend. With everything that had been happening with me lately, and with Beau now spontaneously shifting into the Hollerwolf without warning, Patrick had taken on the lion's share of co-op duties. I needed to jump back in and give him a break.

When I went into the room and flipped on the lights, my heart skipped a beat. The back door to the alley was ajar, and there were wet footprints all over the floor. After a quick glance around, I stepped back into the hallway.

Dog had come back inside and was about to walk into the kitchen when he saw me standing there. "Something wrong?"

I pointed to the room. "You didn't come in through the back door when you got here, did you?" Since his truck was parked in front of the bar, it wasn't likely.

He shook his head and came down the hallway, sticking his head in the room to look around. "Wasn't me."

The sun was just starting to set. Still light enough outside to rule out a vampire standing in the alley. But in this town there were plenty of other threats. Of course it could have been old-fashioned breaking and entering. Wouldn't be the first time someone tried to jack the co-op only to realize we didn't keep product in the bar.

Dog grabbed my arm when I started walking toward the back door, taking the lead as a growl slipped from his mouth.

"Wait," I said, tasting the adrenaline creeping up my throat as my palm started to heat up. I opened the desk drawer and pulled out a pistol.

Dog glanced at it. "Where'd that come from?"

It was my mother's. "I dug it out of the filing cabinet last week and decided to keep it in the top drawer as a deterrent. It's just to scare people off." The perpetrator was probably long gone by now, but those wet tracks looked awfully fresh.

Dog scoffed. "I don't need it." He reached the door in two long strides, but before he could grab the handle, it swung open and hit him in the chest.

I leveled the gun at the intruder, a stack of boxes concealing his face. "Stop right there!"

Beau peered around the boxes he was carrying and dropped them, sending two liters of club soda, a crate full of limes, and enough drink stirrers to last a decade all over the floor. His back hit the wall as he threw his hands up, his eyes morphing from green to amber as he started to shake.

Dog snatched the pistol out of my hand and then got within inches of Beau's face. "Calm the fuck down."

I thought we were about to have a repeat of the night Dog's beast was introduced to the Hollerwolf in the kitchen, but after a few steadying breaths, Beau managed to get himself under control. I guess he was starting to get the hang of it, which was a big plus for job security.

Still a little shaky, Beau shoved Dog out of his face and glared at me. "What the hell, Charley?"

"Sorry about that." I looked down at the mess on the floor and remembered why he was coming in late tonight. We were running low on supplies that couldn't wait for delivery day, and I'd asked him to pick up a few things on his way in. But I didn't ask him to get a year's supply of limes, and I'd be finding those little red stirrer things under the filing cabinet for the next decade.

Beau looked at the gun in Dog's hand. "Where'd you get that thing?"

I grabbed it from Dog and stuck it back in the cabinet where I'd found it. "It's not even loaded."

"Goddamn calamity around here," Dog grumbled, reaching for a pack of paper towels in the corner that Beau must have dropped there on his first trip inside. "I'll be in the kitchen."

I bent down and grabbed a lime off the floor. "You'd better start pushing margaritas at the bar." That's what I got for not specifying a bag of limes instead of the entire orchard.

"Got a discount on a crate," he said, "if that helps."

Not if half of them went bad before we could use them up.

Beau went to shut the door and reached for something taped to it on the outside. "What's this?" It slipped through his fingers and fell to the floor. As he bent down to pick it up, something flew over his head, barely missing him and slamming into the wood.

My eyes flew wide as I stared at the shiny blade protruding from the door.

Beau grabbed the card and straightened back up, his eyes fixing on the knife embedded in the exact spot where the card had been taped a moment earlier. "That could have been my head!"

I yanked him out of the doorway before running into the alley. There was no sign of anyone. It was barely dusk, but I knew who had done this.

When I went back inside, I grabbed the card from Beau's hand. It was the ace of spades, and it had a bright red bull's-eye drawn in the center of it. Shane Ronan had just confirmed Samuel's fear. He was coming for us, and Beau had nearly been collateral damage by delivering that message.

FOUR

Dog eyed me when I barged into the kitchen and headed for the stove.

"What are you doing?" he asked when I turned on one of the burners.

I'd had enough of that damn magic card, and while it wouldn't help matters, it would satisfy me immensely to destroy it once and for all. As I was about to incinerate it, Dog snatched it out of my hand.

"Hey!" I yelled.

"Look, little Ms. Pyro, I'm not gonna let you start a fire in my kitchen." He studied it for a second. "What's this?"

With Beau narrowly avoiding an early demise moments ago, I figured it was as good a time as any for a staff meeting. "Lucy!" I yelled through the order window. "Get in here!" She flinched at my tone and came running. No smart-aleck remarks or anything. "You too," I said to Beau as he lingered in the doorway, still looking a little shell-shocked from what had happened in the back room.

Lucy walked in and stood silent near the door, that strange look still on her face.

"Everything okay now?" I asked her, holding my breath as I waited for her to speak.

"I'm fine, so quit looking at me," she muttered, averting her eyes from mine.

I focused on Beau next. "That knife that almost took your head off back there. It was Decker who threw it."

Dog shook his head. "What knife?" Then he glanced at the card in his hand. "What's going on, Charley?"

"You left the room just before the show began. Decker sent me a message tonight, and he used Beau as target practice to do it. Good thing Beau is clumsy and got out of the way."

Beau's frazzled look turned confused. "Decker? The new guy?"

The bar was about to open, so I needed to make this fast. "His name isn't Decker. It's Shane Ronan, and he's one of Victor Steele's progeny."

Dog stared at me blankly for a few seconds. "You mean he's a vampire?"

"Yes. A dangerous one."

He tossed the card on the counter. "Fuck."

"Fuck is right. He's the vampire who delivered Samuel to Steele the night he was turned."

Lucy's eyes flew wide. "You're shitting me?"

"No one's *shitting* anyone," I said, making her flinch when my eyes snapped to hers again. "So pay attention because the first person who sees Tucker needs to fill her in on everything. This vampire is here to avenge his maker's death. To kill Samuel."

Beau started to pace. "This is bad. Real bad. I ain't no expert on vampires, but I don't think they take it very well when you mess with their maker."

"Well, you're part vampire now," I said to him, "so you might want to become an expert."

"Yeah, that's right." His brow twisted. "Wait a minute.

Victor Steele was the vampire who bit me. Am I... 'related' to this Ronan guy?" The revelations kept coming as a lightbulb seemed to go off in his head. "Now that I think about it, does that make me and Samuel bros too?"

Now wasn't the time for squabbling, so I shot Lucy a warning look to keep her smart-ass comments to herself. Beau's questions were valid, though, but we didn't have time to get into it. "Not now, Beau. Customers will be knocking on the door in a minute."

"So get on with it," Dog said. "What exactly are we dealing with?"

I took a deep breath and got to the part I'd just learned. "Ronan isn't just a vampire. Samuel said he's something called a mimic. It means—"

"I know what the hell it means." A snarl rolled over Dog's face. "I've just never run into one before."

Beau put a hand on his hip and gave Dog a pointed look. "Mind telling the rest of us what it means?"

"It means he's a shapeshifter," I said. "He can 'borrow' someone else's face."

Lucy's mouth curled down like she'd eaten something sour. "Like a doppelganger?"

"What?" I shook my head impatiently. "Look, all I can tell you is that Shane Ronan had us all fooled. Decker doesn't exist. It was just a facade. But if he does walk in here again, I need to know about it immediately."

"I'm more concerned about him walking in here with a different face," Dog said. "We won't even see him coming."

I was worried about that too, but Samuel seemed to think Ronan had gone to ground and was now waiting for him to make a move. But tell that to Beau after he'd almost gotten a knife in his head.

"Samuel said this vampire likes games," I continued. "Likes to play with his prey before he strikes."

Dog picked up the card and handed it back to me. "And being Samuel's woman makes you and the people you care about convenient pawns."

Lucy snorted. *"Woman?"*

When I shot her a look she lost her smirk and shut her mouth. "I thought you said you were fine?" She wasn't acting fine, and I was starting to miss her usual bad attitude.

"I'll have the pack keep an eye on you," Dog said to me. "That vampire won't get within ten feet of you."

I laughed. "Yeah, if you can pick him out of a crowd blindly." Then I lost the humor. "I appreciate that, Dog, but I don't need wolves breathing down my neck." I was more worried about my bartenders. "Have them keep an eye on Beau and Lucy instead." With Mag around, I was certain Ronan wouldn't get anywhere near Tucker.

Dog flicked his head toward the stove. "You can burn that card now if you want."

I turned the burner on and set the damn thing on fire before tossing it into the sink. After watching it be reduced to a tiny pile of ash, I flushed it down the drain and turned on the garbage disposal for good measure.

"Feel better?" Dog asked.

"Not really, but I'm glad I never have to look at the damn card again."

Beau headed for the kitchen door. "I better go finish cleaning up the mess in the back room."

"Just don't open the door to the alley if you hear a knock," I said.

A nervous laugh slipped from his mouth. "Yeah, right."

I was glad Beau had a hellhound at home just in case that vampire came snooping around his house. To give his Hollerwolf a heads-up.

While Beau cleaned up in the back room, I went to help Lucy behind the bar until he got back up front. On my way out of the kitchen, I looked back at Dog. "Don't mention what happened to Beau to Samuel. He'll be all over me like Velcro, and he needs to worry about himself right now."

He kept his eyes on mine for a moment before getting back to prepping for the night. "It's your ass."

A few customers were sitting at the bar when I went out front. They were probably already lined up when Lucy unlocked the door. Sometimes I wondered what would happen if the Stag ever shut down permanently. Not that it ever would. At least not as long as I was still breathing.

Reed Walker was sitting at the far end of the bar sipping a drink. He'd been a customer since my mother ran the place. When he saw me walking in his direction, he turned his face toward the window.

"Haven't seen you in a while, Reed." I leaned onto the bar in front of him. "How've you been?" I straightened back up when he turned, giving me a look at the right side of his face. A good portion of it was black and blue from a shiner covering his eye, and he had a busted lip that probably needed a stitch or two. And then there was the makeshift splint on his finger consisting of two popsicle sticks and some duct tape.

Lucy walked up behind me and looked at him. "Damn. Who beat the shit out of you?"

Nice, Lucy.

"I think your customer needs a refill." I motioned to a guy with a half-empty glass of beer at the other end.

"He's fine. Still has half a drink." She finally got the message when I gave her a look and disappeared.

Reed shrugged. "It's all right. I know what I look like."

I smiled to lighten the awkwardness. "Either you wrecked your car or Lucy's right."

"Well, my car's just fine," he said, raising his glass to his lips.

That shiner looked painful, and he probably didn't have any health insurance, which would explain the DIY splint on his finger. If I'd had any on hand, I probably would have offered him some vampire blood out of pity.

He waved his hand in the air. "I got into it with some asshole over a parking space."

"Must have been a prime spot."

After downing the rest of his drink, he slid the empty glass toward me. "I'll have another."

As I grabbed it, I saw Patrick walking into the bar. I still hadn't gotten around to calling him, so his timing was perfect. "It's good to see you, Reed. I'll have Lucy get you that drink."

Beau was coming around the bar as I was getting ready to head to the back room to discuss business with Patrick. His eyes wandered to the other end. "Is that Reed Walker? Looks like someone took a tire iron to him."

"Yeah. He got his ass handed to him over a parking space."

Beau squinted at him. "I can see that shiner all the way down here."

"Never underestimate testosterone." I motioned for Patrick to follow me. "We'll be in the back. Co-op business."

His brows lifted. "You need me to join the meeting?"

Beau's involvement with the co-op had been practically non-existent over the past few weeks, especially with the unpredictability of his inner beast. It was good to have him as backup, though. "Right now, I need you behind the bar with Lucy. She's acting weird today."

"That's because she is weird."

"Just keep an eye on her."

Patrick followed me down the hallway. "It's not even dark outside yet," I said when we got to the back room. And Patrick didn't do dusk unless he had to. "This must be an emergency."

He sat down and swung his feet up on the desk. "Does pending catastrophe qualify as an emergency?"

I almost laughed until I saw the dire look on his face. "What are you talking about?"

"It's probably nothing."

Which meant it was *something*.

"Mary Foster is in the hospital."

"*Our* Mary?" It was the only Mary Foster I knew. She had cancer, but she seemed to be doing well these days. She was stable. The vampire blood wasn't a cure, but it made her comfortable and kept the disease from progressing. "Is the cancer getting worse?" It would have surprised me, but what else could it have been?

He shook his head. "When I called to confirm her order for this weekend, her phone went to voicemail. I tried two more times this afternoon with no luck, so I finally called Mabel Gentry to see if she knew what was going on with her."

Mary was like clockwork when it came to confirming and picking up her orders. The blood was too critical to her pain management. It was her lifeline. "And?"

"Mary has hep C."

"Hepatitis? My mind immediately started to work, with the worst scenarios coming to mind. "Did she contract it at the hospital? During a chemo session?"

"Mary stopped chemo a long time ago. You know that, Charley. The blood is the only thing keeping her going."

"What are you saying, Patrick?" But I already knew what was about to come out of his mouth.

"I'm saying we need to test the blood supply."

"We already do." We were careful. Vetted our donors thoroughly. Vampires didn't suffer from blood-borne pathogens, but they could be carriers and pass those pathogens on to humans. That's why we had them tested on a regular basis.

He stared back at me for a moment. "Right, but not all of it. From now on, we need to test every drop of blood that passes through the co-op. The doc is going to be busy."

Dr. Bishop was a local who supported the cause. He was our official blood screener. He'd witnessed the casualties of the opioid epidemic and even referred some of his more desperate patients to the co-op.

I ran some numbers through my head and sighed. "It's going to cost us." Even if the doctor only charged us wholesale for his supplies, we were looking at a major expense.

"It'll cost us a lot more if we don't."

Patrick was right. We couldn't risk other members getting sick. I couldn't live with myself if that happened. We were supposed to be helping people, not hurting them.

"We'll need to increase prices to cover the additional testing," I said. "There's no way around it."

"I'm aware. I don't mind being charitable with my time and talent, but I have to draw the line at dipping into my own pocket. Donors aren't going to drop their fees either."

Most of the vampires who supplied us made their living off donating, so the fee for those donations wasn't going to fluctuate based on the co-op's overhead. Someone had to eat it. Either us or the customers, and Patrick and I were barely covering our own expenses.

"What about the deliveries on Saturday?" I said. "We've got a lot of orders to fill, and people aren't going to like it if we have to cancel."

Patrick nodded. "I'll let the donors know we need delivery a day early. Then I'll have a talk with the doc and see if he can get everything tested by Saturday night."

Perfect. Another step to make the vampire blood business even more time consuming. Either we needed to pull Beau back in, which wasn't the best idea while he was still wearing his Hollerwolf training wheels, or we needed another volunteer.

"In the meantime," Patrick said, "I'll stop by the hospital and see if I can visit Mary. I'll give her some of my own blood."

Ironically, vampire blood might have given her the hepatitis, but it was also the one thing that could ease her symptoms.

Make it easier for her to tolerate the lengthy hepatitis treatment. Maybe even speed it up.

I looked at the time. "Visiting hours are over."

He pulled his sunglasses down and looked at me over the tops of the lenses. "And Mary needs blood. And fast. If they give me a hard time about it..." he snapped his fingers, "...I'll throw some glamour at them."

That was Patrick. Slick and aloof on the outside with a marshmallow of a heart underneath it all. He fooled everyone but me.

He pushed his glasses back up with his index finger and headed for the door. "I'll call you later."

As he walked out, a wave of dread washed over me. Patrick had kept his cool, but this was bad. Really bad. An outbreak of hepatitis could end the co-op and hurt a lot of people. And if we were the source? I couldn't live with that. Throw in a shapeshifting vampire with a deadly agenda and we were all in for a ride.

FIVE

When I came back up front, Candy was sitting at the bar chatting with a customer. She must not have had any private clients scheduled after closing the Cauldron.

She caught me in her peripheral vision and swung around on her stool as I approached. "I was about to come looking for you," she said, winking at Mike Miller who was sitting to her left. "I stopped by to say hi and Mike and I got to talking."

"Don't give him any ideas," I said. His lips curved into a sheepish smile. Mike was a flirt and had wasted a lot of effort hitting on me over the years. It was annoying at times, but he was harmless.

Candy squinted at me, reading my expression. "Something wrong?"

I shrugged. "I'm just tired." I wasn't about to discuss co-op business or the attack on Beau in front of Mike Miller.

She studied me for a moment longer before looking at Mike. "You mind giving us a little privacy? Girl talk."

Mike looked back and forth at us and finally got the message. He grabbed his beer and found a vacant stool at the other end of the bar.

Candy's smile settled into a smirk. "Tired, huh?"

I brightened up and decided to change the subject. "How's business been lately?"

She took a swallow of her drink and sighed. "It's been slow this week. I need to have a sale or something. Maybe put up a sign in the window offering two-for-one tarot readings."

She didn't make much money from her tourist trinkets and readings anyway. "How's your back-room business doing?"

"Fine. The mayor's sessions alone are paying the mortgage."

I laughed. "Thank God for that."

She gave me a flat look. "God? Honey, you should be thanking the *goddess* for that." She took another sip of her drink. "And Mayor Adams's unquenchable thirst for…"

Was I finally about to get something juicy out of her? "Thirst for what?"

A playful grin slid up her face. "That's confidential."

"You're a tease, you know that?"

"So I've been told." She glanced up and down the bar. "Any sign of that card-playing vampire today?"

I'd called her that afternoon and told her about Shane Ronan and what he was up to, and she'd gotten pretty angry about it. Wait until she heard what happened with Beau. I wasn't sure I wanted to mention it, but she'd smell the lie and badger the truth out of me anyway.

"He sent me a message just before we opened." I leaned closer to her. "He took a shot at Beau."

A chuckle came from her mouth. "With a gun?"

"A knife."

Her grin vanished as she glanced at Beau at the other end of the bar. "He looks fine to me."

"That's because Beau was blessed with butterfingers. Ronan left me his calling card. He taped the ace of spades to the outside of the door leading to the alley. Beau dropped it. When he bent down to pick it up, a knife came flying out of nowhere and landed in the door right where he'd been standing. He could have killed Beau."

Her face went from neutral to infuriated in a matter of seconds. "That no-good, sleazy bastard!" Then her eyes narrowed. "Where is it?"

"Where's what?"

"The card. It's got his fingerprints on it, and fingerprints are gold to a witch itching for payback. We'll take it to the Squad's house and throw down a spell that'll make that vampire wish he'd never set foot in this town."

In my frenzy to destroy it, I'd never even thought about that. Some witch I was. "Uh... I burned it."

"Okay. Ashes might work. What did you do with them?"

I scratched the side of my neck. "I washed them down the sink?"

"Is that a question?" She stared at me like I'd failed my Harry Potter test. "What about the knife?"

"I threw it in the dumpster in the alley." I didn't want it anywhere near me after yanking it out of the door.

She pointed to her outfit. "You see this dress and these heels? I don't dumpster dive. Probably wouldn't have worked anyway," she grumbled. "Something tells me that vampire is too slippery to make such an amateur mistake, like leaving his DNA all over that card before delivering it to a witch."

"Lesson learned," I said, eager to change the subject. "Next time I'll remember to think it through."

"Let's hope there isn't a next time." She finished her drink and stood up. "I need to get going. I've got a late session tonight. And I forgot to feed Odin before I came down here. Wouldn't want him to starve to death."

That cat had enough fat reserves to keep him alive for a month.

Samuel came through the door as she was getting ready to

leave. She rubbed her hand up and down his arm when he walked over to us. "How you doing, baby?"

He glanced at me and then back at Candy. "Spectacular. You?"

"Fine as I can be, under the circumstances." After giving him a sympathetic smile, she headed for the door.

"I guess you told her," Samuel said after she disappeared through it.

I snorted. "Of course I told her. It's Candy." Like it was even a question. I glanced out the window. "I'm surprised to see you this early." It had only been dark outside for a few minutes.

"I have some business to take care of tonight." There was a grave look in his eyes that he was trying unsuccessfully to hide. "I won't be home until dawn."

My first reaction was to play twenty questions, but if he wanted to tell me what he was up to, he would. It also got me off the hook from having to tell him what had happened with Beau. It could wait until tomorrow because I had a feeling I knew what he was doing tonight. I didn't want him out there looking for Ronan with a hot head and doing something stupid because that vampire had crossed a major line.

"Then I guess I won't see you after closing," I said with just as much of an everything's-fine facade.

His eyes lingered on mine. "You can still sleep in my bed."

"It's tempting, but I think I'll sleep in my own bed tonight." I was kind of looking forward to it, but I would have preferred to have him next to me.

Lucy snickered as she passed us behind the bar. "I guess your dry spell has ended."

She was a little late with that comment. I ignored it so she'd keep walking.

Samuel took my hand and raised it to his lips, brushing them over my palm as he steadied his eyes on mine. "Be careful, Charley."

I pulled it away. "You're hunting tonight." It wasn't a question. "And why are you looking at me like it might be the last time you ever see me?" I averted my gaze. "You're the one who needs to be careful."

He lifted my chin to bring my eyes back to his. "I know who I'm dealing with, but I have to find him in order to end this. That won't be easy." He kissed me on the forehead, giving me a final look. "I'll be back by dawn."

I absently grabbed Candy's empty glass from the bar. "Then go. Do what you have to do. I'll see you tomorrow."

He left, and I watched him through the window, disappearing into the darkness. A heaviness settled in my chest. If he wasn't back by dawn, I'd go after Ronan myself.

Beau came up behind me, snapping me out of the thought. "You mind helping me behind the bar for a few minutes?" he said. "Lucy's taking a break."

A break? Her shift had just started.

"Sure." Anything to get the dark thoughts out of my head.

I went behind the bar and poured a beer from the tap and slid it to Mike. "It's on the house."

He glanced at it. "For what?"

"For giving me and Candy some privacy earlier," I said with a wink.

His face lit up.

What was I thinking? "Don't take that the wrong way."

I looked up when the door opened. A woman stepped inside and surveyed the room. She looked kind of familiar, but I couldn't place her, which was odd because she was memorable. Especially in a town with few, if any, six-foot-tall gazelles with piercing green eyes. A mane of wavy dark hair cascaded over her shoulders, and she had a lot of tattoos peeking out from under her shirt that also seemed familiar.

A cocky grin slid up Beau's face. "Who is that?"

"Why? You haven't slept with her yet?" If she lived within

ten miles of Crimson and wasn't just passing through on her way down to Atlanta, he probably would have by now. "Put your tongue back in your mouth."

The woman walked up to the bar and sat on the stool I'd just vacated, beckoning us over with her index finger.

Beau immediately started down the bar, but I grabbed his arm. "I've got it."

When I walked up, I found it difficult not to stare at her eyes. It was like they were luring me in. Was she a witch? "What can I get you?"

Her gaze darted around the bar again and came back to the wall of bottles behind me. "Wild Turkey. Make it a double."

As I poured her drink, I noticed Dog looking through the order window. Beau was also catching glimpses of her between serving customers. Most of the men in the bar were shooting her glances, in fact. Like she was on the menu.

"Have we met?" I asked as I slid her drink across the bar.

She reached for it with her long slender fingers and stroked the side of the glass. "I don't think so." Her eyes never left mine as she took a sip. Then they wandered down the bar again. "What do I owe you?"

"Eight dollars."

She set a ten on the bar. "Keep the change."

I grabbed it and walked over to the register, noticing that Beau's eyes were still focused on her. "Jesus, Beau. You're acting like you've never seen a woman before."

"Not one like that."

"Well, quit staring." She was attractive, but it was more than that. The woman had something you couldn't manufacture with makeup, Botox, or a scalpel. It was God-given allure.

He finally pulled his eyes away when someone started snapping their fingers to get his attention. After getting the customer another beer, Beau's nose went up in the air. He sniffed and leaned into me. "Is she one of Dog's pack?"

I looked back at the woman. "Not that I'm aware of." Although I hadn't met every one of the pack's members. "Why? You think she's a wolf?" It would explain her ethereal eyes.

"Either that or she's been rolling around with one."

I caught myself sniffing too. "I don't smell anything."

His shoulders hunched. "Guess it's a Hollerwolf thing. I can't help it if my senses are heightened."

If he shifted in the middle of the bar, he was fired.

Out of curiosity, I walked up to the order window where Dog was still standing and flicked my head toward the woman. "Beau seems to think she's a wolf. Is she one of yours?"

He looked down the bar and shook his head. "Nope."

"Well, *is* she a wolf?" If anyone could smell a wolf in here, it was Dog.

He glanced at her again. "Yep."

There were several wolf packs in North Georgia, but there was a good reason they rarely ventured into Crimson. Wolves were territorial. The last time a pack of outsiders came to town a few years ago, it got ugly.

I was about to tell Beau to go find Lucy when it dawned on me where I'd seen the woman before. How could I have forgotten those eyes? "Dog." I backtracked to the order window. "Isn't she one of the northern pack? From the mountains?" Those were the wolves who started all the trouble a few years back.

Dog's eyes narrowed as he gave her another look. "Yes, ma'am."

"What the hell is she doing in here?"

He shrugged. "I guess she's thirsty."

"I'm serious, Dog. I don't want any trouble in my bar this time." Those northern wolves had left their mark on the businesses around here the last time they blew into town, and Dog's pack had only made it worse.

He looked through the window again. "Do you see any other wolves in the room?"

See any other wolves?

Lucy finally returned from her extended break, so I went to have a word with my cook. "You're awfully cavalier about the enemy showing up in my bar," I said as I walked through the kitchen door.

Dog let out a frustrated sigh. "What do you want me to do, Charley? She's a lone female sitting out there having a drink. If she brought her pack with her to start trouble, do you think she'd announce herself like that?"

"Maybe." He was probably right, though. It was possible she wasn't even with her pack anymore. But the only way a female got kicked out of a pack was if she committed a cardinal sin. Females were too valuable. And if the sin was unforgivable, a female wolf could find herself up in the mountains pushing up daisies from an unmarked grave.

After some grumbling, he threw the bag of hamburger buns he was holding on the counter. "Why don't I go have a talk with her and find out." His words were sharp, borderline sarcastic, his stellar mood blossoming.

"That would be fantastic," I said, taking a deep breath to settle down. The tension between us since I walked in that afternoon had been high, and I didn't like it one bit. A rift between us felt wrong. Unnatural. "I'm sorry, Dog, but I don't trust her. I think that wolf is up to something."

When I started to follow him out of the kitchen, he looked over his shoulder at me. "I don't need any help, Charley."

What was his problem today?

I threw my hands up. "You mind if I go out there and work my own bar?" Dog needed a goddamn vacation. I was starting to feel really guilty about dumping so many hours on him. "You're taking tomorrow off," I said. "I'll deal with the kitchen myself."

A mirthless laugh slipped from his mouth as he walked

through the kitchen door, but when we got out front, the woman was gone.

Dog looked back at me. "Want me to run out there and track her down for you?"

I didn't dignify the comment with a response. Instead, I walked behind the bar and made an announcement. "The kitchen's closed for the night." Then I looked back at Dog. "Go home. And like I said, take tomorrow night off too."

"You're serious?" He steadied his gaze on me for a moment. "All right." Then he went back into the kitchen to grab his things.

"Dog," I said as he came back out and strode toward the front door. He walked out without a reply and gave me a look through the window before climbing into his truck. It seemed so final. There were a handful of relationships in my life that I considered to be sacred. People who I trusted with my life—Candy, Patrick, and Dog. But as I watched him leave, I wondered if my attempt to give him some badly needed time off had just backfired. Driven a wedge between us for some ridiculous reason.

Beau walked up to me as Dog's truck pulled away from the bar. "What's up with him tonight?"

"I don't know." Beau was right, though. Something was definitely going on with Dog. "I'll call him in the morning and smooth things out."

"Well, you better do something," Lucy said. "My tips are going to suffer if there's no food coming out of the kitchen."

I meant it about cooking tomorrow, but I wasn't flipping any burgers tonight. I was rattled and suddenly couldn't keep my hands from shaking from all the adrenaline coursing through me. "I'll be in the back," I said, feeling like I was about to jump out of my own skin.

Beau did a double take when I turned toward the hallway. "What the hell, Charley?"

"What the hell what?"

He was staring at me. "Your eyes... They looked funny for a second there."

I went into the ladies' room and leaned against the wall, closing my eyes for a second. When I finally got up the nerve, I looked in the mirror. Everything seemed normal to me, although I was starting to get some circles under my eyes from not getting enough sleep. After calming down, I reached for the door handle. Before walking out, I caught another glimpse of myself in the mirror, gasping at the dark eyes looking back at me. I blinked, and they were gone. My irises were the same blue they'd always been.

I left the bathroom and hurried down the hallway. "You're okay," I told myself as I went into the back room and shut the door. "It's just your nerves." After letting my imagination run wild for another minute, I pulled it together and walked back out. I wasn't going to get any work done anyway, so I figured I'd make myself useful and help out behind the bar.

On my way up front, I glanced at the kitchen door wondering what had gotten into Dog. The full moon was approaching, which might have had something to do with it, but I'd never been one to believe the old wives' tale about it making people act weird. I was starting to rethink that, though. He'd walked out so fast he probably left a mess in there.

I was about to go into the kitchen to clean up when I heard Candy laughing. She was sitting near the window chatting with Mike Miller again when I walked into the room.

"Go see if the kitchen needs straightening up," I said to Lucy when I went behind the bar.

She let out an exasperated sigh. "Tell Beau to do it. I'm busy."

"You do it," I snapped. I was not in the mood.

My tone must have had just the right amount of bite to it

because she shut her mouth and went toward the kitchen without another gripe.

After watching her disappear into the hallway, I went to the end of the bar where Candy was sitting. "I thought you were going home."

Her laugh trailed off. "Well, I decided to come back. Why? Not happy to see me?" She held my gaze in an almost uncomfortable way. Then she flicked her eyes to her left. "Mike was just telling me a funny story."

Mike grabbed his drink. "I know. Girl talk." He got up and headed a few stools down to give us some privacy.

"That was easy." I noticed her glass was almost empty. "What are you drinking?"

She finished it off and set the glass back down on the bar. "Bourbon. Another double."

"I might have to walk you home." I chuckled, wondering if I should ask what had gotten her so thirsty tonight. She was going to have a hell of a headache in the morning if she didn't ease up on the booze.

Candy's chin lowered slightly as she smiled at me. "I'll take you up on that offer. You can tuck me into bed too."

I gave her a funny look and turned around to grab the bottle. "Did you at least feed Odin?"

She huffed. "That fat old dog can wait until later."

Dog?

Shivers raced up my arms and circled me like tendrils. A feeling that had my adrenaline hitting me square in the chest. "What about your late session?" I said, keeping my back to her as I waited for the strange feeling to settle. "Did your client cancel?" My mouth ran dry as she went silent behind me, the steady pulsing of blood pounding my inner ears.

Beau walked up and looked down at my trembling hands. "You okay, Charley?"

"Stay at the other end of the bar," I whispered. He glanced

at Candy and started to say something else, but I cut him off. "Just do it."

There was a flash in his eyes when he gave her another glance. Then he held my gaze for a moment. "Yell if you need me."

After he walked away, I grabbed the bottle and braced myself before turning back to the bar. Steadying my hand, I refilled her glass, my free hand dangling at my side as the energy started to build in my palm.

Candy's eyes zeroed in on mine. "Better make it a triple."

Beau wandered halfway down the bar again and noticed my glowing hand shaking at my side. He brought his eyes to mine before looking at Candy who was staring a hole through me. Then he went back down to the other end.

A lukewarm smile slid up Candy's face. "Can't get rid of him tonight, can you?"

I almost took a step back but forced myself to hold my ground. To not cower. "Well, you know what they say about keeping your friends close."

The light in her eyes dimmed as her smile flattened. "And your enemies closer."

Candy's lips were moving but suddenly it wasn't her voice coming out of that mouth.

I pumped my fist, a sphere of energy burning hot in my palm, conflicted by the person I saw staring back at me. What if I was wrong and it *was* Candy?

And then all doubt vanished as the facade faded away and I was looking at a stranger. A man I'd never seen before with jet-black hair who towered over me as he stood up. And yet he seemed so familiar. It was his eyes. They were as blue as Samuel's. Blue as Victor Steele's.

"You see me now, don't you?" A smile spread across Shane Ronan's face as his eyes went coal-black.

The customers sitting at the bar were frozen with fear, and

Beau had disappeared when I glanced at the other end. I pumped my fist harder to strengthen the magic, but as I was about to unleash it on Ronan, the Hollerwolf burst into the room. Lucy was right behind, and she was gripping a cast-iron skillet with both hands like she was ready to use it.

Ronan reached for Mike Miller several feet away and gripped him tightly against his chest, stopping the Hollerwolf from being on top of him. Then he lowered his fangs to Mike's jugular. "Give me a reason. Please."

"Wait!" I said, raising my hand into the air to let the energy dissipate, praying he wasn't about to murder a customer in the middle of my bar.

The vampire cocked his head. "Well, now you've ruined all the fun." His eyes filled with contempt a moment before he sank his fangs into Mike's neck with the speed of a viper, tearing at the vital vein. Then he pulled his fangs away to look at my shocked face. "We'll have to continue this another time." He shoved Mike at the Hollerwolf and disappeared through the front door so fast I couldn't even track his movements.

I jumped over the bar and dropped down next to Mike, pressing my hands to his neck, foolishly thinking I could stop the bleeding. "He needs vampire blood!" It was the only thing that could heal the wound and stop the hemorrhage. "Now!" I barked when no one moved.

Beau shifted and stood there looking shell-shocked while Lucy dropped the skillet and stalked up to the only vampire in the room, CJ. "Don't just stand there gawking, you idiot." She shoved him forward. "Get down there and help him."

Finally waking up, CJ bit into his wrist and bent down to drip his blood into the wound. Within seconds it started to heal, stopping the bleeding as Mike's skin sealed. Then he held his wrist to Mike's lips, dripping some into his mouth.

"That's all I can do," CJ said, straightening back up.

A moment later, Mike's eyes fluttered open. For now, he was alive.

"Let's get him in the back," I said when his eyes closed again. "Everyone else needs to leave. Except for you," I said to CJ when he started to follow the others toward the door. Mike wasn't out of the woods yet.

While Beau and CJ carried Mike down the hallway, I looked back at Lucy. "Lock up, and don't open that door for anyone. And I mean anyone!"

SIX

Mike had finally recovered completely an hour after getting a second dose of vampire blood, and I was pretty sure I'd lost him as a steady customer. I was just thankful CJ had been there, and that I didn't have to call Tom Murphy and explain a dead man in the middle of my bar.

I was also oddly relieved that Shane Ronan had finally emerged from under his rock and had made a move, if for nothing more than to torment me. And he'd done a stellar job. It also meant we could get on with the game and end it one way or another. At least I knew what he looked like now. I was sure I'd gotten a glimpse of his real face. There was no mistaking it. Those familiar eyes.

Rex was perched in his favorite tree when I pulled up to the house, keeping watch like a sentinel as I parked the truck underneath it. He seemed calm tonight, his entourage of crows nowhere in sight, which made me more comfortable getting out of my truck.

"Come on," I said as I got out. "Let's go have some cereal." He wouldn't budge from the limb as I walked toward the house, his silhouette prominent against the moonlight. My eyes roamed over the yard before coming back around to him still up in the tree. "I guess you're staying out tonight."

I continued across the yard quickly, looking over my shoulder the whole way. I'd called Candy on my way home to make sure she was okay. When I told her what had happened, she was speechless. Literally speechless on the other end of the line. Then she recovered from the shock of being hijacked by that vampire and vowed to kill the bastard herself.

"Last chance," I said to Rex as I stuck my key in the lock and pushed the door open. Once I was safely inside, I wasn't opening that door again until morning.

Before I could cross the threshold, Rex swooped down from the tree, grazing my shoulder as he flew into the house. He sailed straight into a dark corner, a hiss filling the living room followed by a string of expletives.

When I flipped the lights on, Rex flew to the opposite side of the room, barely escaping Ian Masterson's flailing arms.

"That flying *rat!*" he growled. "He's lucky I didn't rip his wings off."

I tossed my keys on the coffee table and glanced at Rex perched on the back of a chair. "He looks real terrified." Like me, he didn't seem to consider Ian much of a threat anymore. I lived for the day when that vampire's blood worked its way out of my system and he no longer had an open invitation to my house.

Ian flashed his fangs and growled at the bird again. Rex flapped his wings and cawed in return.

"What do you want, Ian?"

"Not happy to see me?"

After a brief staring contest, he finally stated his business. "Have you heard of a man by the name of Shane Ronan?"

That got my attention. "How do you know that name?"

"I'll take that as a yes. Tell me what you know about him."

I squinted at Ian, considering how I wanted to play this. "You first."

We stood there glaring at each other, neither one of us willing to initiate the conversation.

"Fuck." His hostile gaze softened. "You really are stubborn."

"And you just broke into my house uninvited."

He strolled over to the chair, but when Rex refused to budge he detoured to the sofa.

"Don't even think about making yourself comfortable," I said before he could sit down. "You won't be staying long enough."

He slowly turned to look at me. "Testy."

I could get rid of him faster if I told him who Shane Ronan was, but then he'd probably clam up and give me nothing in return. Besides, it was Samuel's business, not Ian's. "You were about to tell me how you know Ronan," I said, hoping he was getting bored and would break first.

He finally relented. "I assume you know he's a vampire."

"I'm aware."

"Well, this vampire has been coming into the Beast for the past few nights, and do you know what he's been doing?"

"Let me guess. Card tricks?"

Annoyance rolled over his face. "What the hell are you talking about?"

"Never mind." Bad guess. "Just tell me."

"Creating problems. That's what. He's been whispering about a rich vampire who bought the old Pullman place and is planning to take over the Beast."

A laugh burst from my mouth. "That's it? You're freaking out because some random vampire is spreading rumors about a hostile takeover of the Beast?" It really was laughable.

"You think that's funny?"

The look on his face had me stifling another laugh. "I think it's tragic that you're so worried about gossip."

Before I could say another word, my back hit the wall and all I could see was Ian's angry face inches from mine, his distinct vampire scent filling my nose. And he was way out of line. "Get off me, Ian."

He gave me just enough breathing room so I could reach for the obsidian amulet tucked under my shirt, the one I'd taken from my father after he'd drained mine and tossed it over a cliff. The stone was charged with the energy of three witches—mine, my mother's, and Fawny Goodman's. "I said, get off me!"

His face froze as he eased his hold on me. Then he flew backward and slammed into the front door. "My, my, you do pack a mean punch. But I like it." There was a twinkle in his eyes.

I glanced down at my glowing palm, but I hadn't even touched him with it.

"I warned you," I said, trying to hide my confusion. Whatever worked.

He rolled his shoulders and smoothed his hair back before coming toward me again, this time stopping a safe distance away. "As I was saying, Shane Ronan is stirring the pot. He has my employees and customers thinking I'm weak and prepared to relinquish my business to your boyfriend." He stepped closer and narrowed his eyes at me. "Why do you think he would do that, Charley?"

I had no idea what Ronan was up to down there. "It's your club. Why don't you ask him yourself?"

"Because that little snake has a knack for disappearing the moment I show up. I've ordered my staff to bring him to me next time he sets foot in Reaperstown so I can rip his throat out, but something tells me there won't be a next time. The damage has been done, and now he's hiding under some rock to watch the fallout." The anger in his eyes flared as he came closer. "Your turn."

And then it dawned on me. "He's trying to start a war

between you and Samuel." They were two of the most powerful vampires north of Atlanta. A war between them was the perfect way to throw Samuel's life into chaos. It was just another one of Ronan's games.

Ian looked at me sideways. "Why would he do that?"

He was caught in the thick of it, so there was no keeping secrets now. And if Samuel couldn't track Ronan down, we might need Ian's help to find him. I almost laughed at the thought of Ian's face when I told him who he was up against.

He raised a brow. "Well?"

No use mincing words. "Victor Steele was Shane Ronan's maker."

Ian went still for a moment and then cocked his head. "Excuse me?"

"You heard me."

I could almost see the thoughts running through his dark mind. A trace of... could it have been fear? After all, he was complicit in Victor Steele's demise regardless of who pulled the trigger that planted that sunlight bullet between the vampire's eyes. And there was nothing more dangerous than a vampire out to avenge his maker's death. Being a vampire himself, Ian was well aware of the visceral need for that revenge.

Ian's cool facade returned. "You mean *my* Victor Steele? The Steele who was also Samuel's maker?"

"Yep." I stared back at him while he put the pieces together. The dangerous pieces driving Shane Ronan to destroy anyone involved in his maker's demise.

A few seconds passed before a grin slid across his face, followed by a chuckle. "So they're siblings."

"I wouldn't say that to Samuel if I were you."

"Let me guess." His grin vanished. "This piece of shit has come to Crimson to avenge his maker's death."

Being a vampire, he knew the drill.

"That's not all," I said. Then I hesitated because the rest of it was personal. But I also knew Ian wasn't going to let me drop it now that I'd piqued his interest. He was going to find out anyway. "Shane Ronan is the vampire who delivered Samuel to Victor Steele the night Steele turned him."

His eyes wandered past me, settling into a curious stare. "Well... this just got even more interesting." He brought his eyes back to mine. "Where is Samuel tonight? I thought you two were keeping house these days."

Not that it was any of his business. "He's hunting. And no one's keeping house. Samuel and I just spend a lot of time together. He's free to sleep wherever he wants, and so am I." I wanted to slap myself for saying that last part, but the words had slipped from my mouth like water.

He glanced up and down my body, stopping at my cleavage as a smile worked its way across his face. "All the cake with no strings. How convenient for Samuel."

Pompous fanger.

"My face is up here," I said when his gaze lingered.

He flicked his eyes back up to mine. "You say Samuel is out hunting? For Shane Ronan?"

"What else would he be hunting? Deer?" If he kept irritating me, he'd be able to ask Samuel himself. Samuel was bound to sense this little meeting between me and Ian and come storming through my front door at any second. I was surprised he hadn't arrived already.

Ian's face went cold. "I don't like your tone, Charley."

And here I thought we were being civil to each other for a change.

"And I don't like you standing in my living room uninvited."

"Oh, I'm invited all right. Your door is always open to me, sweetheart."

I scoffed. "Because of the puny few drops of blood I drank from you?"

The night we went down to the Beast to kill Victor Steele,

that had been the only way to convince Steele that Ian owned me. And it had worked. Steele kept his hands to himself when he smelled Ian all over me. Followed vampire protocol. But so far Ian's blood hadn't run its course through my veins the way Samuel had predicted it eventually would.

Ian let out a snide chuckle. "If I recall, your lips were locked to my wrist like a leech that night. Dog had to pry you away."

I shoved my wrist at him. "Why don't you just suck your blood back out of my body and get the hell out of my house!"

"Lucky for me it doesn't work like that. You'll just have to put up with my company until I grow tired of you, which should be... never."

The vampire was infuriating.

"Get the hell out!" I yelled when he came dangerously close again.

His index finger wandered toward the hollow of my throat. "No."

Before I could put him in his place with the magic burning in my palm, he started moving backward. A look of sheer bafflement fell over his face as the front door flew open and he was sucked outside. He kept moving, across the porch and down the steps, landing on his ass in the front yard.

I slammed the door shut and locked it when he climbed to his feet and appeared on the porch again, astonished by what had just happened.

"Charley!" He knocked forcefully. "Open this door!"

"Nope. If you've got something to say to me, you can do it at the Stag. My house is officially off limits to you." I didn't know how I'd managed to kick him out, but I was thankful.

He peered through the front window, holding my gaze like he was trying to glamour me. It didn't work.

"I command you to open the door, Charley!"

"Lucky for me it doesn't work like that," I said through the glass, parroting his own words back to him.

I took a few steps back when he reached for the edge of the window and pulled it open. I'd done a lousy job of locking it that afternoon before leaving for the Stag. He bent down and looked through it but made no attempt to get inside. He probably couldn't. I was back in control of my own house.

"Touché," he said as he straightened back up.

Then he disappeared in a flash, leaving me standing there in disbelief. I didn't know what I'd done to get rid of him, but I had the oddest feeling as I held my arms out and looked at my veins. Ian Masterson's blood had finally run its course. I was finally free of him.

SEVEN

By the next day, Samuel still hadn't shown up. He wasn't answering his phone either. There were half a dozen reasons why he should have been knocking my door down by now, and I was beyond worried.

I drove into town early to stop by the Cauldron. In addition to Samuel being MIA, I wanted to talk to Candy about a few things and check on her before going to the Stag. When I walked into the shop, she was behind the display case grinding something in a mortar and pestle.

"Cooking up a spell?"

"You could say that. I wish I had that card Ronan delivered to you yesterday so I could hex his balls. Make his tiny little pecker fall off," she spat.

I guess she was still hot under the collar about that vampire borrowing her face.

She continued crushing whatever was in the bowl and nodded to the bookcase next to me. "Hand me that jar."

I glanced at the row of vessels on the shelf. "Which one?"

"The one with the crossbones on the front."

I grabbed the ominous-looking jar and held it at arm's length as I crossed the room to hand it to her. When she opened it, I took a step back and gagged. "Christ, Candy. What kind of science experiment do you have going on there?" It smelled like sulfur. Like rotten eggs.

She dumped a good amount of powder into the mortar and started grinding again. "That damn woman is going to wish she never walked into my shop."

"Who?"

"Adelle Spencer."

I almost gagged again. "What are you trying to do? Kill the woman?"

She glanced up from the bowl. "If I thought I could get away with it." A wicked laugh came from her mouth, but just as quickly, her face started to burn with irritation. "That gossiping heifer has been bad-mouthing me all over town. Telling people I sell nothing but snake oil. Had the nerve to call me a charlatan."

Oh, that was bad. The first rule of doing business with Candy from her back room was that you kept your mouth shut. It wasn't like half the town didn't know about her side hustles, but the half that could make it difficult for her to continue with her "community service" was still in the dark. I'd hate to be Adelle Spencer right now.

"She wants a weight-loss spell?" Candy laughed again. "I'll give her one. That cow will be nothing but a toothpick by the end of the week."

I reached over the counter and gently grabbed her arm. "You don't really want to do that."

"Oh, yes I do."

"No one listens to that woman anyway," I said, letting go of her.

She released a heavy sigh and dropped the pestle in the bowl. "You're right. I'll just slip her some psilocybin next time. Let her show this town what an ass she really is."

Adelle Spencer on magic mushrooms? Even I couldn't resist laughing at that image.

Candy suddenly zeroed in on my face. "What's wrong now?"

"You mean, between that vampire almost killing Beau and then one of my customers?"

"That was yesterday." She kept staring at me. "What's wrong today?"

"I haven't heard from Samuel since yesterday evening, and I'm worried."

She kept looking at me like she expected more to come out of my mouth. "That's it? You haven't heard from your boyfriend in less than twenty-four hours? Honey, be glad he isn't smothering you."

"He's out hunting for Ronan, and he should have sensed that vampire showing up at the bar last night." Not to mention Ian in my house when I got home.

Her brow creased. Since I'd filled her in on Samuel's history with Ronan, she must have had a good idea of what was running through my mind. "Did you check his house?"

I shook my head. "He'd be in his chamber by now, and I'm not exactly sure how to get down there." The staircase leading to it was in the master bedroom, but I had no idea what was beyond those steps. Even if I could get into the chamber, it was risky to sneak up on a resting vampire. "I tried to call him several times but he's not answering his phone, and Samuel always answers my calls on the first ring."

"I don't think you should jump to conclusions, Charley." She shrugged. "Maybe he barely made it home in time before the sun came up. And he left his phone upstairs before going to his chamber."

It was nice of her to try to ease my mind, but it wasn't working. Too many alarm bells were going off in my head, and I knew better than to ignore them.

"Something else strange happened last night. Ian Masterson was waiting for me in my living room when I got home."

"That damn vampire," she grumbled. "What did he want?"

"Shane Ronan showed up at the Beast and started spreading rumors about Samuel trying to start a hostile takeover of the club. Ian asked me what I knew about him."

"Well, isn't that interesting." Candy smirked. "Wish I could have seen his face."

"What's interesting is that while I was being manhandled by Ian, Samuel never showed up."

"Manhandled?" The look on her face could have melted a glacier.

"He got a little handsy with me, that's all. Just Ian being a jerk. But it was like Samuel couldn't sense me." Although I wasn't really in trouble. Putting Ian in his place wasn't that hard for me these days. "Samuel always shows up when Ian's around."

She opened her mouth to say something but suddenly seemed lost for words. "I don't know what to tell you," she eventually said. "It is a little odd."

I recalled the other strange thing that occurred. "Something else happened that I can't explain. You know how me drinking Ian's blood has given him carte blanche to enter my house whenever he pleases?"

Her eyes filled with contempt. "How could I forget?"

"Well, that unspoken invitation ended very abruptly last night."

"I thought you said he was waiting for you in your living room?"

"He was, and he kept taunting me about how he could come and go as he pleased. It pissed me off and I told him I wished he would take his blood back and get the hell out of my house."

She cocked her head. "And?"

"And nothing. But then he started to get handsy again and I

told him to get out more forcefully." I shook my head at the memory of what had happened next. "Before I knew it, he went flying out the door. He couldn't get back in either." A laugh slipped from my mouth. "I think his blood finally wore off."

A curious glint filled Candy's eyes as she gazed at me. "Could be."

"Why are you looking at me like that?"

She continued to study me. Study my eyes. "Has anything else strange like that happened recently?"

Define strange, I wanted to say.

I averted my eyes to the floor. "I need to get to the Stag. Dog is off tonight, so I'm running the kitchen."

"You?" She laughed but quickly stifled it when she realized I was serious. "Just don't burn the building down. And we're not done with this conversation," she said as I was walking out the door.

I was done with it. For now. And I regretted stopping by and bringing any of it up, because I was even more nervous now. I didn't have the bandwidth to deal with any more *strange.* Worrying about Ronan walking into my bar again in someone else's body and Samuel going missing was all I could handle, on top of trying not to lose customers over burnt burgers tonight. If Samuel didn't show up at the Stag before closing, I was going over to his house and getting into that chamber one way or another.

Dog's truck was parked out front when I pulled up. "Damn, that wolf is stubborn," I grumbled as I got out. He didn't know what was good for him. I'd tried to call him that morning, but his phone kept going to voicemail, so I decided to give him space to cool off. But here he was. I just hoped his mood had improved so I wouldn't be walking on eggshells around him all night.

When I got inside, I immediately heard noise coming from the kitchen. It sounded like a power tool. I went to investigate and found Dog standing on a ladder with a drill in his hand.

"What are you doing?" I said.

He finished driving a screw into the ceiling and glanced down at me. "I figured I'd come in early and hang that pot rack you got me."

I'd ordered the rack six months ago because Dog kept complaining about having no place to hang things. The kitchen was pretty tight. But that box had been leaning against the wall in the back room collecting dust ever since.

It was a good icebreaker for the tension between us, though.

"Thanks for hanging it." I'd considered doing it myself.

"Thanks for buying it," he said without looking down at me.

When awkward silence filled the room, I spoke up. "I'm sorry about last night."

"You're not the one who needs to apologize." He climbed off the ladder and set the drill on the counter. "I was being an ass."

"Well—"

He held his hand up to stop me. "Let it go, Charley."

I was just glad I hadn't alienated one of the most important people in my life. I didn't know what I would have done if I'd driven a wedge between us. Probably grovel for forgiveness.

I shook my head. "I've been putting too much on you, Dog. I meant it when I said you should take the night off."

He scoffed. "And do what? Take a nap? You know me better than that."

Well, he was the one who said he needed some time off.

Dog was one of the hardest-working people I knew, but to a fault. His problem was, outside of the pack, he didn't have much of a social life. Not since he'd broken it off with his last girl-friend when he found out she'd been running around on him with some guy up from Tallahassee. A human at that. She'd ended up following the guy back to Florida, and it had turned Dog off to relationships. Anything that went beyond a one-nighter.

"I still think you need some time off." And I needed to put

that sign in the window. I got so distracted when I found that door open yesterday that I forgot about why I went to the back room in the first place. "We'll get you some help in here as soon as possible. I promise. Just let me know which night you want off, and I'll help out in the kitchen until we find someone."

Dog chuckled. "No, you won't."

I stared at him for a second. "What makes you think I can't cook a burger and fries?"

He walked toward the pantry, pointing to the kitchen door. "Out."

"Yes, sir."

I couldn't contain my smile as I left. Dog was back, and we'd made things right between us. Hearing from Samuel was the only thing keeping the afternoon from being perfect. Maybe Candy was right, and he was resting in his chamber without his phone.

Right. And pigs could fly. Something was wrong.

* * *

I couldn't stop looking at the time. It was almost eight o'clock and there was no sign of Samuel. He still wasn't answering his phone either. With my stomach in knots, I couldn't wait any longer.

Beau was off, so Tucker was working the bar with Lucy. On my way up to the front, I stopped in the kitchen. "I need to go over to Samuel's place," I said to Dog. "Keep an eye on the bar for me."

He glanced up from the cutting board. "Everything all right?"

"I haven't heard from Samuel since last night, and he's not answering his phone."

"That doesn't sound like Samuel." He grabbed a towel and wiped his hands. "I'm coming with you."

"I need you here."

He held my gaze for a moment. "I don't like it, Charley."

"Neither do I, but I'm not leaving those two alone in the bar." If Beau had been working I would have felt better about it, but Lucy was unpredictable when left unsupervised. And Tucker was just too green.

Dog nodded. "Okay. But if I don't hear from you within half an hour, I'm coming over there."

"I'm just checking to see if he's home, Dog."

I was on my way to look for my vampire boyfriend who'd been out hunting his vampire nemesis before suddenly dropping off the face of the earth. What could possibly go wrong? For all I knew, he was avoiding me while he shacked up with another woman at his house. All kinds of ridiculous scenarios were suddenly running through my head.

As I went out to the bar, the front door opened and two men walked inside. One of them looked familiar, and they were big. Really big. Another man and a woman followed them in. All four had distinct tattoos running from their necks down the length of their arms, terminating at their wrists. Probably bikers. Club members passed through town sometimes on their way up to the mountains. Mostly they stopped in for a drink and left without incident, but occasionally they stirred up trouble.

The biggest guy headed for the bar, while the woman made her way to the back wall. She looked at the signatures and graffiti the Stag's patrons had started replacing after the wall was destroyed by vandals a while back. Her finger rolled over Mag's name where he'd signed it in bold letters, and then her eyes wandered over to me. "Magnus Ryan?"

"What can I get you?" Tucker asked the one at the bar, but her eyes were focused on the woman who'd just uttered her boyfriend's name.

"I don't think they're here to drink," I said, still holding the woman's gaze. They were wolves, and my intuition told me they were up to something.

The wolf at the bar turned to look at me, and I suddenly remembered where I'd seen him before. Where I'd seen those tattoos. He was one of the northern pack. The same pack as the female wolf who'd walked in here last night.

"Whiskey," he said.

I shook my head at Tucker and she got that deer-in-headlights look, like she didn't know whether to listen to her boss or her customer. Meanwhile, I kept glancing at Lucy, hoping she'd catch on and get Dog's attention through the order window.

"I don't want any trouble in my bar," I said, recalling how much chaos that pack had caused the last time they were in here when my mother ran the place. "You're obviously not here to socialize, so how can I help you?"

With his eyes trained on my nervous bartender, the wolf sniffed the air. "I'm looking for my woman. She's been in here. I can smell her."

My thoughts immediately went back to the day before when that female wolf walked in here. I assumed that's who he was talking about.

After looking around the bar, I brought my eyes back to his. "Do you see her in here?"

The female took a step toward me but stopped, a growl rolling up from her throat as her lips curled into a cruel smile. "Watch your mouth."

"This is my bar." I held her hostile gaze, reminding myself that you never back down from a wolf. Never show submission, unless you want to get your ass handed to you. "You don't like what I have to say, there's the door."

Several of my customers got up from their stools, but there was no leaving with the two wolves blocking the exit, so they grabbed their drinks and headed for a safer table near the wall.

One of them flashed his fangs, but I shook my head for him to stay out of it. A single vampire was no match for four wolves.

Where the hell was Dog?

I pumped my fist, feeling the energy build in my palm as I considered my options. If that female came at me, I'd do my best to make her reconsider. But since I preferred not to spend my evening cleaning up the place, and my time was better served finding Samuel, I decided to try a little cooperation.

"Is she a tall brunette with tattoos?" Of course it was her.

The linebacker of a wolf standing at the bar scowled, his full beard twitching as he turned to look at me with his icy-blue eyes. "Where is she?"

"She was in here last night." I pumped my fist harder as adrenaline crawled up my throat. "She had a drink and left. Haven't seen her since."

From the corner of my eye, I could see Lucy inching her way toward the order window, but she didn't make it there fast enough.

The wolf at the bar reached over it and grabbed Tucker around the waist, dragging her over the top like she weighed nothing. "I'll just take one of yours until you give me mine." He pulled her against his chest, ruining any shot I had at him.

Was he serious? "I don't have her."

He sniffed the air again. "Then you better find her for me." Tucker let out a strangled squeak as his hand slid down her waist and slipped under the hem of her shirt. The wolf ran his tongue along her cheek as his fingers gripped her breast. "Because I'm getting horny."

The front door flew open, but it was a commotion behind me that distracted me long enough for the female to attack. As I jumped out of her reach and hit the ground, another wolf sailed over me and landed between us. It was Dog.

Wolves from Dog's pack funneled into the bar from the hallway while one with jet-black fur barreled through the open front door. It collided with the wolf holding Tucker and knocked her free. Mag Ryan. His wolf was almost as impressive as Dog's.

The female shifted and skidded around Dog, a pair of amber eyes boring into mine as the wolf straddled me, its fangs coming within millimeters of my throat just before it went airborne. The light from my palm had delivered a direct hit to the wolf's sternum.

Dog's wolf growled at me and flicked his head toward the hallway.

"Behind you!" I yelled as one of the northern wolves near the door lunged at him.

I climbed to my feet when Dog turned and met the wolf head-on. There were at least ten of them going at it in the bar and a row of terrified customers pressed to the back wall.

As I was looking for my bartenders, something hit me from behind like a freight train, knocking me back to the floor. The female wolf was staring down at me when I rolled over. Its fangs clamped down on my right wrist and dug them deeply into my skin. To the bone. A scream left my mouth as the pain crippled me.

The wolf suddenly released my arm and stumbled back, shaking its head and spraying me with liquid. Alcohol. Lucy was standing behind it, gripping the end of a broken bottle in her hand. The wolf shifted, and the naked female stalked toward her. "I don't need fangs," she said as Lucy backed away. "I'm gonna kill you with my bare hands and eat your fucking heart." A grin spread across her face. "Then I'll wash it down with one of those bottles on the wall behind you."

I don't know how I did it with the pain radiating through my arm, but I managed to hurl some magic at her when she cornered Lucy near the order window. It hit her square in the head and slammed her into the wall, allowing Lucy to flee down the hallway.

The female shook it off and shifted again. When the wolf leaped at me, another ball of light left my hand, but it only grazed the creature's hindquarters as it sailed over the glowing sphere. The wolf was on top of me before I could summon another one. As I braced myself for... death, Lucy appeared behind it. She had that cast-iron skillet in her hands and raised it in the air. But before she could bring it down, the wolf stopped and cocked its head like a whistle had gotten its attention. It looked up at the door and took off, following the rest of the northern pack out of the bar.

When I looked back up at Lucy, she was staring down at me with her hair in her face and that skillet dangling at her side. "What in the hell just happened?" she said.

I rolled onto my hands and knees to get up. "You just saved my bacon." For once, she'd come through for me instead of the other way around.

She dropped the skillet on the floor with a thud and turned to head down the hallway. "Good. We're even now."

EIGHT

I'd just been viciously attacked, and again Samuel hadn't shown up, which confirmed my suspicion that something was terribly wrong. In his absence, one of my customers was kind enough to spare a few drops of vampire blood after that wolf had used my arm as rawhide. It was already healing nicely.

Tucker nodded to the wolves' clothes on the floor. "What should we do with those?"

Mag's jaw stiffened. "Burn them."

"I don't know," I said with a halfhearted chuckle. "They might come back for them. I'd rather hand them over than give them a reason to start trouble again."

A merciless grin slid up Mag's face. "Let them, so I can rip their fucking hands off for touching Tucker."

Dog settled his eyes on the wolf. "That's not happening."

Mag stepped up to him and looked him dead in the eye. "You're getting soft, Dog."

Oh, fuck.

Dog had Mag slammed against the wall a second later. "You ever call me soft again, I'll castrate you. Got it?"

Mag kept his mouth shut this time. And he was still on probation with the pack, so that was a wise move.

Dog released him and walked over to the bar to make himself a drink. He glanced at me before pouring it, though. "You mind?"

Did I mind?

"You can have the whole bottle." He'd earned it. Most of the customers had cleared out anyway, and it took a lot to get a wolf drunk.

Lucy grabbed the bottle from Dog's hand and poured herself a shot. "I ought to get workers' comp for all the mental distress I get from this place."

"One shot," I said to her. "That's it." She'd earned one too, but I wasn't having an inebriated bartender serving drinks. If Murphy walked in here and caught her consuming alcohol on the clock, he'd dangle the threat of shutting the bar down just to torment me.

We needed to straighten the place up, but I had more important things to do first. "I need to get over to Samuel's house. Can you guys handle this mess without me?"

Lucy shot her drink back and started to pour herself another. "Sure, no problem."

Dog grabbed the bottle from her. "That's enough."

Before I left, I had a question. I looked back and forth between Dog and Mag. "Which one of you is going to tell me about this woman who showed up here last night and why her pack just trashed my bar?" My eyes stopped on Mag. "That female wolf who almost handed me my lunch seemed to know you pretty well." That cocky smile she got on her face when she saw his name scrolled on the wall spoke volumes.

Tucker's brow furrowed as she looked at her boyfriend. "How well?"

"It's nothing, baby. It's a small world up here among packs. I met her a few times, that's all."

That was bullshit, but Tucker was too busy melting from the way he was stroking her back to question it. I decided to keep my mouth shut. Whatever had been between the two wolves was clearly over.

"The one who grabbed Tucker is named Zane," Dog said.

Mag growled, his pupils dilating. "I should have killed the bastard."

"Not in Charley's bar." After staring at Mag a moment longer to solidify the warning, Dog continued. "He's their pack leader."

I snorted. "So that's why he was such an asshole."

He looked at me sideways.

"Not that all pack leaders are assholes," I said, walking it back.

Dog finally got around to the tall brunette from last night. "If I recall, the woman's name is Tempest. She belongs to Zane. Or rather, she's been promised to him."

"It's the twenty-first century, Dog. Women don't *belong* to men."

Lucy snickered. "They do if they're wolves like my brothers. Wes and Richie act like cavemen when one of them's lucky enough to find a woman who'll let him get within five feet of her."

Bad example. Lucy's brothers were uncivilized mongrels, but somehow Richie had managed to find a wife, which baffled me. Out of politeness, I held my tongue.

I gave Dog a curious look. Like every other outsider, I didn't know the intricacies of wolf social dynamics other than how strong the bond was between mated pairs. I'd never asked, and Dog had never had a reason to discuss it with me. "You don't own your women, do you?" I said, referring to the pack.

Dog chuckled. "You've met Coda." Then he glanced at Mag. "I'd like to see any wolf try to harness that woman."

Mag and Coda had a turbulent history—and a child

together. The day she found out Mag was back in Crimson, she charged into the Stag like a hurricane to confront Dog to see if it was true. There was nothing submissive about her.

He nodded to Tucker. "But ask your bartender over there."

She gave me a meek look when my eyes wandered over to her. Then her brow pulled tight. "I'm nobody's property." A smile slid up her face a moment later when she glanced at Mag. "But I'm not going anywhere."

Tucker was also human, so their relationship was bound to be different. Maybe even more complex.

"The northern wolves live by their own rules," Dog said. "You saw them. They're a bunch of goddamn Neanderthals."

"Well, if this Tempest woman shows up here again, get rid of her. I don't want any more trouble in my bar." I needed to get over to Samuel's house, so I headed for the door. "I'll be back as soon as possible."

"I'm coming with you," Dog said.

I didn't refuse his offer this time. I was actually relieved because I didn't know what I'd find when I got there. "Do you mind sticking around?" I asked Mag.

"We don't need a babysitter," Lucy said.

I looked at the shot glass on the bar in front of her. "Yes, you do. And just in case those wolves decide to come back."

"Pick up the phone if they do," Dog said to Mag on our way out.

Samuel's house was only five minutes away, but that handful of blocks felt like miles as we drove, with every horrific scenario working its way into my head. Part of me wanted to find Samuel safe and sound at home, but that meant he couldn't have cared less that I'd been neck-deep in trouble for the past twenty-four hours. Or that his nemesis had shown up at my bar. And then there was another scenario. The one where I found his ashes piled in a mound on his living room floor. I'd been through that before when

Victor Steele tricked me into thinking Samuel had met his ultimate death. The memory of that night still left a lump in my throat.

"You missed all the excitement last night," I said as we turned onto Samuel's street. "Shane Ronan came into the bar."

Dog turned to look at me, incredulous. "What?"

"I got a firsthand look at his mimicking skills. And let me tell you, he had me fooled." Just the thought of it infuriated me. "And guess who he mimicked?"

"Just tell me."

"Candy."

Dog shook his head. "Christ. What happened?"

I pulled into Samuel's driveway and parked. "I'll tell you everything after we check the house."

"Great," he said as he got out. "Tell me Ronan showed up and then leave me hanging."

"Calm down. No one died." Well, Mike Miller almost died, but he didn't.

The place was dark when we pulled up, which wasn't unusual for a vampire's house. It didn't feel right, though. Samuel usually left a light on in the living room. Though my gut was telling me not to go inside, I needed to know if he was in there.

Dog motioned to the door. "You want to knock, or should I break it down?" He raised a brow when I pulled a spare key from my pocket and stuck it in the lock. "Wow. I guess you two have taken it to the next level."

"It's just a key," I said, borrowing Samuel's words from the night he gave it to me.

A sliver of light coming through the door illuminated the pitch-black hallway as we walked inside. I startled when I saw two glowing eyes staring back at me from the other end. "You scared the hell out of me, Sebastian." The cat raised his tail in the air, the tip swinging back and forth as he walked toward us.

Instead of stopping when I bent down to pet him, he hung a left and went up the stairs. "Where is he, boy?"

I was about to follow the cat but Dog grabbed my arm. "Let's look around down here first."

"I'll check the kitchen." Of all the rooms in the house, I doubted I'd find him in that one, but I needed to put some food out for Sebastian anyway. He must have been starving. Another reason this all felt so wrong.

"Yell if you need me."

A funny little laugh escaped my mouth. "Right."

I flipped the light switch in the foyer and continued down the hallway while Dog checked out the living room. When I reached the kitchen and looked around, it was pristine. Like it always was. The only person who ate in there was me. The back door was locked when I checked it, and just for good measure, I held my breath as I pulled the refrigerator door open. I'd seen my share of horror movies, and you never knew what you'd find on one of those shelves. A sigh of relief rushed out of me when I saw the lone carton of coffee creamer inside.

After dumping some dry food in Sebastian's bowl, I went back out to find Dog. He was standing by the staircase when I came down the hallway. "The kitchen is empty and the back door is locked."

"There's nothing in the living room or the study either," he said.

There was a look on his face I knew well. "What's wrong?"

He glanced up at the top of the stairs. "I don't know, but there's a smell in the air."

I sniffed. "I don't smell anything." Other than dust and mildew because the house still needed a good airing out. Samuel and I had been busy lately and hadn't had time to give it a thorough top-to-bottom cleaning yet.

Dog shook his head. "You wouldn't." He started up the steps

and looked back at me. "Are you coming?" My brow furrowed as I sniffed again. "Why does everyone smell things I can't?"

"Because you're not a wolf."

I didn't know why it was so hard for me to put my foot on the stairs. The thought of what I'd find up there. That mysterious smell in Dog's nose that could lead us to my worst nightmare. But I did, and my heart sped up when I reached the top step.

Dog turned around and gripped my arm. "Maybe you should wait downstairs."

I shook my head. "I can't." I went into the first room and looked around. Nothing was disturbed. It was the same with the rest of the rooms.

When Dog tried to enter the master bedroom, I stopped him. If there was something in there, I needed to see it first. I couldn't bear the thought of watching his face shift into a stone-cold gaze if...

With my heart beating out of my chest, I walked ahead of him, my eyes traveling around the empty room. There was nothing to see. I almost sank to the floor with relief, but then I saw Sebastian sitting next to the closet door with his tail swishing back and forth. The door that led to the area below the cellar. It was suddenly difficult to swallow around the obstruction forming in my throat.

"We need to check Samuel's chamber," I said with my eyes fixed on the door. It felt like a violation to go down there without Samuel's permission. But fuck that. I was desperate.

"You want me to go down first?"

"No." I walked past him and slowly pulled the door open. Sebastian slipped inside and disappeared down the stairs. It was so dark in there I couldn't see past the first two steps, so I pulled out my phone and used the flashlight. "Careful," I said to Dog as he followed me. I didn't even know if there'd be enough room in the chamber for the two of us. For all I knew, it was no bigger than a coffin.

After descending two flights to what must have been the cellar, I spotted another door directly in front of me. I pulled it open and continued down another flight of stairs that terminated at a concrete floor. The space was damp but surprisingly warm. When Dog made it down behind me, I shined the light on a room that looked to be about the size of the bedroom we'd just come from.

Dog glanced around. "Shit."

Shit was right. So much for being coffin-sized. I'd imagined a crevice hollowed into the ground with dirt walls and hard earth for a pillow, but this was no hole under the cellar. This was a vampire suite.

I got back to the reason we were there and reached for a light switch on the wall. The room lit up in a soft yellow glow, revealing a king-size bed against the wall. It had a dark mahogany headboard adorned with claw-shaped finials, a blood-red velvet comforter, and matching pillow shams. To the right of the bed was a contraption I couldn't quite identify, but there was no mistaking the leather restraints at the top of two boards or the chains in the middle where they intersected to form a giant X.

"When I told Samuel I wanted to come down here with him, he said this was no place for me. Now I know why." I was beginning to wonder if I knew Samuel as well as I thought I did.

"Don't forget who built this house. Cliff Pullman had a reputation, so I'm sure he built this chamber too."

I cocked my head. "What reputation?" Other than Pullman being filthy rich and a bit of a recluse, I'd never heard about a reputation.

He nodded to the medieval-looking torture device. "For that."

It took a second for it to sink in. "No way."

Dog chuckled quietly. "Different strokes..."

At least he'd eased my concern that Samuel was leading a double life. I was open to a lot of things, but that contraption wasn't one of them.

"I'm sure it came with the place." He glanced around the room. "Samuel's obviously not here, so let's go. I'm getting claustrophobic down here."

Sebastian jumped up on the bed and meowed. He clawed at the red velvet and looked at me, a steady growl coming from his mouth.

Dog and I looked at each other, and then he walked over to the bed and grabbed the edge of the comforter. As he pulled it back, I saw a look on his face I'd feared seeing earlier when we walked into the master bedroom.

My heart started to beat faster. "What is it?"

He just stared down at the bed.

When I forced myself to go over and look for myself, a sharp pain sliced through me. Near the pillow were four teeth. Canines. The roots were attached, and the sheet was soaked with blood. "Are those...?"

Dog brought his eyes to mine. "A set of fangs."

My breath hitched, an invisible hand reaching into my chest and twisting my heart until I couldn't breathe. Blood pounded in my ears as the reality of what Dog had just said sank in.

He caught me when my legs started to give out. "Breathe, Charley."

"I knew something happened to Samuel. Why did I wait so long? I should have checked on him this morning." I knew last night when Ronan showed up at the bar and Samuel didn't appear. And later when Ian Masterson slammed me against the wall in my living room.

"We don't know who they belong to," Dog said. "Someone wanted you to find them. To get a reaction out of you just like the one you're having now." He grabbed my arms and made me look at him. "Samuel could still be alive."

Alive?

My stomach turned. I thought the contents were about to spill all over the floor, but then a moment of clarity hit me, and I pulled myself together. Forced myself to use my head. To wipe away the tears that were brimming in my eyes and do the only thing I could. "You're right. We'll find him. Then I'm going to kill the bastard who did this." It was Ronan, and I was going to hunt him down and rip his heart out the way he'd just ripped out mine.

"Wait," Dog said as I was headed back toward the stairs. "There's something else here." He reached for something sticking out from under the velvet comforter. A piece of paper with rust-colored stains along worn edges.

"Is that a note?"

Dog shook his head. "It looks like an old flyer."

"A what?" I went back over to the bed and took it from his hand. The font was faded, and the stains looked like dried blood. Printed in large letters at the top were the words FIGHT CLUB. Underneath were details of an event, but there was no address. Just the words WATERFRONT WAREHOUSE. "What the hell is this?"

Dog snatched it back from me and looked at the date. "1887. Someone's playing a game with you, that's what it is." He sniffed the paper. "It's that same smell I picked up at the bottom of the stairs. A vampire, and it isn't Samuel."

I already knew it was Ronan. When I looked back at Sebastian on the bed, I confirmed it. Underneath his paw, sticking halfway out from under the comforter, was the card that seemed to haunt me at every turn. It was the fucking ace of spades.

NINE

On the way back to the Stag, I told Dog everything that had happened when Ronan showed up last night. He was kicking himself for walking out, but I reminded him that I'd told him to take the night off. Pretty much ordered him out. It didn't make him feel much better, though.

When we pulled up to the bar, the place was packed, which was not what I was expecting this late on a Wednesday night. Especially after those wolves pulled that stunt earlier. What people would put up with for a drink in this town. But we needed to find Samuel, so we were shutting down early.

Lucy expressed her annoyance about the kitchen being closed the second we walked inside. "We've got customers bitching left and right about not being able to order food."

They were really going to be unhappy when I told them all to get out.

"Start settling tabs," Dog said. "We'll clear the place out in ten minutes and get down to business."

It might as well have been ten hours the way I was champing at the bit to get out there.

While I went behind the bar, Dog motioned for Mag to

follow him into the kitchen, hopefully to come up with some kind of plan because I didn't have a clue where to start. But who was I kidding? I knew exactly where, and I wasn't looking forward to it. We needed to start at the epicenter of vampire depravity. The Beast.

"We're closing early," I announced to the bar.

Groans filled the room and Lucy gave me the stink eye again. "I'm not making up for your lost tips tonight, if that's what you're thinking."

She kept her mouth shut when she saw the seriousness on my face and walked away.

"Is everything okay?" Tucker asked.

"Not by a long shot." I watched her fidget with the napkin in her hand, and she had that nervous look on her face she usually got when she was having one of her visions. "Why? Did you see something?" Her *episodes* usually came out of nowhere and without warning.

She shook her head. "No. I just figured something was wrong since we're closing early." She continued past me and muttered, "And your nervous energy is bleeding all over the place."

I looked down at my hands, half expecting to see light "*bleeding*" out of them. "Just start settling up with your customers."

When I looked down the bar, I saw Becky Simms sitting at the other end. She had a busted lip and a bandaged wrist. As I walked over to her, I got a good look at her right eye. The white was filled with blood. "Who did that to you?" I asked, lowering my voice. Becky was a little rough around the edges, so it didn't surprise me to see her looking like she'd gone three rounds with someone's fist.

She huffed and looked away from me. "I got into an argument with someone."

I dropped it and looked at her glass. "Finish your drink."

The front door opened as I was walking away. "We're closed," I said over my shoulder.

From the corner of my eye, I saw Becky hop off her stool and head toward the door. A second later, her fist landed square in the jaw of the customer who'd just walked inside. By the time I turned around, the two were going at it, and we hadn't even finished straightening up from the brawl earlier that night with those wolves.

"Damn fools!" I growled, moving to break it up. But before I made it around the bar, Dog and Mag came running out of the kitchen and separated the two.

Mag grabbed the man while Dog wrestled Becky away from him. It was Will Pickens, one of the Stag's more agreeable customers. Or at least he used to be. Like Becky, he was knocked up good, but he didn't get those bruises from her just now.

Becky narrowed her eyes at Will. "How's that for payback, you piece of shit!"

Lucy rested her elbows on the bar to watch the show. "You two idiots did this to each other?"

"Shut up, Lucy." No one needed her commentary. Then I focused on said *idiots*. "What the hell is happening around here?" I glared at Becky before turning my attention to Will. "You're the third customer in two days to walk in here looking like you've had a run-in with a wrecking ball."

Dog grabbed Becky's wrist to examine something on the back of her hand. A raised mark that looked like a brand. A circle with a random symbol in the center. Then he turned to me. "What did you just say?"

"Reed Walker came in here last night looking like he'd been in the same train wreck as these two."

"Let go of him," Dog said to Mag.

Mag shoved Will forward, and Dog grabbed the man's arm. There was nothing on his hand, but then Dog's eyes focused on

Will's neck. "Where'd you get that mark?" Will was still seething at Becky, but he clammed up tight when Dog asked the question. He wouldn't even look him in the eye.

Dog shook his head and went back into the kitchen. He came back out a moment later with his phone and keys, glancing at me on his way to the door. "Let's go."

"Where?" We had a plan to put together, and I didn't feel like going down to the Beast by myself tonight.

"To the compound. I need to have a talk with one of my wolves."

* * *

Mag was waiting for us when Dog and I arrived at the compound. The wolves lived several miles outside of town at the edge of the woods, in a secluded fortress where only a fool would venture without an invitation.

I climbed out of Dog's truck and went up to Mag. "That was fast." Dog had barely given me enough time to ask Mag to clear the bar out and lock up, or he was going to leave without me.

A grin spread across Mag's face. "You might have a few pissed-off customers tomorrow after I kicked them out, but the place is locked up tight."

I was glad he'd decided to join us. The more the better if it helped us find Samuel.

He glanced at Dog. "Wouldn't want to miss all the fun."

The pack's compound had definitely grown. I hadn't seen the place in a while. Couldn't even recall the last time I was here. The wolves liked their privacy, and an invitation was rare. There was no dropping by for a casual visit or just to say hello. It required a specific purpose, like the reason Dog had brought me here tonight. Although being the pack leader, Dog could do whatever the hell he wanted.

There was an ominous bonfire raging in the distance, a

marker that told anyone coming across it that they'd strayed into wolf territory and needed to go in the opposite direction. And for those who weren't from around these parts and didn't know the drill, an encounter with one or two sentinel wolves was the next deterrent.

As we walked toward the fire, I noticed how much work they'd done to the camp. All the new structures that had been built around the edge of the woods. But Dog's house, which was really just a cabin, stood out. It was larger than the others and had a front porch. There was a bold symbol of a wolf painted on the door, matching one of Dog's tattoos, that gave notice to anyone entering the compound that the pack leader lived there. The cabins weren't much to look at, but the wolves spent most of their time outdoors anyway.

Halfway across the clearing, we were met by Loki and several other members of the pack. Coda was standing next to him. She looked at me and then settled her gaze on Mag. "What's he doing here?"

Nadeen, or Nae as everyone called her, stepped out from behind her mother and wrapped herself around Coda's legs and waist, her striking green eyes wandering to her father as a smile worked its way up her face. Mag had only recently acknowledged his ten-year-old daughter, but the bad blood between him and Coda made it difficult to co-parent. I understood her anger toward him. He'd disappeared and slut-shamed Coda when she got pregnant. Refused to acknowledge he was the father. But he was back now and making a genuine effort. That didn't excuse his shameful behavior in the past, but she needed to tone it down when Nae was present. Kids picked up on crap like that, and it scarred them for life.

Dog gave her a warning look. "Not tonight, Coda."

She let up on the glaring, but the underlying hostility in her eyes was unmistakable. She didn't fool me, though. That woman was still under Mag's spell. Suffering from a love-hate that would probably never fade.

Mag dropped down on his haunches and smiled back at Nae. "How's Daddy's little girl?" He reached into his pocket and pulled out a candy bar. "I brought you this."

Coda gripped Nae's shoulders when she tried to reach for it, but she loosened her hold a moment later. "All right. You can have it."

Slick move, Mag. What kid didn't love chocolate? At least he was trying.

Nae plucked it from his hand but kept her distance, like an unsure puppy. But that little smile was still there as she stepped back.

Coda squeezed her daughter's shoulders again. "What do you say?"

"Thank you." Her voice was barely a whisper.

Mag stood up. "You're welcome."

I glanced at Dog, waiting impatiently for him to move it along. It wasn't my place to walk into the compound and start throwing my weight around, but we didn't have time to spare, and it was ticking by fast.

Dog finally looked at Loki. "Where is he?"

Loki flicked his head toward a smaller cabin at the other end of the clearing. "He's in his cabin."

"I'll be out here with my kid," Mag said. "Holler if you need me."

Dog had filled me in on the way over. Max, one of his top wolves, had shown up at the compound a few days ago looking worse than my two customers at the bar earlier. He claimed he'd gotten busted up by a couple of wolves at some bar two towns over. Dog was skeptical, but when Max stuck to his story, he let it go. Until he got a look at that mark on Becky's hand and Will's neck tonight. It was the same mark he'd noticed on Max's left cheek. It was already fading by the time Dog saw it, and it looked like it could have been the imprint from a ring the other guy was wearing when he punched Max in the face.

"Try not to kill him,' I said to Dog as we headed for Max's cabin. "We need him to talk."

Pack discipline was brutal, and knowing Max had lied to him, Dog was likely to take the wolf's head off.

Dog didn't bother to knock. He pushed the unlocked door open and went inside. By the look on Max's face when he saw us, he knew his fate. There wasn't a mark on him now, but that didn't surprise me. Wolves healed fast. Once they shifted, almost as fast as vampires. I was surprised Dog even got a look at Max's wounds the other night before they disappeared. It was almost as if he wanted Dog to see them.

Dog stalked up to the wolf and stuck his finger in his face. "We're gonna have a conversation, and this time you're going to tell me the fucking truth."

Max took a step back and brought his gaze up to his pack leader's eyes. A bold move that could have gotten the shit kicked out of him in the middle of his own living room. After glancing at me, he wisely averted his eyes to the wall behind Dog. "Conversation about what?"

It happened so fast, I didn't see it coming. Dog landed his fist in Max's jaw, snapping his head to the side with such force I thought I heard a bone crack. A spatter of blood painted the air as Max stumbled backward and crashed into a shelf behind him before hitting the ground. As he rolled onto his knees to get up, Dog kicked him in the side, sending him flying a few feet back.

"Stop!" I said to Dog when he was about to kick Max again.

"Back off, Charley. This is pack business." His eyes never left the wolf. "If you can't handle it, wait outside."

"He won't be able to tell us anything if you break his jaw."

Then the voice of reason must have kicked in. Dog took a deep breath and growled, "Get up!"

Max climbed to his feet and planted his hand against the

wall to steady himself. After wiping blood from his mouth with his sleeve, he finally decided to talk. "I placed a few bets and lost."

"You were gambling?" I said. The closest casino was almost two hours north of here. Unless he was doing some illegal betting.

"There's a card game over in Adlersville. Invitation only. I couldn't cover my losses, so they tried to convince me to get the money. Beat the shit out of me." He cocked his head at Dog. "Satisfied, or do you want to take another shot at me?"

Dog held his gaze for a moment and then went through a door to his left. He came back out a minute later with a duffel bag and threw it at Max. "Pack your shit."

A clipped laugh came from Max's mouth. "You're kicking me out for placing a few bets?"

"I'm kicking you out for lying through your teeth." Dog headed for the door, throwing me a look to follow him.

"Don't you think that was a little harsh?" I said when we walked outside. I'd seen Dog discipline his wolves before, and he had his reasons for it each time. Mistrust within the pack could get wolves killed, so loyalty and trust were gospel. Truth was non-negotiable, so lying to his pack leader was probably the stupidest thing Max could have done. But to banish him?

Dog's face was filled with anger, but I could also see the conflict in his eyes, reminding me of the immense responsibility that came with being pack leader. I guess it wasn't that different from me running the Stag, but I didn't have to kick the crap out of my employees to keep them in line. Although with Lucy it was tempting.

"He knows how to make it right," Dog said. "The ball is in his court."

We made it about twenty feet across the clearing when Max came out of his cabin, and he didn't have his duffel bag in his hand.

Dog turned to face him. "You got something to say?"

"Not out here." Max motioned Dog inside but stopped me when I tried to follow them in. "Just Dog."

"I don't know what the hell is going on," Dog said, "but I have a feeling all the shit happening around here is related to whatever you're about to tell me. Charley needs to hear it too."

Max stepped aside to let me pass, his face clouded with shame. At least that was what it looked like to me. If I wasn't so desperate for a lead on Samuel, I would have stayed outside to spare him any more humiliation.

When Max stalled, Dog got in his face. "I don't have time to coddle your ass, so start talking."

"It's a club," he finally said. "I got caught up in it and couldn't stop."

"Caught up in what?" Maybe I should have kept quiet and let Dog handle the conversation, but we didn't have time.

Max shifted his eyes to the window. "The blood." He flexed his fists and swallowed hard. "The fighting. When I heard about it, I just wanted to watch. Be a spectator. But then I got..."

"For fuck's sake!" Dog growled. "Get to the point!"

"I got hooked on the shit!" he growled back. "Are you happy now?"

Dog backed off and narrowed his eyes at the wolf. "You're talking about vampire blood? Some kind of club handing out vampire blood?"

Holy shit!

"Max?" I waited for him to continue as a horrible pressure started to build in my chest. "If he shuts up now," I said to Dog with my eyes still fixed on Max, "I'll make him talk myself." I was already manifesting a ball of energy in my palm to do it if necessary. The wolf hadn't told us the half of it, and his mention of vampire blood had triggered me.

"Take it easy, Charley." Dog stepped between us when he sensed the shit show I was about to start.

I stepped around him. "What club are you talking about? And what did you mean by fight—" The air left my lungs as it hit me. "The flyer in Samuel's chamber. Fight club."

Max squinted at me. "How do you know about it?"

"I don't, but you're going to tell me."

Dog stepped up to Max, making the wolf's shoulders curl into submission. "Yeah, he is. Start from the beginning, and then we're going for a ride."

TEN

Max kept dancing around the truth until Dog finally had enough. He came eye to eye with the wolf. "You better get that bag packed because I'm about to drive you to the county line myself. There's no coming back after that."

"All right!" Max paced the living room, smacking himself in the side of the head with his palm, muttering about how stupid he was. Then he finally came clean. "Like I said, it's a fight club."

"How'd you hear about it?" Dog asked.

He hesitated and then mumbled, "Some vampires down at the Beast."

Dog glared at him. "Come again."

Max suddenly got up the nerve to look directly at his pack leader with a trace of defiance in his eyes. "I said I heard about it from some vampires at the Beast."

Dog's eyes narrowed. "And what the hell were you doing down there?"

"What do you think?"

When he just stared at Max like he was genuinely

perplexed, I spelled it out for him. "He's going down there for the women. Isn't that right, Max?"

A sneer crawled over Dog's face as he shook his head at the wolf. "Idiot."

"What do you expect?" Max said. "The females in the pack are off limits, and no offense, Charley, but the women in town aren't exactly my type."

"You mean young and trashy." I guess he hadn't met Mary Ellen Mitchell, although she'd changed her ways drastically since her near-death experience with that demon, Atticus Devereaux, a while back.

He shrugged. "Got to ride something around here."

"Get back to this fight club," Dog said. "Who's running it?"

"We know who's running it," I said. "It's Ronan."

Max shook his head. "I don't know anything about this Ronan. I just pay the cover at the door and watch the show. At least that was how it started."

Dog snickered. "From what I saw the other night, it looked like you were doing more than just watching. Looked like you were part of the show." He kept his eyes on Max, making the wolf more uncomfortable by the second.

"Are humans involved in these fights?" I asked, knowing damn well they were.

Max glanced at me sheepishly. "That's how it starts. They put two humans together in the ring. Whoever wins moves on to the next round." He lowered his chin slightly and seemed to have difficulty looking at me. "Round two is human against vampire."

"What?" My anger flared. A human going up against a vampire was slaughter. Even the mainstreamers who didn't hunt to feed and relied on donors could take down a human in an instant. Hell, even Jake who owned Midnight Auto Repair could rip a human's throat out if he wanted to.

"Here's the deal," Max said. "There's no biting allowed

during the fights. To even things out and make it a little more interesting, the human gets to choose a weapon. No guns. It's usually a knife."

"And you think that makes it a fair fight?" Dog said.

Max chuckled. "You'd be surprised at what a human is capable of when they have their eye on the prize."

"Prize?" I said. "What kind of prize?"

"The winner gets to take a bite out of the loser. A nice long drink." He leaned closer to look me in the eye. "You know what it feels like to drink directly from a vampire's vein?"

Actually, I did. It was pretty damn amazing.

"The vampires get a free meal and I suspect a cut of the bets placed on them. And if a human manages to win, they get a real taste for that blood. They chase it. Can't get enough of it and keep coming back for more."

Dog rubbed the bridge of his nose. "I guess that explains the busted-up customers at the bar this week."

"Wait a minute," I said. "Vampire blood isn't addictive." That was why we started the co-op in the first place. Vampire blood was safe. It didn't affect the brain pathways like opioids did. But it was euphoric, and people did use it recreationally.

Max's tongue ran along his lips as if he could taste it. "I didn't think it was either, until I got a taste of it myself."

"Maybe they're spiking it with something else," I said.

Dog raised a brow. "He said they're drinking it straight from the vein. How do you spike a vampire?"

I looked at Max. "Good question. Are they selling vials of it at this club as well? Vials that can easily be laced with something that is addictive?"

Max's face hardened. "Son of a bitch. They're not selling it, but they're handing it out to the winners. You get it straight from the vein, and then you get to take a vial home as a souvenir, to hold you over until the next fight." He ran his fingers over his cheek where Dog had said he'd seen the raised mark. "They also give you a nice little brand when the fight's over. Your badge of honor for making it through a round. Winner or loser."

"So that's what that mark is," I said to Dog. "Becky and Will must have been put in the ring together, which explains why she wanted to rip his face off tonight." Will must have won the round, and it pissed her off. "I guess this club has no problem with throwing men and women together in the same ring?" I was all for equality, but that was just wrong.

Max shrugged. "You wouldn't catch me in the ring with a female, though."

Dog gave him a firm look. "Which brings me to my next question. How did you end up in the ring?"

A touch of humiliation returned to Max's face. "I wasn't lying when I said I lost a bet. Another strict rule of fight club is, if you lose a bet and can't pay up you work it off in the ring. I got thrown in with a vampire, and guess who won?" He glanced at me and then back at Dog. "I'm not proud of it, but I kept going back for more. It's over now, though. I'm done."

"Damn right, you are." Dog's eyes were firm. Unwavering. "I'll put you out of your misery myself if I find out otherwise."

Max's taste for fighting may have been nixed, but by the way he was fidgeting, it was obvious his taste for that tainted vampire blood was still under his skin. "We should get him some clean blood to wean him off that poison they've been feeding him." A few days on it would probably do the job.

Dog shoved him in the chest as an extra warning to clean up his act. "Good idea."

"Where is this place?" I asked.

"A warehouse a couple of miles outside of town."

Dog's brow tightened. "The old tractor warehouse?"

"Yeah, that's it."

I knew the place. Every teenager in Crimson had attended a high school party in that old building. It had been built to repair tractors and other large farm equipment, and part of the warehouse doubled as a storage facility for straw and hay. But it had been abandoned for over a decade because the structure wasn't sound. I figured it had caved in on itself by now.

"Let's go." I headed for the door.

"Wait," Dog said. "The last thing we need to do is rush in there without a plan. There'll be a lot of people in there, including vampires on Ronan's payroll."

Max held up his phone. "A notification goes out a couple of hours before a fight. I didn't get one, so there's no action tonight."

I looked back at him. "He sends invitations via *text message?*"

"Yep. First time in a week I haven't gotten one. No text, no fight."

"Then it's the perfect time to go in there." Fewer innocent people who might get caught in the line of fire.

"No, it's not," Dog said.

I was incredulous. "Are you crazy? Samuel is in there. I know it."

"Probably. And so is Ronan."

"Then we kill him." I stared at the two of them when they stood there silently. "Tell me you're with me, Dog."

He rubbed his forehead and groaned. "Look, Charley. We don't know much about this vampire, and if he was able to get to Samuel, he damn sure isn't your average bloodsucker."

"I'm well aware of that. I came face-to-face with him last night just so he could show me how above average he is." And I was looking forward to doing it again so I could kill him.

"Then you should know better. I'm not getting you or one of my wolves killed because we didn't think this through." He took a deep breath and let it out slowly. "He left you clues to lead you straight to that warehouse, and there's a reason he isn't holding a fight tonight. Ronan just cleared the deck to strike when you go storming in there with your emotions running on high. So we wait until morning."

"And do what? Wrap Samuel in a blanket and hope the sun doesn't kill him when we pull him out of there?"

Dog said nothing, letting the logic of his argument sink in. I wanted to find fault in it, but I couldn't. We'd be playing right into that vampire's hands if we went in there tonight. But what if... "What if you're wrong, Dog?" I shook my head. "I couldn't live with myself if he kills Samuel tonight."

"If Ronan just wanted to kill him, then we're already too late. He wouldn't have wasted his time leaving those clues in Samuel's chamber. He's looking to avenge his maker, Charley. He wants Samuel to suffer." His gaze leveled on mine. "I think he plans to kill you in front of Samuel. Or kill Samuel in front of you. Either way, he gets his pound of flesh while twisting the knife."

"Then what are you suggesting we do?"

"Like I said, we go in as soon as the sun comes up. Confirm Samuel is in there and get the lay of the land. Then we go back with an army at sundown and end this."

I couldn't even think about the hours until then. The wait. Or what Ronan may have already done to Samuel. But Dog was right. Samuel was a skilled hunter. An average vampire wouldn't have gotten anywhere near him, so we needed to be smart about this. Now I just had to fight the unbearable itch driving me to do something reckless. But when the sun came up, it was game on.

ELEVEN

I didn't even offer Dog and Mag a cup of coffee when they got to my house at dawn. I just grabbed my keys and met them on the porch. "Let's go."

Dog threw his hand up to stop me. "Take it easy, tiger. Five minutes to discuss a plan might be a good idea."

"We can do that in the truck." I stepped around him and headed for the steps. "Where's Max?" Since he wasn't with them, I assumed he was meeting us there.

"He isn't coming."

"Why not?"

"Three people is conspicuous enough. Four really increases our chances of some unwanted attention."

"What's the matter?" Mag said when I shifted my eyes to him. "I'm not wolf enough for you?"

He was wolf enough, but Max had an insider's perspective. "Max has been in that place."

Mag chuckled. "We've all been in that warehouse. I doubt it's changed much over the years. Maybe some bloodstains from those fights."

True.

"He was a goddamn mess this morning," Dog said. "More trouble than he would have been worth."

"We really need to get him some clean vampire blood as soon as possible." I continued down the steps. "Let's just talk about the plan on the way over."

We took Dog's truck because the muffler on mine would have notified every person within a four-block radius that we were coming. The warehouse was three miles south of town at the end of a dirt road. We parked on the other side of the state highway and crossed over on foot, cutting through the trees to the building. STOKES TRACTOR was still visible on the side, stirring up fond memories along with all the chaotic nerves dancing around in my stomach.

There were plenty of broken windows to climb through, but they were too high up to get to without making a lot of unnecessary noise. Noise we couldn't afford to make. When I peered through one of the lower ones, I saw a large open space, just like I remembered, and a hell of a mess. There were bottles and trash everywhere. And rust-colored stains all over the floor. We were definitely at the right warehouse.

A bird whistle at the other end of the warehouse got my attention. Dog could mimic just about any animal in these mountains, and it came in handy when discretion was required. He waved us over and pointed to a door on the side of the building. "It's open."

"How convenient," I said.

"A little too convenient," Mag said, following me through it.

I got a sick feeling we were walking straight into a hornet's nest. But it was light outside, and all those windows let in enough early morning sun to stave off a vampire attack. It was the rooms at the back of the building that worried me. The ones I remembered as being pitch-black inside. We used to call them the dungeon rooms because of their concrete floors and lack of windows. Urban legend had it that old man

Stokes ran a human-trafficking operation under the guise of a tractor repair business. But that was probably just kids telling stories.

"Charley," Dog whispered. "Wake up."

I snapped out of the memory and followed him deeper into the building. Except for twice as many busted windows and the obvious mess from the place being taken over by a rogue vampire, it hadn't changed much. There was old straw and hay strewed around the floor and a two-story-high ceiling to accommodate the large agricultural equipment it used to house. I estimated the place could hold a few hundred people if you squeezed them in like sardines. But I doubted Ronan's gatherings had gotten to that level yet. News of something that big would have spread through town, and Crimson PD would have been out here by now. I suspected by the time the police got wind of it, Shane Ronan would be long gone.

Something fluttered up from the floor in front of me, and I caught a gasp escaping my mouth. The bird flew into the rafters, and Dog gave me a stern look, his index finger pressed to his lips.

We continued toward the back of the building, toward those dungeon rooms. If Samuel was in here, he had to be in one of them. About halfway across, a sound started to fill the place. It started low, like a distant radio. Music—if you could call it that— that left your eardrums barely intact. It kept getting louder, like someone was cranking up the volume as we got closer.

Death metal.

"Where's it coming from?" I whispered to Dog.

He nodded toward a door to one of the rooms against the back wall.

"He's fucking with us," Mag said as it kept getting louder.

I kept looking over my shoulder to make sure something wasn't behind us. There was too much light streaming through the windows for vampires to descend from the rafters, but I couldn't shake the feeling that something was watching us. And someone was cranking up that music.

Dog reached for the knob of the first door. He turned it and pushed it open, letting a sliver of light stream into the room. Samuel was standing in the center with his back to us. He let out a strangled scream when the light crawled up his backside, but he never flinched. He just stood there like a statue while the ray seared his skin.

I panicked and stepped inside, slamming the door shut to block the light.

Dog yanked on the knob. "Open the door, Charley!" I could barely hear him over the music blaring. It was so loud that my head was starting to pound.

I tried the door but it wouldn't budge. "It won't open!" I yelled.

My back hit the wall when I saw something sparkle through the darkness. It was coming from the center of the room. From Samuel. A veil of shimmering light covered him as if he'd been showered with millions of tiny crystals, each one reflecting sunlight. But there was no light in the room.

Feeling my way along the walls, I came around to face Samuel. His eyes were ruby-red, and his gaze was fixed on mine. "What did he do to you?" I didn't even know if he could hear me over the loud music, but I knew he could see me through the darkness.

I stepped closer and reached for him, bringing my hand within inches of the strange light. When his lips moved, I stopped.

No, he mouthed, his eyes glowing brighter.

Without thinking, my fingers grazed the veil. A spark lit up the space between us, and a flash of light raced up my arm. It traveled across my shoulders and down my torso, shocking me like the sting of a jellyfish. The pain crescendoed, so strong now that it brought me to my knees.

I fell to the floor and everything faded to black, the pain radiating through me like fire. When it mercifully subsided and my vision returned, someone else was in the room and staring down at me with glowing eyes.

Shane Ronan.

The music suddenly stopped, replaced by pounding on the door and growls coming from the other side. A high-pitched sound filled my ears as Ronan vanished, and all I could hear were the wolves yipping and howling in the distance.

After climbing to my feet, I steadied myself and made my way along the wall, yanking on the door. Light flooded into the room when it opened. After stumbling out, I slammed the door shut to protect Samuel from the rays and fell to the floor. The cold nose of a wolf against my cheek was the last thing I remembered before falling into darkness again.

* * *

Candy helped me sit up and stuffed another pillow behind my back. "How you feeling, honey?"

I was in the spare bedroom at the Cauldron, and everything started to rush back: the warehouse. The dark room. Samuel.

"We have to get him out of there." I tried to climb off the bed but stopped when my head started to spin.

Candy grabbed my shoulders to steady me. "Slow down, Charley, or you'll face-plant on the floor."

Dog came into the room carrying a cup of something hot and steaming and approached the bed.

"Is that coffee? Bless you," I said, reaching for it.

Candy grabbed it from his hand. "It's tea, and it's for me." She took a sip and smiled at Dog. "Thank you, sweetie. Would you mind getting Charley a cup too?"

"Never mind." I could have used some coffee, though. "What time is it?"

"It's almost five o'clock," Candy said.

"In the afternoon?" I started to panic and tried to get up again, attempting it slowly this time. I managed to sit on the edge of the bed.

Dog frowned. "Where do you think you're going?"

"Where do you think? I can't believe you let me sleep all day." Had they lost their minds? "Samuel's in that room. And he's got some weird... sparkly stuff floating around him."

Dog and Candy glanced at each other. "Maybe I should get her some coffee," Dog said with a raised brow.

"I'm not crazy." Neither of them seemed to agree with me. "Didn't you see it?" I said to Dog.

"I didn't get a chance. When you started screaming in that room..."

Screaming?

"...we tried to break the door down. That's when that damn whistle kicked us in the head."

My brows scrunched together. "I didn't hear any—" Then I remembered a shrill noise filling my ears just before Ronan vanished, and the sounds the wolves had made on the other side of the door. It was awful.

"That frequency hit us hard. By the time Mag and I shifted and shook it off, you stumbled out of that room and slammed the door shut behind you."

"Are you telling me Shane Ronan used a dog whistle on you?" I asked. His tense jaw ticked as a growl snaked up from his throat. "I'll take that as a yes."

Dog's lips curled into a snarl. "It took us off guard, that's all. It won't happen again. That vampire will have to come up with a better trick next time."

"Samuel is in that room," I said. "And what the hell was that music all about?"

"Torture."

"No kidding. I felt like my head was going to explode."

Candy narrowed her eyes. "What kind of music?"

"Death metal," Dog said. "The kind that makes you want to stab yourself in the head. It's meant to disorient. Keep a person awake for days until they start to break. Ronan was probably using it to weaken Samuel."

I couldn't get the look in Samuel's eyes out of my mind. It was like he was trapped. "Samuel was just standing there like a statue in the middle of the room with this... I don't even know how to describe it. He had this shimmer around him. When I touched it, it was like electricity was racing through me. Like I was burning inside." I shuddered from the memory. "It hurt like a mother."

"Well, it knocked you out good," Candy said.

"Any idea what it could have been?"

"Honey, I'm a witch, not an electrician. But here's some advice. If you see something like it again, don't touch it."

Mag came through the bedroom door, grinning when he saw me sitting up. "Welcome back, sunshine."

"I don't feel very sunny."

He handed me a paper bag. "Thought you might be hungry when you woke up."

There was a chocolate donut inside. Probably from the deli on the next block. Who would have thought Magnus Ryan could be so considerate? And I was hungry. "Thanks."

I took a bite and looked at Dog. "We're going back."

He nodded. "As soon as the sun goes down. Neither one of them is leaving that warehouse until then."

It made my skin crawl just to think about waiting, but we didn't have a choice. We couldn't get Samuel out of there until after dark. "Then take me home." We had about two hours until dusk.

"You can stay here," Candy said.

"No, I can't." I needed to take a quick shower and change clothes. The ones I was wearing were starting to stink. "I'll meet you back at the Stag in an hour so we can figure out how to get Samuel out of there."

I managed to stand up and headed for the door, but my phone rang before I reached it. It was Patrick. After a brief conversation, I hung up.

"Everything all right?" Dog asked when I stood there for a few seconds.

"No. Everything just went to hell."

TWELVE

After Dog dropped me off, I climbed in my truck and made it to Patrick's house in record time. The news wasn't good, but we needed to have the conversation fast so I could get to the Stag. This latest fire would have to wait until after we got Samuel out of that warehouse.

When I walked inside, he was sitting in the corner with his sunglasses on. "You want to shut that door before I light up like an emergency flare?"

"Sorry." I slammed it shut.

The blackout drapes did an excellent job of making the place feel like a funeral parlor. A dim lamp on the table next to him was the only source of illumination for the entire living room. "Do you mind?" I pointed to the light switch next to the door.

"Be my guest."

I flipped the lights on and got a better look at his chartreuse psychedelic robe. It had hints of neon-pink swirled in the pattern. "Now I know why you're wearing sunglasses."

He stood up and looked down at it. "Got it on Etsy."

"Obviously."

When he bent down to grab an envelope from the coffee table, his ass peeked out from under it.

"Jesus, Patrick. Ever heard of underwear?"

The sunglasses dipped down his nose. "No."

All righty, then.

He handed me the envelope. "It's all in there."

Patrick had summarized the test results over the phone, but I needed to see them for myself. After reading the report, I tossed it on the table with a heavy sigh. Glen and Marta, two of our donors, had tested positive for hepatitis C. "Have you shown this to them?"

"Not yet. I just got the results an hour ago. The doc sent someone by to drop them off."

"How did you get blood samples this early? Donors won't be dropping off until tomorrow night." We collected from the donors the night before customer delivery, priding ourselves with supplying fresh product. The only way to get it fresher was to get it straight from the vein, and that was a whole different kind of service.

Patrick stroked his chin. "Like I said the other night, we need to take delivery a day early. Friday morning at the latest so the doc can test it all by the end of day." He nodded to the results on the table. "Those came from samples collected last night. I had a bad feeling I was right about how Mary got hep C, and I wanted an extra day to sort this shit out."

"So you had the donors deliver samples," I said, knowing where he was going with this. "And you were right."

"Delivered? I had to chase down the donors and collect those samples myself." He pointed his finger at me. "Next time, you're going to have your boy, Beau, do it because my time is precious."

"There won't be a next time. Like you said the other night, we need to test every drop that comes through the door, and that means taking delivery earlier."

He nodded. "I'll make sure everyone delivers before dawn tomorrow so I can drop it off at Bishop's office. You can pick it up with the results on your way to the Stag and drop it here so I can get it packaged."

His house wasn't exactly on the way, but he couldn't go out in the afternoon to do it himself. "This is going to suck, especially when we have to tell customers the price is going up." To make it worse, we needed to short the orders because of the bad blood this week. We were down two donors.

"I'll notify Glen and Marta to let them know we're severing ties."

"Don't you think that's a little extreme?"

He deadpanned me. "Those reckless assholes infected our blood supply. They're gone."

"Right. What the hell was I thinking?"

He grabbed my keys from the coffee table and handed them to me. "Now get out of here. I need to get some rest."

"By the way," I said on my way to the door, "did you stop by the hospital to see Mary?"

"I did. Slipped her a little blood, so she should be feeling better by now."

I wished I'd had time to go over there to see her myself, but I'd been busy. "I'll try to give her a call and see how she's doing."

"Don't worry about it. I'll check on her." He held my gaze for a moment. "I know you've got some shit going on. Want to tell me what it is?"

That man knew me better than I knew myself. I wanted to tell him what was happening with Samuel, but I didn't have time, and it would only worry him. He didn't need the distraction. He needed to hold the co-op together because I couldn't.

I shook my head. "It's nothing."

After reading my bullshit, a weak smile crossed his face. He pulled his eyes away from mine and started walking toward his bedroom. "I'm sure you'll be boring the hell out of me with it when you decide you need a shoulder."

As I was walking out the door, I stopped and looked back at him. "Do you think they know?"

"Do I think who knows what?"

"Glen and Marta. Why would they give you blood samples if they knew they'd come back positive for hepatitis?"

He shrugged. "Maybe they were rolling the dice and praying for faulty test results."

"But they're not bad vampires. I can't imagine either one of them intentionally infecting humans with something like hepatitis C. It doesn't make sense."

"I don't know, Charley." He grabbed his phone from the side table on the way out of the room. "But I'm about to find out."

* * *

Beau was already at the Stag when I got there. He was opening tonight, and I was about to tell him he was in charge for the evening. I'd also asked Tucker to come in so we'd have three bartenders working instead of two, seeing as how Dog and I wouldn't be around tonight.

I didn't see Dog's truck when I pulled up, but he was supposed to be here by now so we could discuss the plan for getting Samuel out of that warehouse. "Have you seen Dog?"

"Yeah, he's in the back with Mag." Beau started wiping down the bar. "Something going on tonight?"

"You could say that. In fact, you're in charge."

"Yeah?" There was a slight smile on his face as he bobbed his head. "I can handle it."

Thursdays had been busy nights lately, so it made me nervous just to think about it.

"Tucker and Lucy are both coming in," I said. "Just in case. But the kitchen is closed."

That seemed to dampen his joy. "Two nights in one week? Customers are going to bitch about that."

I nodded to the order window. "Feel free to flip burgers if you feel like it." I wasn't serious, but I could see the wheels turning in his head as he considered it. "Don't even think about it, Beau. Dog will kill you. The kitchen's definitely closed."

I headed down the hallway to find Dog and Mag. When I walked into the back room, the two of them were strategizing. "Have you come up with a plan, or are we going in there blind and obliterating anything with fangs?" Except for Samuel, of course. If he still had his fangs. That bloody warning that Ronan had left in Samuel's chamber still weighed heavy on my mind.

"We're waiting to hear if Max got that text or not," Dog said. "Two very different scenarios depending on whether we're walking into a crowded warehouse or an empty one."

Dog had told me the pack was coming with us for backup, so one way or another we'd be well prepared to kill that vampire.

"Any preference?" I asked.

"A crowded one. One with a whole lot of distractions."

Dog was about to call Loki to see where they were when there was a knock on the back door.

Max was standing in the alley with Loki and Lux when he opened it. "About damn time."

"Where's the rest of the pack?" I licked my lips because suddenly they felt very dry.

Dog motioned them in. "We don't need the others."

"You sure about that?"

He came closer and looked me in the eye. "These are my best wolves, Charley. You know that. Besides, this place is going to have security. I don't think we'll get a dozen wolves past the front door."

He made a good point, and I trusted his decision.

Max's phone dinged. He pulled it out and looked at it. "Guess what I just got?"

The gods were looking out for us. "There's a fight tonight?"

"Yes, ma'am. We just got lucky."

* * *

"We can't just stroll up to the door and walk in there," I said. After Ronan had left that trail of breadcrumbs to lead us here this morning and then manipulated us once we were inside, I was thinking more along the lines of a sneak attack. Maybe we could go in through that back door again.

"Why not? He knows we're coming." Dog started walking toward the building. "Let's just get this over with."

Perfect. We were strolling right back into Ronan's waiting arms.

I took a therapeutic breath and followed him. "You'd think a bunch of wolves and a witch could outplay one vampire."

Dog glanced back at me. "That's your problem, Charley. You're underestimating that vampire. Don't."

I'd looked into Ronan's eyes the other night. Seen the cunning in them. The darkness. So Dog was right.

He glanced back and forth between Mag and Lux. "I bark, you come running." They were staying outside because he determined that even getting two wolves past the front door was going to be a challenge for Max.

The area around the warehouse was packed with cars wherever there was an empty spot. We'd parked at the far edge of the lot, just in case some asshole decided to block us in and hinder a smooth getaway. Had the place been visible from the road, someone would have probably reported suspicious activity to the police by now.

There was no music coming from the warehouse when we

approached the entrance, but it would have been hard to hear it over all the noise coming from inside. The crowd cheering. You would have thought it was a UFC fight taking place in there.

A guy stepped in front of us at the door. The bouncer, I assumed. His eyes were completely black, and he was just as big as Dog. He glanced at the phone in Max's hand displaying the text message. The golden ticket to enter. "You," he said, motioning him in.

Max looked back at the three of us. "They're with me?"

The guy shook his head. "Only you." Then his eyes wandered to me, his grin revealing a set of fangs.

As his tongue played with the corner of his mouth, I forced myself to smile back. "And I was really looking forward to seeing a little blood tonight." I lowered my eyes to his fangs. "I'd be grateful."

You brainless piece of meat.

The vampire's gaze softened, his pupils shrinking to reveal a set of blue irises. Then he stepped aside.

That was easy. I just prayed he didn't come looking for me before we found Samuel and got out of there.

He held his hand out when I tried to walk past him. "Twenty. Each."

Twenty?

Everyone reached into their pockets, but I beat them to it and handed the guy eighty bucks. I'd grabbed some cash from the register on my way out, just in case. And there went my spending money for the week.

We continued inside. The place was packed, and I could barely see across the warehouse to where that room was located. I had no idea if Samuel was still in there, or in the other room next to it, but I was going to find out.

"We need to work our way down there," I said to Dog, nodding toward the other end.

"Slow down, Charley." His eyes surveyed the crowd. "We can't just walk in there and escort Samuel out."

"Sure we can. Who's going to stop us? A bunch of locals?" Most of the crowd was probably human, with a few vampires mixed in to make the fights more interesting. They were no match for the wolves.

"Are you forgetting what happened this morning? I guarantee you Ronan knows we're here, and he's got something planned for us." Dog looked at the other end. "And those vampires standing near the door of that room aren't locals."

"Vampires? Where?" I couldn't see over the growing crowd.

Dog lifted me off the floor like a child and pointed. "Right there."

I spotted them. "How do you know they're vampires?"

"Trust me, they are."

They looked like the type that hung out at the Beast. "Okay, you can put me down now." I straightened my shirt when my feet touched the floor again. "Next time, warn me before you do that."

He ignored me and continued to stare at those vampires. "They're gonna be a problem."

"To the left." Max nodded toward the center of the room.

Adrenaline hit me square in the chest when I saw a chair on a platform on the side of the makeshift ring. Shane Ronan was sitting in it. His legs were crossed, and he was balancing a metal rod against the floor with one hand as his eyes focused on two men in the ring. His fake facade was long gone. The vampire sitting in that chair was the dark creature I'd come face-to-face with the other night. The formidable vampire who sent a wave of fear through me.

"There he is," I said.

Dog followed my gaze. "That's Ronan?"

"Yep. The real Ronan."

What I would have given for one of those sunlight bullets at that moment. Samuel had introduced me to the rare weapon. He'd described them as something to incapacitate a vampire, but when he used the last one in existence on his own maker, on Shane Ronan's maker, it had done far more than just slow Victor Steele down. That bullet had incinerated the vampire from the inside out.

My skin began to crawl as the vampire's head slowly turned, his eyes catching mine from across the room. He gripped the end of the rod tighter as a smile slid up his face.

"He definitely knows we're here." A slight gasp escaped me when I felt something like a tendril work its way around my body, similar to the feeling I got the other night when he showed up at the bar. When Ronan's eyes locked on mine again and the sensation grew more intense, I backed up and hit a wall of cool, hard flesh. When I turned around, a pair of dark eyes was peering down at me.

"Well, hello there," he said.

I flinched. "What are you doing here?"

THIRTEEN

"I could ask you the same question." Ian Masterson glanced at Dog and his men. "Girls' night out with the wolves?"

I ignored him and looked back across the room. Ronan had shifted his attention to the fight taking place in the ring. "I think we're here for the same reason."

He followed my gaze. "So that's the bastard. I'm here to find out what he's up to."

"Way ahead of you, Ian. I already know what he's up to."

"Are you planning to tell me?"

The warehouse went up in a roar when one of the fighters flew backward and fell. The one still standing went in for the kill, pummeling his opponent with savage blows to his head and face. The man on the floor finally went still, and his opponent threw his arms in the air triumphantly, his smile revealing a mouthful of bloodstained teeth.

Ian watched the spectacle and groaned. "That was anti-climactic."

"You're into this crap?" It shouldn't have surprised me.

His eyes settled back on mine. "I had money on the dead guy."

When I looked back at the ring, the man on the floor wasn't moving. "He's dead?" Max hadn't mentioned that the fights escalated to murder.

Ian's eyes wandered back to the man. "He's still breathing."

Ronan got up from his chair with that rod gripped in his hand. He approached the loser and flipped it upside down, the tip smoldering and glowing bright orange. Then he flipped it again and pressed the hot tip to the man's forehead, searing that mark into his skin as his semiconscious body writhed.

Two men emerged from the crowd and grabbed the man to haul him away. Then Ronan turned his gaze on the winner and crooked his finger. The man backed up but met a very large roadblock standing behind him. He struggled as a vampire manhandled him back to the center of the ring.

Ronan cocked his brows and brought the hot tip to the fighter's eyes. "You know the rules." Then he lowered the iron to the man's neck. The fighter screamed as it seared his skin, and the vampire released him as he fell to his knees.

A shudder ran through me. "This is barbaric."

"They know what they're getting into when they walk in that ring," Max said.

Ian threw him a glance. "Speaking from experience?"

"Fuck off," Max growled.

A cold smile barely raised Ian's lips. "Is that a yes?"

Max looked like he was about to shift and jump Ian, but Loki stepped between them. "Not now."

The noise picked up again when Ronan addressed the crowd. "And now for the main event." He pulled the winner back to his feet and shook him violently. "Wake up. It's time for the second round." Then he motioned to the other side of the room.

"Hmm..." Ian mused. "I wonder what's next?"

I already knew what came next. That human winner was

about to face off against a much more powerful opponent—a vampire.

A commotion started up. It was coming from the direction of that room at the other end of the warehouse. Suddenly I couldn't breathe as Samuel was led out and practically dragged toward the ring. My heart was thundering all the way into my throat as we locked eyes for a moment. His gaze was dull and lifeless, and that strange shimmer of light was gone. Samuel looked like he'd been drugged.

Dog stepped in front of me. "Don't watch."

Ian's face perked up. "Well, this should be interesting."

"Shut up!" Dog growled.

A wicked grin crawled up Ronan's face as I ran toward Samuel, my palm on fire with building energy.

Dog grabbed me and pulled me back. "This is what he wants. Don't give the bastard the satisfaction."

I stared at him for a second. "So we just watch?"

Dog went silent. Loki and Max had nothing to say either.

To my surprise, Ian was the most comforting of all of them. "I think Samuel can take a human."

"Look at him! He's been drugged!"

"That doesn't work with vampires," Ian said without a trace of concern.

"Well, they've done something to him."

"No one's killing Samuel," Dog said, glancing at his wolves before looking back at me. "This is our opportunity." He nodded to Samuel as they shoved him forward. "He's right there waiting to be plucked from that ring. When the moment is right, we're going to grab him and get the hell out of here."

Ian shifted his eyes to the left and then to the right. "Not with all those vampires positioned around the room."

Dog followed his gaze. "*Fuck.*"

"Fuck is right. I know what they're capable of. Most of them were on my payroll before they defected and went to work for

Victor Steele. Seems they're still working for the vampire in a roundabout way."

I glanced at the army of vampires poised to stop us. "You mean they're loyal to his progeny now. The one who didn't kill his maker." They were on Shane Ronan's payroll now, and we were royally fucked.

The crowd started to stir again, restless for blood. I could see it in their eyes. When the *fight* was over, the winner would get to take a bite out of the loser, and Samuel had obviously been set up to fail. And if Ronan had extracted Samuel's fangs, he was a sitting duck. There'd be no stopping the winner from bleeding him dry. Then I'd become the final pawn in Ronan's game. The knife in Samuel's chest as he was forced to watch *me* watching him die.

That wasn't going to happen.

I pulled myself together and looked at the wolves. "What do we do?"

Dog kept his eyes on the ring. "We wait."

"For Samuel to be pulverized?" If he thought I would stand there and watch that happen, he was out of his mind.

The frenzy was building as Samuel's opponent stepped back into the ring. He wasn't a local. Must have been from a nearby town. There were a lot of people in that warehouse I'd never seen before, so news of Ronan's fight club must have spread beyond Crimson.

Ronan stood up and strolled toward Samuel who was standing like a zombie in the center of the ring, and he was still gripping that metal rod.

"This is insane," I said to Dog. "We have to stop this." When I took a step toward the ring, he grabbed me again.

The anger in my eyes gave him pause, but he refused to let go. "You need to trust me, Charley. We rush that ring and it'll be raining vampires."

I glanced around the warehouse again. At the arsenal Shane

Ronan had recruited to keep his criminal enterprise running. As usual, Dog was right.

The crowd roared. When I turned to look, Samuel was stumbling across the ring. He was shaking his head, and blood was coming from his split lip. The man came forward and landed his fist in Samuel's jaw. Samuel was knocked off his feet, his head snapping back at a gruesome angle as he hit the floor.

I couldn't watch any more of it. "Tell me you have a plan." It was difficult to breathe with the tightening of my chest. "Because if you don't, I do." I had a clear shot at Ronan, my hand glowing as I focused on that vampire who had pure blood-lust in his eyes.

Dog snatched my wrist, careful not to get too close to my hand and suffer my wrath. "You do that and none of us are getting out of here."

Loki was texting on his phone, and Max was watching the ring with his own bloodlust. The wolf was jonesing for a taste. And Ian had wandered off or maybe even left the building. They were all acting like nothing was happening. Like Samuel wasn't about to get his head bashed in.

And why wasn't Samuel healing? He was still a vampire.

As I looked back at the ring, Samuel slowly turned, his eyes fixing on mine. I could see clarity in them for the first time since he was led out. While he was distracted, his opponent came at him again.

Ronan whistled to get the fighter's attention. He tossed the metal rod to him as a vicious grin played on his lips.

"Samuel!" It was a whisper that felt like a scream when I watched the man raise the rod in the air. As I yanked my arm free from Dog's grip, a ball of light haphazardly escaped my hand and sailed across the room.

A flash of life filled Samuel's eyes when he saw the magic hurtling toward him. He stepped out of its path and threw his hand up, catching the metal rod as it came down toward his skull.

Ronan's fists clenched as his head snapped in my direction. There was pure hatred in his eyes, which quickly turned back to Samuel. Then he gave a signal to his hired vampires, and they converged on us from every direction.

The sound of breaking glass filled the warehouse as wolves flooded in through the windows. Most of the pack had shown up, distracting the vampires. When the crowd panicked and people funneled past me toward the exit, I caught a familiar face in my periphery. It was one of the co-op donors. He saw me looking at him and quickly disappeared into the flood of people trying to escape.

I pushed against the flow of the crowd, trying to view the ring. Through the chaos, I saw Samuel grab his opponent by the neck and lift him off the floor. Then he lowered the man back down and sank his fangs into his neck. His fangs! My breath hitched when Samuel dropped him to the floor and brought his sapphire eyes back to mine, his mouth glistening with blood.

The crowd suddenly engulfed me, and Samuel slipped from view. I was trapped and couldn't breathe from the powerful crush. As I started to lose consciousness, the bodies around me began to part as Samuel plowed through them. He grabbed me and forced us through the thick crowd until we came out on the other side.

After catching my breath, I took his face in my hands and searched his eyes. "You're okay." Then I looked at his mouth. "And you've got fangs!"

He frowned. "Why wouldn't I?"

I shook my head. "Never mind. We need to get out of here."

Samuel glanced up. "I'll shove you through one of those windows." It was at least six feet off the ground. "Then you need to run."

"I'm not going anywhere without you and Dog." Speaking of which, I couldn't see the wolves anywhere.

His eyes turned nearly black. "I need to find Ronan."

Before I could argue about it, he lifted me off the ground. "Put me down, Samuel!"

"Damn it, Charley! He'll use you against me." With that nugget of information, he shoved me all the way through the window.

I hit the ground on my ass and winced as my tailbone began to throb. When I finally climbed to my feet, I tried to reach the window to get back inside. It was too high up, so I hobbled around front, barely avoiding getting trampled by people still fleeing the building. It was like watching bumper cars in the parking lot as vehicles tried to make it onto the dirt road to get out of there.

Around the corner, I found a window low enough to look inside. All I could see through the dirty glass were wolves and vampires going at each other. The rest had finally cleared out. I considered going back in, but besides Samuel giving me an earful, Dog would tan my hide—if I made it back out alive. And Samuel was right. I'd be a prime weapon for Ronan to use against him. But something needed to happen soon because that battle taking place inside seemed to be in a dead heat. A distraction was necessary to break it up.

Through the window, I looked up at the fragile ceiling and wondered if I could bring a section down with a strategically thrown light bomb. It was risky, though. The heavy rafters could kill a wolf or decapitate a vampire.

As I was anguishing over my options, I heard something in the distance. Something familiar.

I glanced up, but it couldn't be. "Don't be ridiculous," I muttered, pulling my eyes away from the sky.

Inside the building, a body slammed into the wall next to the window, jolting me out of the absurd thought. The vampire pressed his hands to the glass and looked out at me, running his bloody tongue along one of the panes with a lewd grin. I backed away from the window and glanced at Dog's truck parked at the edge of the empty lot, seriously considering driving it into the side of the building. That would create a major distraction, although I'd be on the hook to buy Dog a new truck. Even if I had the nerve to do it, the keys were in his pocket.

The eerie sound I'd heard a moment earlier came again, only this time it was louder. I looked up at the sky when suddenly it was all I could hear. It was all around me. Everywhere.

The crows flew overhead like a black cloud of death, circling the building until they narrowed into a tight formation above it. I searched for Rex, but it was too dark outside and impossible to spot a single white feather among what must have been thousands of birds. He was in there, though. I could feel him.

In that moment, I knew without a doubt that Rex was my familiar.

As I was beginning to wonder if they were waiting for me to give some kind of signal—a wave of a hand or an order I wasn't aware of—a single crow dove toward the building and through a broken window. Another one followed, and within seconds, the entire cloud funneled into the warehouse. It was spectacular and terrifying.

I stepped away from the building when I heard an ungodly commotion coming from inside. Screams and howls echoed through the windows as a horde of vampires exited through the front door, each covered with flapping crows anchored to their skin by sharp talons. They ran toward the woods, the birds letting go as they disappeared into the forest.

While the crows sailed over the trees in pursuit, Rex came back around and did a flyby over my head. He came to perch on top of the building and stared down at me, his white feather catching the moonlight.

"I guess we need to have a talk," I said to him, wondering how one communicated with a familiar. I had no doubt that crow understood every word I said. I just wished I had a clue how to read what was in his mind.

He flew back into the sky and followed the other crows when the wolves started emerging from the building, most of them taking off into the woods. Dog and Loki came out a minute later fully dressed. Thank God Samuel was right behind them, and walking by himself.

Ian Masterson stumbled out last, with no crows clinging to him but covered with small gashes. "Fucking flying rats!"

"I guess they assumed you were one of the bad guys." The attack wasn't severe enough to drive him into the forest with the others, so it was probably just a little payback for his bad behavior at my house the other night.

He glanced at Samuel. "I don't see any damage to your vampire boyfriend over there."

"Where's Ronan?" I asked, ignoring Ian's whining. Samuel hadn't dragged him out, so either he was a pile of ash on the warehouse floor or he'd escaped and we were back to square one.

"He's gone," Dog said. "The fucking vampire disappeared."

I rubbed my sore backside and groaned. "Now we have to start looking for him all over again."

"We'll find him," Samuel said, looking a little unsteady. He grabbed Loki's arm when he started to sway. Then he went down like a sack of potatoes.

"Samuel!" I dropped to my knees next to him, with no clue what to do. He was a vampire. It wasn't like I could check his pulse.

Ian bent down and forced one of Samuel's eyes open. "I don't know what Ronan did to him, but you might want to get him out of here before those vampires come back." Then he straightened up and extended his hand to me.

He was being awfully chivalrous this evening.

After helping me up, he glanced back down at Samuel. "I suggest you get him to wherever he rests and leave him to recover. A few days should do the trick."

We didn't have a few days. Ronan would make another move quickly.

"Let's get him out of here." Dog hoisted Samuel over his shoulder and headed for the truck.

While he and Loki got in the cab, I climbed in the bed of the truck with Samuel and rested his head in my lap while we drove back to town. I'd seen him like this before. The night Victor Steele nearly killed him. But Samuel had come back with a vengeance, and I'd make sure he did it again, even if I had to feed him half my blood. The gloves were off. The next time I came face-to-face with Shane Ronan, that vampire was dust.

FOURTEEN

Candy hovered over Samuel for a few more seconds and then straightened up. "I'm no expert on vampires, but I think he'll be fine. He just needs some serious rest."

Dog and I had somehow managed to carry Samuel down those narrow stairs to his chamber, only dropping him once. After putting a fresh sheet on the bed and disposing of those mystery fangs, we got his bloody clothes off and tucked him in. He hadn't so much as blinked an eye since. I'd started to think Ian was wrong about Samuel's prognosis and decided to call Candy over to take a look at him.

"Thanks for coming," I said. "I know it's late."

She smirked. "Since when has a clock ever stopped you?"

That was the truth. I'd shown up at the Cauldron many a night at an ungodly hour needing her help, and she'd never batted an eye.

She glanced back at Samuel. "Give him time. But if he hasn't opened his eyes within twenty-four hours, you might want to call someone a little more qualified to assess his condition." She frowned. "Like Ian Masterson."

"He already told me the same thing, only he suggested I wait a few days for him to come around."

Candy turned thoughtful. "You said Shane Ronan is running some kind of illegal fight club outside of town?"

"Was," I corrected. "I'm pretty sure we shut him down. We drew a lot of attention to that warehouse tonight, and I doubt folks around here are going to jeopardize their jobs and reputations to watch their neighbors get the shit kicked out of them again."

Candy snickered. "What reputations?"

For all I knew, that fight club would be back up and running again by tomorrow night. I had a feeling its only purpose had been to stage this whole confrontation, though. To trap, torture, and kill Samuel right in front of me. Now that he was safe and sound down here in his chamber, the whole damn town could go out to that warehouse and get their depraved kicks for all I cared.

"Speaking of reputations," Candy glanced at the wooden device against the wall, "I wouldn't go showing that contraption over there to anyone else, if you want to keep your own intact. Don't get me wrong. I'm not a prude." A playful grin spread across her face. "It's not the first time I'm seeing one of those things."

It took a few seconds for her comments to register. "Wait. You think—"

"What you and Samuel do in private is no one's business, but you know how people talk in this town. You'll have the preacher over at the church planting signs in the yard warning people about the devil who lives here."

"That thing came with the house," I said. "It was here when Samuel bought the place."

"Oh." She narrowed her eyes at me. "Well, then forget I said anything."

Gladly.

"Come on. I'll walk you out."

She started up the narrow steps and looked back at me. "You might be putting me in that bed next to Samuel if I break my ankle maneuvering these god-awful stairs. You'd think a hobbit lived in this house."

I glanced down at her shoes. "Why are you wearing high heels?"

"I didn't expect to be performing a death-defying descent into a dungeon. And I was in the middle of something when you called."

That was fair.

"And why do we have to climb all the way up to the bedroom to get out of there? Isn't there a shortcut through the cellar from the first floor?"

That was a good question. "I guess." It was only the second time I'd been down there, and I didn't have a clue where the cellar door was, if there was one. Clifford Pullman had built that chamber, and since a vampire was most vulnerable when resting, he'd probably sealed off the cellar door for security reasons.

After making it up to the bedroom and coming back down to the foyer on the first floor, Candy nearly tripped over Sebastian lounging on the bottom step. "If I don't break an ankle going down to that chamber, I'll break it tripping over that damn cat." She looked up at the peeling wallpaper and the creepy painting hanging to her right. "This is a house of horrors."

"Then I better get you out of here." I reached for the door. "Thanks again for coming over."

"Now, wait a minute." She waved me off and peeked into the living room. "I've been wanting to see the inside of this house since I moved to Crimson. Why don't you give me a tour?"

What I really wanted to do was get back to Samuel. But I'd

appease her curiosity. It was the least I could do since she came over here at such a late hour.

Candy followed me into the living room, her eyes assessing the furniture. "Kind of dreary, isn't it?"

"The place came furnished. Samuel wants to redecorate eventually."

She pointed to a doorway. "That must be the study." After going inside and looking around, she stopped at one of the bookcases and ran her fingers along the spines of the books. "Did the place come with all of these too?"

I shrugged. "I guess. I don't think Samuel came to town with much more than a suitcase of clothes."

She continued to peruse the titles, and then her eyes flicked up to the top of the shelf. "There's something up there." There was a sliding ladder against the bookcase, so she climbed it and reached for whatever had been shoved against the wall at the top. "Well, isn't this interesting," she said as she stepped down to the floor with it.

I looked at the oversized tome in her hands. It had a black cloth cover with a red symbol on the front. "What is it?"

She flipped to the table of contents. "Looks like a manual."

"A manual for what?" There was no title on the front. Just that strange symbol.

"A bunch of people who like to wear robes out in the woods and pretend they know how to conjure spirits." She flipped the pages and pointed to a picture of a naked woman tied to a device similar to the one in Samuel's chamber. "Looks like they also practice sex magic. I guess the rumors about Pullman were true."

"That's what Dog said when he saw that contraption in the chamber. How come I never heard any of these rumors?"

She continued to flip through the pages. "You were only a child when Cliff Pullman bit the dust."

I snorted. "I wasn't that young."

"You were young enough." She closed the book and set it on the table. "Of course, I moved here right after he died, but I got an earful from the Squad. A lot of people in this town were glad to see him go because he made us all look bad."

"You mean witches?"

She shrugged. "Witches, conjurers. Anyone who knows how to wield a legitimate spell."

That was interesting. Made me want to snoop around the house myself to see what other secrets this place held. "You want to see the kitchen?"

She looked at the time and started walking toward the door. "It's past my bedtime. You can show me the rest of the house next time I visit."

After seeing her out, I went to the back of the house and started looking for that mystery door. The stairs from the master bedroom led to the cellar and a second set continued down to the chamber. There had to be a door leading to the cellar. But every door I opened in the hallway and kitchen turned out to be a closet. Maybe I was right and Pullman had sealed it off.

I went back up to the bedroom and opened the closet door, taking the stairs back down to the chamber. Samuel was still out cold, and Sebastian was lying on the bed next to him. "How did you get down here?" The closet door in the bedroom was definitely closed before I came down just now, and unless I was losing my mind, Candy almost tripped over that cat on our way down to the foyer earlier. Now I was convinced there was another way in here.

"Move over." I got undressed and turned the lights off, nudging Sebastian aside so I could curl up next to Samuel. There was no way I was leaving him here alone until morning, while he was so vulnerable. Especially with Shane Ronan still out there. I reached for the obsidian stone around my neck and clutched it tightly. If that vampire came for Samuel tonight, he'd have to go through me first.

* * *

When I woke, I forgot where I was for a moment. The chamber was so dark I couldn't even make out shapes in the room. The feel of the velvet comforter draped over me brought it all rushing back.

I sat up and fumbled for my phone on the nightstand, panicking about the time. But before I could find it, I was struck from the side so hard it knocked the wind out of me. My back hit the bed as I fought to free my arms from the hands pinning them, but the weight on top of me was crushing. And then I felt something digging into my shoulder, causing a sharp pain to radiate down my arm.

A familiar scent filled my nose. "Samuel?"

The weight lifted off me, and the lights came on. Samuel was standing next to the bed, naked, his eyes filled with horror as he gazed at me. "I've hurt you."

I shook my head. "I'm fine."

He came closer and tilted my head to the side. "I bit you."

"What?" My hand went to the spot where I'd felt the pain. It had blood on it when I pulled it away. It shook me. The thought of what *could* have happened if even a few more seconds had passed before he realized it was me. "You were a little aggressive this time, but you've bitten me before, Samuel."

He kept staring at my shoulder. "Not like that."

The color of his eyes darkened as his lips parted slightly. They were fixed on the wound, and I could see the hunger in them. His need to feed and heal from whatever Ronan had done to him. I'd seen that look once before. The night Victor Steele tried to kill him and I brought him back.

Samuel stepped closer, a low moan coming from his throat. There was something both exciting and unsettling in the way he was looking at me, and it had me moving away from him on the bed until my back hit the headboard.

"Don't be afraid of me."

I shook my head slowly. "I'm not, but the way you're looking at me is making me a little nervous." There was that hunger on his face again. It was my blood driving it, so I tilted my head and offered my neck to him. "You need to feed, Samuel."

He continued toward me. "I love you for that, Charley, but right now I need something else from you." His eyes flicked to the wooden contraption next to the bed. "Do you trust me?"

I glanced at it, suppressing the sudden pang of fear racing through me before looking back at him. "Yes."

Before I could catch my breath, he pulled me off the bed and had my back pressed to the device. He bound my wrists with those leather straps. Then he parted my legs and bent down to tie my ankles as well.

My heart was beating wildly. "You'd untie me if I asked you to, wouldn't you?"

He got to his knees and pressed his lips to my stomach, wrapping his fingers around my waist as his thumbs stroked the curves of my hips. "You'll have to trust me, Charley," he whispered against my shivering skin.

A blast of heat hit me in my core when he began to rise and his mouth continued up my body, lingering on my breasts, his fangs teasing my very sensitive nipples. I tried to yank my arms free from the leather, to pull him into me, to relieve the ache building between my legs. But I was completely at his mercy.

Samuel pulled back to look at me, his eyes glassy with desire. I gasped when his fingers slid inside me, and I saw my own desire reflected in his dark eyes. I wanted to spread myself wider for him, but all I could do was squirm against the restraints. Then he dropped back down to his knees and brushed his lips against my inner thigh before sinking his fangs into my skin, the ache inside me growing painful as he fed.

His hands gripped my hips as his fangs finally released me. "Look at me, Charley," he said with a deep, commanding voice.

My head fell forward to look down, my back arching as a rush of pleasure shot up my torso when his tongue slipped between my thighs. The sensation kept building, but just as I was about to explode, my ankles were suddenly freed and Samuel was back on his feet and gazing into my eyes. "Trust," he whispered into my ear as he untied my hands.

As my arms fell free, he picked me up and carried me to the bed, driving himself into me the moment my back hit the mattress. I rolled my hips, raising them to meet his forceful thrusts. I couldn't get enough of him. Couldn't get him deep enough. And just when I was about to come, he sank his fangs into my neck and gave me the orgasm of my life. I screamed as it rolled through me, collapsing against the mattress when it finally reached its peak and began to fade. Then we lay there, sated and exhausted.

I had a lot of questions for Samuel about what happened in that warehouse, but right now I was more interested in discussing what had just happened between us. We needed to talk about it before the euphoria faded away completely.

I lifted my head off his chest to look at him. "That was really intense, Samuel. What was all that stuff about trust?"

"Your blood does things to me." He stroked the back of my head, holding my gaze until my body started to heat up again. "I guess I needed more from you tonight than just sex. I needed all of you. Intimacy. And there's nothing more intimate than making yourself completely vulnerable to someone." He brushed his thumb over my bottom lip. "I'm a vampire, Charley. My needs will surprise you at times."

It was a little scary, but it was also exhilarating. I'd let him tie me to that contraption again in a heartbeat. But if Samuel expected all of me, I wanted all of him. "You never finished telling me what happened between you and Shane Ronan the night you were turned? I trusted you completely tonight, so now you need to trust me."

Samuel ran his fingers up and down my back with a featherlight touch, gazing at me for a moment. "Are you sure you want to hear this?"

"I want to know everything." I wasn't letting him shut me out tonight. No more secrets. "It's time for you to finish your story."

FIFTEEN

SAMUEL

Boston, 1887

Perfect. I was in a questionable part of town after dark, apparently lost, and now I was being accosted by a stranger eyeing my expensive watch.

The man nodded to my wrist. "Let's have a look at the fancy watch you got there."

"It was a gift, so I'd rather not." I took a step back when he reached for it.

He glanced down at my shoes and inspected my suit as he brought his eyes back up to my face. "You look like you can afford to buy a new one, so let's have it."

"I'd *really* prefer not to give it up." Under the circumstances, it was stupid of me to challenge the man, but I was feeling reckless.

A blow to the back of my head sent me lurching forward. The man demanding my watch caught me and shoved me to the ground, the air escaping my lungs when his boot made contact with my rib cage. As I rolled over, a fist caught me in the face. I lay there half dazed as my watch slipped from my wrist while the other man rifled through my pockets and found my wallet. I heard a scuffle, and the assault abruptly stopped. One of the thugs escaped down the street while the one holding my watch flew against the building.

Still shaky, I managed to climb onto my hands and knees as a dark figure came into view and approached the wall, a shadow engulfing my attacker. A scream followed, and then there was nothing but eerie silence.

"We need to get out of here, Samuel."

I looked up at the man hovering over me. "Ronan?"

"Come on." He offered me his hand. "Get up."

I grabbed a hold of it and pulled myself to my feet. "What are you doing here?"

"Who gives a shit?" A smile flashed across his face. "Just be glad I showed up."

I glanced back at the building, but there was no one there. "I got turned around trying to find my way out of this hellhole. No offense," I quickly added just in case he lived around here.

"None taken. It is a hellhole." He turned around and started walking down the street.

"Where are you going?"

He glanced over his shoulder. "O'Malley's. You want that drink now, dontcha?"

There was nothing I wanted more, except maybe to start the night over.

I touched the back of my head and winced. "I should probably get this checked out."

"At this time of night?" He chuckled. "You really do need a drink."

I caught up to him when he picked up the pace. "What happened to your friend back there?"

"Friend?" He glanced at me sideways. "Maybe you *should* have your head checked out."

"There was someone else back there," I said, but he just

shook his head and kept walking. "I saw him corner one of those men against the building."

I dropped it when a sign for O'Malley's came into view on the next block. The street was so quiet, I thought the place was closed, but when Ronan pulled the door open, I was surprised to see the establishment was full. There was a bar that ran the length of the room and several small tables toward the back, each surrounded by patrons who looked like they'd been cut from the same cloth as those thugs who'd just attacked me.

"Maybe this wasn't such a good idea," I said, feeling every eye in the place turn as we approached the bar.

Ronan let out a sharp laugh. "Don't worry about it. Paddy doesn't go for roughnecks in here."

"Who's Paddy?"

He motioned to the bartender heading our way. "Him."

Paddy tossed a rag over his shoulder as he leveled his heavily lidded eyes on me. Then he turned to Shane. "What're you drinking?"

"Whatever you have on tap." He nodded to me. "He'll have the same along with a shot of whiskey. Better make it a double."

I grabbed a stool and winced as I sat down. "I think the bastards broke my ass."

He snickered. "Wait until you wake up tomorrow."

When Paddy returned with our drinks, I reached for my wallet and remembered it had been stolen back there.

Ronan pulled it from his pocket and handed it over. "I guess you'll be wanting your fancy watch back too, but I wouldn't go flashing it around in here," he warned, slipping it to me under the bar.

"How did you get these?" I stuffed the expensive gift from my father into my pocket. To my recollection, he hadn't gotten anywhere near either of the men who'd helped themselves to my property. But his imaginary friend had.

His eyes lingered on me for a moment. "The watch was

lying next to you on the sidewalk along with your wallet. The bumbling idiots must have dropped them."

"Right..." I said before downing my whiskey and chasing it with the beer. "I appreciate your help tonight, but I should get home. I'll be worthless in the morning if I don't sleep off this headache."

"You're not going anywhere." Ronan took a swallow of beer and smiled as he turned. "We just got here." Then he motioned for Paddy to bring another round.

"Fine. One more, but then I really have to go."

Paddy slid a second shot of whiskey toward me and held Ronan's gaze for a moment before heading down to another customer. He was a big man, and I had no doubt there was a baseball bat on the other side of the bar that he used to dispatch troublemakers swiftly.

With the throbbing in my head getting worse, I grabbed the glass and swallowed the shot. "You still haven't explained how you managed to find me while I was getting the shit kicked out of me back there." Either I had a guardian angel, or he'd followed me from the fight club. The latter seemed more feasible and made me uneasy.

"I live around the corner." He shrugged. "I guess you got lucky tonight when I stumbled on you getting a rough welcome to the neighborhood."

"I guess so." My vision suddenly started to blur, but it sharpened quickly when I thought I caught something in Ronan's eyes. A strange flicker. "What the...?"

His chin lowered as he leaned closer and cocked his head. "You okay, buddy?"

I squeezed my eyes shut, blinking several times after they reopened. His irises looked perfectly normal. "That's some powerful whiskey."

"Well, it ain't for the faint of heart." He leaned back to give me some room.

After tossing some money on the bar, I stood up and grabbed the edge to steady myself. "I need to leave." My window of opportunity was closing fast.

Ronan finished his beer and got up, slowly turning his head to the bartender with a grin. "See you around, Paddy." When he refocused on me, his smile was gone. "I'll walk you to the edge of the neighborhood. Wouldn't want a repeat of earlier tonight." While the color of his eyes looked normal, there was something in them that made me uneasy. Brought on a visceral urge to get the hell away from this place.

I held my hand up to stop him. "I can manage." After stumbling out the door, I struggled to get my balance as I headed up the street. When I glanced over my shoulder, Shane Ronan was leaning against the wall outside of O'Malley's, watching me as he lit a cigarette. If I could just make it a few more blocks north, I stood a chance of getting a carriage to take me the rest of the way home. Then I'd forget I'd ever met the man.

Two blocks up, my vision started to blur again. I was far from being a drunk, and I usually held my whiskey well. I was starting to think something had been slipped into my drink. Suddenly I was turned around again with no idea which way was north. I was walking in circles trying to catch a glimpse of something familiar beyond the buildings. A beacon to lead me out of this godforsaken part of town.

"Careful there," I heard Ronan say from behind me when I stumbled again. "Concrete makes for a nasty pillow."

I hit the ground a second later and rolled onto my back, barely able to focus my eyes. "Why?" I slurred, figuring I'd been his mark since walking into that fight club. "Why didn't you get it over with earlier tonight?"

He took a drag of his cigarette before flicking it into the street and crouching down next to me. "That wouldn't have been any fun, would it?" Then his eyes turned a shade of dark blue, sapphire, and his sandy-blond hair was now jet-black and framed a face I'd never seen before.

I tried to scurry away, but I could barely move. Then he hoisted me over his shoulder like I weighed nothing and carried me up a flight of steps. Next thing I knew, I was lying on a wood floor in a damp and musty room with this stranger standing next to me.

"What are you?" I said as I tried to get up but fell back down. "Are you going to kill me?" I was too confused and exhausted to give a shit anymore.

A smile crossed his face as he planted his feet on either side of my head and looked down at me. "I'm not going to kill you, Samuel." His eyes shot to a doorway. "But he is."

Through the haze that was still obstructing my vision, I could make out someone walking toward us. A tall man dressed all in black. A shadow.

"Well done," the man said.

Ronan bent down and cocked his head, patting my cheek roughly to get my full attention. "I've enjoyed our little game, Samuel." There was a red flicker in his eyes. "But all fun must come to an end eventually."

The dark figure stepped closer and loomed over us.

Ronan straightened up but kept his eyes fixed on mine. "Allow me to introduce you to my maker."

"Your what?" The shadow came closer, his shoes stopping inches from my face. "What do you want from me?" The fog was starting to clear from my head. "Money? I have plenty of that. I can get it for you."

The figure crouched down next to me, revealing his black eyes. "Money? I'm afraid it's too late for that." As the rest of his face came into view, a set of fangs glistened in the moonlight coming through the window. "I want revenge."

I was frozen with fear. Felt like I was glued to the floor. "This isn't real!"

Ronan peered down at me, his lips parting to reveal his own set of fangs. "Oh, it's very real, Samuel."

The shadow leaned closer to whisper in my ear. "I've been watching you, Mr. Cain. Waiting to take my pound of flesh."

I shook my head weakly. "I don't understand."

"But your father will." He lifted my shoulders gently and pulled me against him, brushing his lips along the edge of my jaw until they reached my neck. Paralyzed in his grip, I felt his fangs sink into my throat, my screams filling the room when he dug them deeper. They tore at my flesh as he drained the blood from my veins.

When it was over and I felt my life slipping away, he dropped me to the floor and stood up. "When you see your father in hell," he said, wiping my blood from his mouth with the back of his sleeve, "tell him Victor Steele killed you. His debt has been paid."

SIXTEEN

Now I understood the deep-seated hatred Samuel had for Shane Ronan. That vampire was just as evil as his maker.

"I haven't told you the worst part," Samuel said.

I rolled onto my stomach to look at him. "It gets worse?"

He chuckled. "I'm afraid so. Steele attempted to kill me for revenge. For something my father did."

Samuel hesitated, but I wasn't letting him stop now. Not when we were so close to finally resolving any secrets between us. "You can tell me anything, Samuel. You have to know that by now."

There was conflict, or maybe it was shame, in his eyes when he continued. "It seems my father wasn't the upstanding citizen everyone thought he was. When Steele attacked me and drained me within an inch of my life, he gave me a message to deliver to my father when I saw him in hell. He said to tell my father that Victor Steele killed me and that my father's debt had been paid." His brow furrowed. "I had no idea what he meant at the time. The next thing I knew, I was waking up to a whole new world. The reality that I was a vampire, and I was starving."

"You never found out what Steele meant by that message?"

Samuel laughed bitterly. "Oh, I found out. When I ran into Shane Ronan in New Orleans, I tried to kill him for what he'd done to me. And to force him to tell me where Steele was hiding. I was about to drive a stake through the bastard's black heart when he offered me answers to that burning question in exchange for his life." He shrugged. "So I agreed."

I didn't push Samuel when he went quiet this time. He was too close to shutting down on me again. I just took his hand and held it tightly. Whatever Ronan had told him obviously still weighed heavy on his mind. It was written all over his face.

He finally continued. "It seems my boring, unassuming father had a secret. The man known for philanthropy and running one of the most successful companies in Boston was the opposite of what he presented himself as. No better than Victor Steele." He pulled his hand away from mine. "My father was a monster."

"What do you mean by monster?" Was I about to find out my boyfriend was more than just a vampire? That he held the genes of something terrifying?

He sat up and rubbed his hands over his face. "He trafficked people."

I gaped at him for a moment wondering if I'd heard him right. "Your father sold people?"

"Well, not people. Supernaturals."

Was that supposed to make it better?

He was clearly uncomfortable with coming clean about his family secrets, and my shocked reaction wasn't making it any easier for him. But how was I supposed to react? It was shocking.

"Despicable, isn't it?" He gave a mirthless laugh.

I knew without a doubt that some of us were chips off the old block, destined to repeat the sins of our parents. But others didn't hold a flicker of their parents' light or darkness in their souls. Samuel was nothing like his father.

"My father looked like a science professor," Samuel continued. "He was all business. No hobbies. No interests outside of work." He laughed quietly. "At least that's what I thought. I never detected an ounce of evil in the man. And trapping and selling supernaturals takes a fair amount of evil."

I shook my head in confusion. "I still don't understand what any of this has to do with Victor Steele?"

Samuel got up and headed for the stairs.

"Where are you going?" I asked, grabbing my shirt from the chair.

"I need a drink for the rest of this."

I quickly got dressed and followed him up to the bedroom. After he changed into some clean clothes, we went down to the living room to continue the conversation.

Samuel went straight to the bureau and grabbed a bottle of bourbon. "Are you having a drink?"

"Might as well." After this night, we both needed one. Probably two.

He came over to the sofa and handed me a glass, his energy palpable. Then he downed his drink and went to pour himself another before continuing. "My father was in business with Victor Steele."

I snorted. "Selling fabric?" Cain Industries was in the textile business, but I doubted Steele made his living hawking cotton.

He shot me a dry look. "The business of abducting shifters and vampires, or anything non-human, to be sold to wealthy clients." He glanced over his shoulder at me. "Freak shows were very popular during the Victorian era, so you can imagine what an oddity like a shifter was worth. Vampires brought top dollar, though. For obvious reasons."

"Like what Victor Steele was doing in the basement down at the Beast," I said. Before Samuel killed him, Steele had been selling female vampires to the highest bidder. It was one of his side hustles, along with his plan to hijack the blood co-op.

"Exactly. And a century later he was still getting away with it. Until we stopped him."

"How did your father get involved with Steele?"

He shook his head. "I have no idea. Ronan only gave me the details about their sordid business and told me that my father betrayed Steele. You know the rest."

I wanted to ask how his father had crossed Victor Steele, but when Samuel chose not to continue, I decided not to push it.

"You're not your father," I said, just in case he was thinking I'd start looking at him differently now. "I think I'm qualified to say that because my own father was just as much of a monster."

He finally came back over to the sofa and sat down next to me. "I guess we both have skeletons hanging in our closets."

I smiled. "We're a regular pair of misfits."

"The only thing Ronan told me was that the betrayal had something to do with a vampire my father had tortured. When I asked for more details, he politely told me to fuck off." He leaned back against the cushions and stared straight ahead as a memory seemed to take hold of him. "I decided I'd have to confront my father if I wanted to know the whole truth, which wouldn't be easy considering I never told him I was a vampire. I left Boston a week after I was turned and didn't see my father again for years."

"You just walked away?"

"I thought it was for the best. Better to disappear than disgrace the family name with my new reality." His pupils expanded. "Had I known what my father was, I would have shown him my fangs and dared him to do to me what he'd done to others like me."

I stroked his hand with my thumb. "There's more, isn't there?"

He nodded and got that distant look again. "It took me four

years after that to finally go back to Boston. My father was surprised to see me after all that time, but he didn't lash out as I expected him to. I wouldn't have blamed him for it. Then I got the nerve to show him what I was and demanded to know why Steele had attacked me. Why he wanted revenge. Who this tortured vampire was that Ronan had mentioned." Samuel looked at me. "You think your father was fucked up? Wait until you hear about mine. But first I have to tell you about my mother."

My brow furrowed. "Okay." It was the first time he'd ever mentioned the woman.

"My memories of her are... faint at best. I didn't have a doting mother like other children. She was always sick with something. Fevers. Weakness. Always in bed. She slept endlessly."

"What was wrong with her?"

He shook his head. "I don't know. When I'd ask my father—and I did, many times—he'd just say she was tired."

"She slept through your entire childhood?" It was a miracle he'd turned out as normal as he did, being a vampire aside.

"Most of it. There were periods when she seemed to be getting better, like right before I left for college. But by the time I graduated, she was completely bedridden. My father moved her to our house in the country. In those days, fresh air was medicine."

I was starting to get nervous with where he was going with all this. "You're not about to tell me that your father killed your mother?"

"No, but her condition is relevant to the story. My father agreed to tell me everything. He owed it to me after what Victor Steele had done. My mother was dying, and my father was desperate. He ended up abducting a young vampire and locking her in a cage."

I gasped. "A child?"

"Young as in recently turned. A newly made vampire is easily manipulated because they're still learning how to *be* a vampire. He kept her in that cage and drained her nightly which made her weak." Samuel stopped and glanced away from me. "He fed her blood to..."

"To your mother," I said when he seemed to be having trouble saying it.

He nodded. "Small daily doses. Just enough to keep her alive because he was afraid too much would turn her." His brow pulled tightly together. "I remember going to visit her a few years before I was attacked by Steele. She was comatose. My father wouldn't let me near the bed, and I remember thinking how cruel it was for him to keep me from touching her. My own mother."

"Samuel..." I chose my next words carefully. "If he was feeding her vampire blood, shouldn't she have been getting better?" It was a legitimate question. I ran a blood co-op, so I considered myself a bit of an authority on its medicinal benefits. And being a vampire now, Samuel should have been wondering the same thing.

"The doses were too small. They kept her breathing, but they weren't enough." When he turned to look at me, his eyes were dark. "She was already dead when I went to see her that day. That's why he wouldn't let me touch her. By the time he realized his mistake and started transfusing her daily, it was too late. All it did was keep her flesh from rotting."

My blood ran cold.

A weak smile returned to Samuel's face. "You see, Charley, my father had lost his mind." He recounted the events as if they belonged to someone else's life. "He'd gone completely mad. Killed himself a few months later by slitting his own throat." His expression turned puzzled. "Do you have any idea how difficult it is to cut your own throat?"

I didn't know what to say. It had happened a lifetime ago, but scars like that never really healed. "I'm so sorry, Samuel."

"Don't be. My father confessed. During a moment of lucidity, he recounted every dirty detail of what he'd done over the course of years." There was no bitterness in Samuel's eyes now. Just a hollow gaze. "My father was evil. He got what he deserved."

I still didn't make the connection. "But why did Victor Steele try to kill you?"

"It was the vampire. The young woman my father abducted. She was one of Steele's progeny. Steele never knew because my father kept her so weak she couldn't even call out to her own maker." He rolled a shoulder. "As I said, she was newly made and easily manipulated. He was sane enough to realize he had to get rid of her. Hide the evidence." Samuel's jaw tightened as his eyes sharpened. "He severed her head and threw her body into the bay. But death is like a beacon for a vampire. Steele felt it instantly and was drawn to that house." His lips curled as a dark laugh slipped from his mouth. "Just like Shane Ronan was drawn to Crimson the moment I destroyed Victor Steele."

I slowly nodded. "So that's why Steele did it."

"An eye for an eye. An offspring for an offspring. He took his time exacting his revenge, though. Years. If he had waited a few more weeks, I would have been long gone."

The night Samuel told me about his family's wealth, he'd mentioned that he'd always been planning to leave Boston. And yet he was rich. "So your father never cut you out of his will? Even after you disappeared?"

"I'm sure he did. But when I returned to Boston to confront him about what Ronan had told me, he must have had a change of heart. A year after his death, I was tracked down in New Orleans by an estate agent." His eyes flashed wide for a moment. "Went from rags to riches overnight. That's when the real trouble began."

"What kind of trouble can a boatload of money bring?" Come to think of it, sudden wealth did have its drawbacks, like distant relatives and long-lost friends coming out of the woodwork.

He groaned. "Let's just say I attracted a lot of women looking for benefactors."

"I don't want to know about any of that," I said. The image of Samuel with women crawling all over him made me cringe. The past was the past, and stuff like that usually didn't bother me. I had no intention of letting it get under my skin now.

He glanced at me sideways. "Good. Ronan was the worst of them, though. He thought I owed him restitution for my father killing his *sister*." Disdain washed over his face. "Fucking leech."

This whole progeny-maker thing brought up something I'd been curious about for a while, and I needed to ask the question perched on my lips before I lost my nerve. His response could have consequences.

"Have you ever turned someone?" I wasn't sure I was prepared to deal with *progeny* if one of them showed up on his doorstep one day. Would I find myself at the mercy of jealous family dynamics? I had enough vampires to worry about these days, and I never signed up for any of that. But by the way his face froze when I asked the question, I assumed I'd hit on a subject he wasn't eager to talk about.

He eventually turned his eyes to mine with a faint smile that quickly vanished. "Yes," was all he said.

"And?" I gestured for him to elaborate.

"What would you like to know?"

I leaned back and cocked my head. "Should I expect a plus-one at the holidays?" An expression was growing on his face. Annoyance or possibly impatience. "I'm sorry, Samuel, but I think I have the right to know if you have little vampires running around out there who could show up at any time."

"You're right, and I answered your question. There should be no secrets between us."

He was making me nervous. "Any more secrets you'd care to tell me?"

"I've been a vampire for over a century, Charley. There will always be more. But right now, I'd prefer to keep you blissfully ignorant." He stood up and offered me his hand. After helping me up, he gave me a deep kiss and pulled me against him.

I nuzzled my cheek into the hollow of his throat. "You can tell me anything, Samuel. Anything."

He tensed slightly. It was barely the tightening of his chest, but I felt it, the secrets buried in there.

"What time is it?" I said, searching for my phone.

Samuel glanced at the clock on the bureau. "It's almost eight."

"In the morning?" I looked out the window and realized it was too dark outside to be eight a.m. When I finally pulled my phone out, I almost had a heart attack. I'd turned the volume down last night so it wouldn't disturb Samuel while he recovered, and there were multiple missed calls from Dog, Candy, and Patrick. I was surprised one of them hadn't shown up here by now looking for me. "How did I sleep through an entire day?"

"I guess I wasn't the only one who needed rest," Samuel said.

I shoved the phone back in my pocket. "We have to go."

"Go where?"

"To the Stag to debrief about what happened last night." Then we needed to start hunting. Between me, Samuel, and a pack of wolves, we were going to flush out Shane Ronan and send him straight back to hell.

SEVENTEEN

When we arrived at the Stag, Lucy gave me a meek smile and brushed past me on her way down to the other end of the bar. Not a single comment came out of her mouth about where I'd been all evening.

"Why is she being so pleasant?" I asked Beau. Something must have been going on.

He glanced at her and shrugged. "She probably wants something from you."

"Since when has that ever stopped her from opening her mouth?"

Beau leaned closer and lowered his voice. "And by the way, I picked up the blood from Doc Bishop's office and dropped it off at Patrick's house."

I closed my eyes and cursed. I was supposed to pick it up along with the test results and deliver it myself to Patrick that afternoon. "Thanks, Beau. I completely forgot."

"He called me when you never showed up and weren't answering your phone. Where've you been all day?"

"I got tied up with Samuel." Literally. "Thanks for picking it up."

Dog peered through the order window when he heard my voice. "Back room. Now."

"Yes, sir."

Samuel and I followed him down the hallway and through the door, into the room where Mag and Loki were playing a game of cards at the desk.

"You have no idea how much those cards trigger me," I said. "Get rid of them." And if an ace of spades magically appeared in the top drawer, I was going to lose it.

Mag dropped his cards and Loki collected them, stuffing the deck into his pocket.

Before we got into what happened in that warehouse last night, I had another question for Samuel. It had been on my mind, but we'd been distracted with other things for the past few hours. Now seemed like the right time to bring it up. "What happened to you in that room yesterday morning? You seemed paralyzed, and you had that strange light around you."

Loki glanced from me to Dog. "What's she talking about?"

"I'm right here, Loki. Dog doesn't need to interpret for me."

"It was a weapon," Samuel said.

"I could see that." He was standing in the middle of that dark room, barely moving his lips and eyes. "What kind of weapon?"

"Let's just call it a net laced with magic," Samuel said. "It's used to stun vampires."

"Damn," Mag drawled. "I could use one of those."

I recalled the shock it gave me. "I may not be a vampire, but it stunned the hell out of me when my fingers grazed it."

Samuel trained his eyes on mine. "With the magical current running through your hands, it could have done a lot worse."

So that's why he warned me with that look when I reached for it. "Where did Ronan get it?"

"From the same witch who gave me that sunlight bullet."

"Wait a minute." I was confused. "Shane Ronan knew this

witch too?" When he went quiet on me, I knew I needed to give him a nudge. "What are you leaving out, Samuel?"

Dog leaned against the wall and crossed his arms. "By all means, elaborate."

Samuel locked eyes with me, and I felt an uncomfortable story on the edge of his tongue. "I've seen you at your worst, Samuel. Just tell me."

"No, you haven't."

I swallowed the obstruction that was forming in my throat. "Okay, then rip the Band-Aid off and tell me now so we can move past it."

Samuel glanced at the wolves in the room. "How about a little privacy?"

I shook my head. "We're way past that, and we don't have time."

"All right." He walked over to the desk and absently fiddled with a pencil, his eyes focusing on it. "I told you about the scam Ronan was pulling in the French Quarter when I ran into him in New Orleans."

My stomach started to sink. "Yeah?"

"Well, it wasn't just him." He dropped the pencil and looked back at me. "We were partners."

Okay. I could handle that. I didn't like the idea of Samuel being a thief, but it was over a century ago, and he had to survive. And there were worse things than swindling tourists out of their vacation money.

After gauging my reaction, he continued. "We didn't just steal money from tourists."

It was like he'd plucked the words right out of my head. "Then what was it?"

"Ronan and I were caught up in a twisted, reciprocal alliance. We lured victims to a house where we feasted on them. Then we took their money." His eyes were filled with a mix of defiance and shame. "Still like what you see?"

Mag blew his breath out slowly and sat back in his chair. "Fuck."

I didn't know how to feel. And then I thought about his opponent in the ring last night and the look on Samuel's face when he tore into the man's neck and dropped him like a stone. "Keep going."

Samuel zeroed in on my gaze and held it captive for a moment. "I'm not the same vampire I was back then. I was young. Hungry. I had no one to teach me how to survive."

He'd said those words to me before. The night he told me how he was turned. Victor Steele had attacked him and left him to die. Abandoned him in a strange new world to fend for himself. But at the heart of it, Samuel was a powerful vampire. Just as capable of killing as any of the wolves in the room. I'd killed myself, but never the innocent.

Samuel came closer and looked me in the eyes, stirring thoughts of our very intimate moments together just hours earlier. "You know me, Charley."

My skin flushed from the memory of baring myself to him. The things he could have done to me while I was completely at his mercy. I did know Samuel, and he wasn't that vampire from New Orleans.

"Tell me I haven't lost you," he whispered.

His scent had me flushing again. "Of course not." And I was suddenly acutely aware of the fabric brushing against my nipples.

Dog cleared his throat. "If you two are finished, we need to move on."

I shook it off and took a step back from Samuel. "Just tell us about Ronan."

His eyes lingered on mine for a few more seconds. "As I said, the witch he was working with was the same witch who created the sunlight bullets. Turns out, she was working on another weapon as well. That substance you saw around me was colloidal silver, which is at worst an irritant to our skin. But when mixed with the powdered bones of..." A dark laugh escaped him. "Let's just say it's a very effective straitjacket for vampires."

"The powdered bones of what?" Dog said.

"If I knew that, I would have created it myself by now. It could be anything: a dead demon, a cypress corpse."

"A cypress corpse?" I muttered.

"I suspect Ronan killed her for it when she wouldn't give it to him." Samuel shook his head slowly. "Why would she give a weapon used against vampires to a vampire?"

"But she gave you the sunlight bullets," I said.

"Because she trusted me. I finally got control of my blood-lust and left Shane Ronan behind. I became a hunter. That's why she gave them to me. To take down rogues like him. I only wish she'd given me all her weapons."

"It's too bad she's dead," Dog said. "Those bullets and that substance would come in handy right now."

We had to find the vampire first. "What do we do now?"

Samuel gave it some thought. "Nothing."

"Excuse me?" Loki looked at him like he was short a few marbles.

"Shane Ronan isn't your average vampire. We won't find him until he wants to be found, so we wait until he drops us a lead." He pulled his eyes away from Loki and looked at the rest of us. "And we better be prepared when he does."

"So we just wait like sitting ducks?" I said.

"We don't have a choice."

Since we were playing the waiting game, I decided to go check on my bar. "When you guys find this *lead*, let me know. I'll be up front running my business." And making sure my bartenders knew to stay alert. That target on Beau the other day still had me worried, although Ronan had my attention now.

As I was walking into the bar, Candy came through the

front door. I scrutinized her face carefully, making sure it was actually her, although the other night I had no clue it wasn't.

She stared back at me for a moment before walking over to the bar, convincing one of my regulars to give up his stool with a mere look.

I went over and leaned against the edge. "Quit intimidating my customers."

"He was just being a gentleman."

"He's scared of you, Candy."

"Well, he should be." She straightened the hem of her shirt and barked at Lucy when she breezed past us. "Hey!"

Lucy stopped and let out a rushed sigh before turning around. "What?"

So much for pleasantries.

"Don't *what* me, Little Miss Sunshine. I'll have a club soda." It was definitely Candy.

"You're in a good mood tonight?" I said. "What's wrong?"

"Just stopped by to see if you're still alive." She sized me up. "Looks like you are."

I texted her as soon as I realized she'd been calling me all afternoon. "I messaged you an hour ago." By the look on her face, you'd have thought I'd dropped a postcard in the mailbox.

She huffed. "Anyone could've gotten a hold of your phone and sent me that text. Next time I leave you with an unstable vampire, do me a favor and pick up the phone." She settled down when Lucy delivered her drink. "I was worried about you."

"I'm sorry, I wasn't thinking. And it was Samuel you left me with." Although, he did attack me before nearly bringing me to my knees with pleasure.

She patted my arm. "I'm just glad you're okay. How is Samuel?"

"Better. He's in the back with Dog discussing our next move. How to find Ronan."

"That's good." She leaned closer and lowered her voice. "I was just wondering if I could borrow that book we found in his study?"

"Why do you want it?" I whispered back, although I didn't know what all the secrecy was about.

"Not me. I mentioned it to your aunt, and the Squad wants to take a look at it."

The word *aunt* didn't sit right with me. "I'd appreciate it if you didn't call her that." I may have recently found out that Katherine Belltower was my blood relative, but I wasn't ready to plan any family gatherings yet.

"Too soon?" she said.

"A little. Just call her Katherine."

Candy sucked in a deep breath. "All right. But you know you're in line to inherit that big old house out in the woods, so you might want to get used to the idea."

It had occurred to me, but I wasn't going to bring it up. Turns out, Katherine Belltower's brother was my biological father. These days, he was swimming with the trout in that river in the mountains I'd sent him crashing into. But he tried to kill me first, so I had no choice.

Candy chuckled. "Desiree is going to shit when she finds out you're her new landlord."

Another reason I didn't want to think about it. "You mean if she outlives Katherine."

"That stubborn witch is never going to die."

I shuddered at the thought of having to look at Desiree Dubois's bitter face for the next fifty years.

"Anyway," Candy continued, "the Squad wants to see that book."

"Are they worried about a little competition in town?"

"Hardly." She took a sip of her club soda. "Pullman's dead anyway. They're just curious about what he was up to when he was alive."

I didn't buy it. Those witches were looking for something. "I'll ask Samuel, but I'm sure he won't mind. I doubt he even knows that book exists."

She finished her drink and got up to leave. "I better get back to the Cauldron. I've got a tincture brewing in the back room. If it infuses much longer I'll be scraping guts off the ceiling."

"Eww! What kind of guts?"

She gave me a sly grin. "That's for Adelle Spencer to find out. Let me know about that book."

Samuel came back into the bar as she was walking out the door. "Was that Candy?"

"She stopped by to make sure I was still breathing. She came by to check on you last night, by the way."

His brows hiked. "In my chamber?"

"Yeah." The word came out more like a question. "Is that a problem?"

"I feel strangely violated knowing that half of Crimson has been in my private quarters."

In my opinion, it was no different than having people in your bedroom, and he'd been in Candy's spare room before. "You're overreacting, Samuel. It's not Candy you need to worry about." Shane Ronan had been down there too.

"You're right. It's not like she was snooping around my house."

"Uh... speaking of which. I did give her a tour last night. We didn't go through your drawers or anything, but we did look around the study. She found a book on one of the shelves she wants to borrow."

He smiled. "It's okay. She's welcome to it. In fact, she can take all of them if she'd like. Saves me from having to weed through them."

"Thanks. I'll ask next time before giving her any more tours."

"Don't be ridiculous. Candy's always welcome in my

house." He gave me a look that threatened to have me flushing again. "Are you coming over after work?"

What I needed to do was get up super early. Well before the crack of dawn. "I think I'm going to stay at my place tonight. You need some serious rest, and I have co-op deliveries in the morning with Patrick." If those test results were good.

There was a look of concern on his face. "Then I'll see you tomorrow night." As he was walking out, he looked back at me. "Lock up tight when you get home tonight."

I knew what he was worried about, but Shane Ronan wasn't getting in my house. Not without an invitation. Not now, not ever.

EIGHTEEN

I fought back a yawn and pulled up a chair next to Patrick while he unpacked his briefcase on the desk. "Remind me again why we're doing this at six a.m.?"

"Because I've got a life."

Setting up shop in the evening was preferable, but Patrick had been booked on Friday and Saturday nights lately, and members weren't crazy about having to pick up their blood on weeknights. A lot of them worked during the week and others were in bed by nine p.m., so Saturday mornings before dawn seemed to work for everyone except me. But I made myself available to make people happy.

"Your boyfriend keep you up last night?" Patrick said when I finally gave in to a yawn.

"I slept like a rock." If anything, I'd gotten too much sleep over the past two days, which was probably making me even more tired.

When he went quiet and got a strained look, I knew something was up. "I can see it all over your face, Patrick. Might as well tell me what's wrong before people start knocking on the door."

He pulled the last few vials out of the briefcase and shut it. It was only about half of what we usually delivered every week. "We've got a problem."

"Not another one." I wanted to bang my head on the desk. "What is it?"

"I got a call from Mabel Gentry last night. She canceled her order."

That was strange. Mabel was one of our most dependable members. The woman never missed an order. In fact, she was usually the first person in line. "Maybe she's running low on funds this week." She was a widow and lived on a tight budget. It wouldn't be the first time she'd struggled to pay for an order. I'd helped her myself in the past when she couldn't afford her blood.

His expression told me it was much worse than that, so I braced myself when he swiveled in his chair to look at me.

"She's not the only one," he said. "I got a call from three others who also canceled. Word's getting around about Mary. She's doing okay, by the way. They released her, so I went by her house last night."

So it had finally happened. Hysteria was starting to break out about the co-op's blood supply. "I guess people figure living with pain is better than living with hep C." I probably would have felt the same way if I were in their shoes. "What about the test results?" None of that blood on the desk was leaving this office unless they were good.

He turned his pointed gaze to me. "If you'd picked them up instead of me having to call Beau yesterday, you wouldn't have to ask."

And here I thought I'd skated by and he wasn't going to bring that up.

"Sorry. I got busy and it slipped my mind."

"Slipped your—"

"Just give me the results," I practically snapped at him, but I had good reason to be on edge.

After staring at me for a moment, he looked back at the row of vials on the desk. "Most of them are good."

"Most?"

"Another sample came back positive."

My stomach bottomed out. Everything was falling apart, and we were minutes away from hearing a knock on the back door. There'd be a line of people in the alley expecting us to deliver a miracle cure for their pain. And then I got an even worse thought. "Was it Newt Daniels's sample?"

Patrick pulled his eyes away from the desk. "How the hell do you know that?"

"I have to tell you something first." Patrick had no idea what was going on, so he needed some context before I answered his question. I spent the next few minutes telling him about the war between Samuel and Shane Ronan.

"And I'm just hearing about this now?"

He hadn't heard the half of it. "I was going to tell you, but I haven't had time. And you've had other things to deal with this week." Like tracking a hep C outbreak.

"Was this vampire emancipated before Samuel offed his maker?" he asked.

There are two kinds of vampires: those released by their maker to live independently and do whatever the hell they wanted, and those who would never know freedom. Inextricably bound to their maker for eternity. Samuel was the former by default when Steele abandoned him.

"If you mean released, I think you know the answer to that." Victor Steele never gave up control of anything. Samuel won the lottery when Steele left him for dead.

"Then you best say bye-bye to your boyfriend," he said with a snicker.

I glared at him. "That's one of the shittiest things you've ever said to me."

"Have I ever lied to you?" There was no apology in his eyes. "I'm a vampire, Charley. I know how this ends. Hell hath no fury like a vampire who lost his daddy."

I couldn't believe he was saying these things to me. "You're supposed to be my ride or die."

"Meaning I tell you the shit you don't want to hear. But if it makes you feel any better, this asshole is gonna have his work cut out for him to kill a vampire like Samuel."

"Thanks, I feel so much better now."

He got serious again. "What does all this have to do with Newt Daniels?"

"Shane Ronan is running a fight club in a warehouse outside of town. Or at least he was. At the old Stokes Tractor building."

Patrick nodded. "Yeah, I heard something about it. Humans going up against vampires." He shook his head. "Nothing but a damn bloodbath if you ask me."

"I went out there the other night with Dog and the pack and saw Newt. He ducked into the crowd when he caught me looking at him."

"Jesus, woman, what the hell were you doing out there?"

"Stopping Ronan from making Samuel's murder the main event. I'll tell you everything later," I said when he started to ask more questions. We didn't have time to get into it. "As an incentive, they're handing out vials of vampire blood to the fighters. One of Dog's wolves has gotten himself caught up in this mess. He's also gotten himself hooked on that blood they're giving out. But since vampire blood isn't addictive, I think Ronan is spiking it with something that is."

Patrick's brow twisted. "With hep C? That doesn't make any sense."

I shook my head. "I think they're spiking it with a drug. Something to keep people coming back for more."

"You're still not making any sense, Charley."

"Just hear me out. Samuel said Ronan wants to torture him. Really make him suffer for killing Steele. What's a good way to do that?"

"Fuck, I don't know." Patrick shrugged. "Kill you?"

"I'm sure he'd like to, but what if he found a way to drag it out? Mess with me slowly while Samuel watches. What if he went after the Stag or the co-op?" Then I got to my theory. "When one of the human fighters wins the first round, they get pitted against a vampire in the second round. Do you know what the prize is? The winner gets to take a bite out of the loser."

Patrick's face froze. "Son of a bitch. He's giving blood infected with hepatitis to the humans before the fights."

"And guess who almost always wins the second round?" I said.

"The vampire."

I nodded slowly. "I think Shane Ronan made it his business to find out who our donors are. How much do you want to bet Newt Daniels has been more than just a spectator at those fights? The fool got himself infected with hep C by biting one of the infected humans in the second round."

"You think Glen and Marta are involved with those fights too?" Patrick scoffed. "I doubt it. Neither one of them is the type to get their hands dirty."

"I didn't think Newt was either," I said, "but I saw him in that warehouse with my own two eyes. Now his blood is testing positive."

We couldn't take a chance with any of that blood on the desk. Even the clean vials because there was always a slight risk of a faulty test result. "I hate to say it, but we need to make an announcement when the members get here. The co-op is suspended indefinitely."

Patrick looked at his phone when a text notification went off. There were several of them stacked on his home screen. "I don't think that's going to be a problem." He read a few more and looked back at me. "Orders are dropping like flies. It's over, Charley."

I glanced at the time. Members should have been knocking by now. When I went to the door and looked outside, the alley was empty. Patrick was right. The co-op was officially radioactive.

* * *

I hung up the phone and stuffed it back in my pocket, digesting what Patrick had just told me. He'd interrupted his date to call and give me the news. He'd gotten a hold of a few members who said word had spread like wildfire that Mary Foster had caught the virus from the co-op's blood supply, which was probably true. It wasn't like she went around soliciting strange vampires. The main reason people came to us in the first place was for safe, high-quality product, and we'd failed them. The co-op was dead in the water.

Dog looked at me through the order window. "You okay?"

"No, I'm not. We had to shut the co-op down this morning." Or rather, the members shut it down, sparing us the unpleasant task of making the announcement.

"What happened?"

I went into the kitchen to continue the conversation because too many ears were perked at the bar. "The blood supply is contaminated with hepatitis C."

Dog's face turned to stone. "You want to repeat that."

"And Shane Ronan did it."

"You're sure about this?"

"About the contamination or about that vampire being responsible?"

"Both," he said.

I couldn't have been any more convinced. "Mary Foster contracted it. To be safe, we tested all the blood donations we collected yesterday, and several came back positive." I shook my head as anger swelled inside me. "I don't have any hard evidence that Ronan did it, but I saw one of our donors at that warehouse the other night. One of the donors who tested positive. I'd bet my bar that those vials they're handing out to the humans are infected with it."

Dog sneered. "And some of your donors have been partaking in those fights and winning." A growl slipped from his mouth. "Fuck. So we've got vampires running around town carrying hep C."

I hadn't even thought about that yet. Others were at risk too. Humans who voluntarily serviced vampires in exchange for a few vials of recreational blood. Thank God Samuel didn't rely on that anymore. "We're on the verge of an epidemic in this town if we don't do something." Although hepatitis C was curable, the treatment was long and expensive, and a lot of people around here didn't have insurance.

"We'll keep an eye on the warehouse to make sure that fight club doesn't ramp back up for business."

"The damage is done, Dog. We need to discreetly get the word out." If the less-than-open-minded citizens of this town found out, or God forbid the pastor of the church, we'd be right back where we were not too long ago. The humans around here would be sharpening their pitchforks and trying to run every vampire out of town.

"I think we both know where to start," he said.

I pulled out my phone and flipped through my call log to find one from Ian Masterson. Technically we had a relationship, so I reluctantly went ahead and added him as a contact. His number could come in handy in the future. Then I dialed it, but it went straight to voicemail. "What the hell?" I stared at my phone. "I think he blocked me. And his mailbox is full."

Dog chuckled. "I guess that means you're going for a drive."

"*We're* going for a drive."

He shook his head. "It'll start a riot if I walk in there with you, and you know it."

Right. Wolves weren't welcome in Reaperstown, let alone the Beast, but I wasn't going down there by myself. I wasn't scared of the place anymore, but it still made my skin crawl. I needed to talk to Ian, though, and it couldn't wait. Every minute that slipped by was an infection waiting to happen, with all those seedy vampires down there mingling with humans. And then there was Ian's own side business of peddling blood. Unless contained, the situation was about to explode into a colossal clusterfuck.

"Take Beau with you," Dog suggested. "We've got an extra bartender working tonight, so we'll be fine. I'll jump in if they need help."

"No, you won't." Dog was a disaster behind the bar. "Besides, they'll smell the Hollerwolf and have the same reaction as if you walked in there with me."

He scoffed. "Don't compare me to a Hollerwolf. Personally, I've never smelled anything like one. It'll probably just confuse those scumbags and make them keep their distance."

Not too long ago, Dog would have blown a gasket if I'd even suggested going to the Beast without a full entourage. His faith in my magic skills had shifted drastically.

"You can take Samuel with you."

I couldn't think of a worse idea. "That's not going to happen." Taking him with me to the Beast was a fight in the making, especially if one of those lowlifes hit on me.

"He's not going to be happy when he finds out you went down there without him."

Last time I checked, I didn't need anyone's permission. "He'll get over it."

"Then Beau's your man. Just make sure you find Masterson before those vampires get too curious about what he is."

Now I needed to convince Beau to go with me.

As I was walking out of the kitchen, I noticed the sounds coming from the bar had gone silent. I could hear the TV Dog had installed near the ceiling, with the volume turned down low, but there was no other noise. Not a voice or the clink of a glass. When I came out of the hallway, Zane, the northern pack leader, was standing in the middle of the bar. He surveyed the room, his eyes stopping on me as I ventured closer to him.

"I don't want any more trouble," I said. "What do you want now?"

He cocked his head. "I want my woman."

I glanced around the room. "Do you see her in here?"

A growl rumbled up his throat. "No, but I can smell her."

Gross.

"She's not here, so if you don't mind, I'd like you to leave."

He stepped closer to me. "And if you don't mind, I'll just take a look in the back."

Jesus, what was wrong with this wolf? Did he think I was hiding her under the bar? "Actually, I do mind. But if it will put an end to your showing up here, be my guest."

As he entered the hallway, the kitchen door flew open and nearly slammed into him. Dog stepped out and barred the wolf from going any farther. "Employees only." He was bigger than Zane and not budging an inch.

"It's okay," I said. "Let him look around. Then you can escort him out."

Dog slowly shook his head, meeting Zane's gaze with equal hostility. "Nah. He's just going to have to take your word for it that she's not here." A growl came from Dog's throat.

After a tense second or two, Zane began to retreat. He

sniffed the air and smiled at Dog. "Sure, but I'll be seeing you again soon." Then he walked out, throwing us both a glare over his shoulder.

After he disappeared down the sidewalk, I finally let my shoulders drop. "You should have let him look," I said to Dog. "I don't like the idea of that wolf nosing around the back room, but if it got rid of him..."

Dog's eyes remained on the front door. "See, that's the problem, Charley. You give that son of a bitch an inch, he'll keep coming back for more. That wolf is nothing but a predator."

I hadn't seen such hatred in Dog's eyes in a long time. "This seems personal."

"Oh, it's personal." Dog finally pulled his eyes away from the door, shaking off whatever had ignited him. Then he walked over to the bar and nodded to Beau. "You're taking a drive with your boss."

Beau's mouth gaped as he looked back and forth between us. "A drive where?"

It wasn't the best idea, but I sure as hell wasn't taking Lucy or Tucker with me. "To the Beast. You're my escort for the night."

NINETEEN

"Your vampire boyfriend should be going down there with you, not your bartender," Beau said the second we climbed into the truck.

"Relax, Beau. We're going to have a quick conversation with Ian Masterson, and it'll be over. Piece of cake."

His face curled with disgust. "That vampire hates me."

"I wouldn't say that. He probably doesn't want to sit down and have a beer with you, but I don't think he hates you." I patted him on the thigh. "You're safe with me."

I wasn't worried about Ian, though. It was the rest of the vampires who hung out at the Beast.

On the drive over, I gave Beau a recap of everything that had happened: Shane Ronan and the fight club, the co-op closing down indefinitely, and the reason we were looking for Ian.

Beau gazed out the window as we approached Reaper-stown. "Hep C? You think I should get tested?" His foot tapped nervously against the floorboard.

"The way you sleep around, it's not a bad idea." Although not as common, you could get it through sexual activity. It was better to be safe than sorry. "Cheer up, Beau. It's just a blood test."

He finally relaxed. "Thank you, Jesus. I thought it was one of those tests where they stick a probe up there."

I glanced at him sideways. "Different kind of test, Beau."

We came to the four-way stop at the corner of the club, and I noticed the sign with red lacquered letters that Victor Steele had erected on the building was gone. The words THE BEAST painted above the door in black was the only signage now.

After parking in the back lot, I turned to Beau. "If anyone stops us at the door, let me do the talking. Especially if the bouncer gets nosy about the way you smell."

He lifted his arm and took a whiff. "Why, do I stink?"

"Not to me, but I'm not a vampire. I'm talking about the Hollerwolf."

We got out and headed down the side of the building. When we rounded the corner and walked up to the entrance, a vampire stepped in our path. He was very large and had a shiny bald head. I couldn't stop staring at his hazel eyes. They had a translucent quality. Very hypnotic.

"Can I help you?"

"We're looking for Ian Masterson," I said.

A lopsided grin slowly slid up his face, revealing his fangs. "Everyone's looking for Ian. I might be able to arrange an introduction."

When his gaze dropped to my chest and his index finger wandered toward it, I stepped back. "We don't need an introduction. He's a friend." Friend might have been a stretch.

His eyes shifted to Beau as his nostrils flared. "Who's your pet?"

Beau huffed. "Pet?"

"Beau..." I gave him a warning look and grinned at the vampire. "He's a friend of Ian's too, so why don't you let him know we're here. Tell him Charley Underwood needs to see him, and it's important."

The vampire's fangs retracted as he stepped back. "Wait here."

"Why is it so damn difficult to get into this place?" I said as he walked inside. "Come on. We're going in."

Beau wouldn't budge. "That vampire said to wait out here, and he had some pretty big fangs."

"We're *friends* with the owner, Beau, and I need a drink before having that conversation with Ian."

He let out a frustrated sigh and followed me into the small entryway, staring at the condom dispenser against the wall.

"What's the matter, Beau? Running low on supplies?"

"As a matter of fact," he muttered.

I pushed the second door open and went inside, stopping when I saw a pink-haired vampire come through the archway behind the bar. "Irina?"

When she saw me, a playful smile tugged at her lips. "Charley Underwood. Imagine that." She came over to us when we walked up to the bar. "Taking a walk on the dark side tonight?"

"Hardly. We're here to see Ian."

Her nostrils flared when she looked at Beau, the same way the bouncer's had. "Who's he?"

Beau just stood there gazing at her, tongue-tied.

"He's one of my bartenders. And a friend."

She bent over and rested her elbows on the bar, giving us both a thorough look at her impressive cleavage. "Does your *bartender* want a drink?"

"We'll both have a shot of tequila."

She didn't bother to ask what kind. She went straight for the good stuff. "It's on the house," she said, sliding them across the bar. "I owe you."

For playing a part in saving her life when Victor Steele tried to traffic her? She was right. I'd earned that drink. "Thanks."

I downed my shot and turned around to survey the club. Beau was gawking at the stage in the adjoining room. Dancers had been part of Victor Steele's business model after he bought the place, but now there were both men and women sharing the stage. "I see Ian decided to keep the entertainment."

Irina slid me another shot. "Money is money. Whatever sells."

The bouncer returned and glared at Beau. Then he had the nerve to grab my arm. "I told you to wait outside." His face seized up as a strangled sound rushed from his mouth. Light sparked from the spot where his hand was gripping me and crackled all the way up his arm. After letting go, he stumbled and hit the ground, his eyes filling with rage as he climbed back to his feet.

I had to admit, the vampire was scary looking, but I held my ground. "Next time you touch me, you won't be getting back up."

His jaw clenched. "You bitch!"

In a blink, Irina was standing between us, glaring at the vampire. "Don't even think about it."

He lowered his chin and glared back. "Who the fuck made you the boss?"

"Really?" A cocky grin slid up her face as she glanced at a camera near the ceiling before bringing her eyes back to his.

That was all it took for the vampire to back off. "Ian's door is shut," he said. "He's busy."

"Then I guess you can go now." She was half his size, we all were, but there wasn't a trace of fear on her face.

After shooting me another vicious look, he walked out the door.

Relieved to see him go, I looked to my right. "Where's Beau?"

He was standing at the other end of the bar, his eyes glowing amber, and there was a feral look in them as he started to vibrate.

Irina groaned. "A fucking shifter?" Then she approached him but kept her distance. "Not in here!" she barked. "You want to shift, do it outside."

I walked up to him and slowly reached for his arm. When he pulled it away and growled, an army of vampires was suddenly flanking me. "Take it easy," I said. "He's just protecting me."

"He's got a funny way of showing it," Irina said, calling off the vampires who were ready to pounce.

"Yeah, he's still new at this." I finally managed to touch him, and his eyes immediately faded to green. "I'm fine, Beau. The big bad vampires are gone."

Irina snorted and went back behind the bar. "Not if he pulls that shit again."

Beau shivered, shaking it off. "Sorry."

"Don't apologize. You weren't the instigator."

With things under control—for the moment—I decided to move it along before something else set him off. "I really need to talk to Ian," I said to Irina. "It's important."

She glanced at the camera again. There were several positioned all around the club, and I was surprised Ian hadn't come out yet. Surely me and Beau walking into the Beast had whetted his curiosity.

"Come on." She flicked her head toward the hallway. When Beau started to follow us, she shook her head at him. "Not you. Watch the bar."

His eyes flew wide. "What?"

"You're a bartender, right? So deal with the bar until I get back."

"I ain't staying out here alone with all these vamps!"

She smiled at him. "Don't worry, big boy. I'll be right back to keep you company."

"I'll hurry," I said, trying to ease his growing panic.

As Beau cowered at the bar, I followed Irina down the infamous hallway that led to the even more infamous basement. Or dungeon. It was where Steele had kept the female vampires he was trafficking, and all the other illegal product he dealt in. The place where it all ended when Samuel killed him. It was also where I met Diablo, the hellhound that now lived with Beau.

Instinctively, I went straight for the door on my left.

"Where do you think you're going?" Irina said, stopping at a door on the right.

"Isn't his office in the basement?"

"It's in here." She motioned for me to go inside. "I better get back out there before your bartender gets himself into trouble." A wicked smile rose up her face as she backed away from me. "Have fun."

"Fun?" I muttered, hesitant to reach for the doorknob. But the sooner I got this over with, the sooner Beau and I could get out of here.

The door opened to a hallway that was on the same side of the building as the stage, and I could hear the music coming through the walls. "Ian?" There was no answer, so I started walking toward another door at the end. It was ajar and had a dim light streaming through the crack. As I got closer to it, the music picked up, and there were strange rhythmic sounds getting louder with each step. When I came within a few feet of the door, I realized they were coming from inside the room.

I pushed the door open and got an eyeful of Ian's naked ass as he drove himself into a woman who was draped over a desk, her grunts growing louder with each of his steady thrusts.

From the corner of his eye, Ian caught me standing there and slammed into the woman harder, nearly knocking her over the edge of the desk.

"Jesus!" I walked back out to the hallway, a rush of warmth rolling through me. My mouth suddenly felt dry, and my skin was heating up. What the hell was wrong with me? If Samuel hadn't figured out where I'd gone to yet, he would now.

A minute later—could have been two—the sounds of slapping flesh and moaning came to a crescendo and then abruptly stopped as the woman let out a guttural scream. She walked out a moment later, dressed but with her stilettos dangling from her fingers. Her hair looked like she'd gotten caught up in a windstorm, and her lipstick was smeared beyond the edges of her mouth.

On her way down the hall, she glanced back at me with a smile. "He's all yours, sweetie."

Irina's words came back to me. *Have fun.*

"Oh, hell no!" I sucked it up and went back inside. If anyone should have been embarrassed, it was Ian. He was shirtless and zipping his pants up when I walked in.

After taking a seat behind the desk, he glanced at a row of monitors in front of him showing every angle of the club, including that hallway outside. "Sorry. Did it make you uncomfortable?"

He'd probably timed it perfectly. "Really, Ian. I swear you enjoy making me uncomfortable."

"Every chance I get. But surely you've seen a naked man before." His cocky gaze turned curious. "Are you a virgin?"

"Shut up, Ian."

He grinned. "I didn't think so. Not when you're shacking up with that stud of a vampire."

I let it go, because engaging would only encourage him.

He pointed to a chair on the other side of the desk. "Sit."

"No thanks. I won't be here very long."

His eyes wandered over my face. "Why are you here?"

"Because we have a problem. Shane Ronan isn't just running an illegal fight club outside of town."

"*Was*," he corrected.

At least *he* was confident about that. He was also getting on my last nerve, and I'd been in his presence for less than five minutes. "He's infecting the blood supply." I suddenly had his undivided attention. "With hepatitis C."

He relaxed again. "You had me nervous for a second. I thought it was something serious."

"Are you kidding me?"

"It's curable, Charley. Hep *B* is another story."

"You're not going to think it's so benign when people start ghosting your blood business," I said with a smirk. "The co-op has been shuttered. At least temporarily."

He frowned as the implications seemed to work their way into his thick head. "That's not good."

"No, it isn't." I pointed my thumb over my shoulder. "And once those humans out there start testing positive, this club will be half empty." If there was one way to light a spark under that vampire's ass, it was to make a dent in his bottom line. Ian was an opportunist, and money was his love language.

He squinted at me. "How do you know Ronan is responsible? Maybe your customers have been acquiring blood from shadier sources."

You mean like you? I wanted to say. But I needed his cooperation, so I kept my mouth shut. Granted, I didn't have any proof that it was Shane Ronan, but I'd get it.

"One of my infected donors was at that fight the other night. I saw him. And I know for a fact that Ronan has been handing out free vampire blood to the human winners of the fights to keep them coming back for more. Infected blood."

The revelations seemed to keep coming. "And the vampires who win the next rounds get to take a bite out of them." His face began to harden. "That sleazy son of a bitch."

"This isn't just your reputation, Ian. Ronan is about to cut into your revenue streams. And if the virus spreads to the

Beast..." I let that sink in good and deep. "Let's contain the problem before he burns us all to the ground."

Ian's eyes suddenly snapped to the monitors on the desk. "That fucking moron!"

"What?" I looked at the screen and then ran out of his office, the sounds of a brawl getting louder as I raced down the hallway. The Hollerwolf was backed into a corner near the bar, lashing out with its long claws as a horde of vampires blocked the exit. The bouncer had the telltale marks of those claws running down the side of his face. They were healing before my eyes, but he looked like he intended to return the favor.

Ian came up behind me to watch the spectacle. "This should be interesting." There wasn't an ounce of urgency on his face.

"Call off your vampires," I said as they moved closer to the Hollerwolf, "or I will."

"Have at it," he said, his amusement growing.

Calling his bluff, I focused, manifesting a ball of energy in my palm. It continued to grow and quickly flared into a bright sphere of angry magic. But when I looked back at the vampires, I realized I didn't have a clean shot. Then my hand started to shake. If I landed it a few inches in the wrong direction, Beau would take the hit and those vampires would tear him apart. However, the result would be the same if I didn't take the shot.

Ian grabbed my wrist when I took aim. "Wait!"

Something streaked across the room, and Irina was suddenly shielding the Hollerwolf. But one of those bloodsuckers was already in motion, lunging for Beau before she could stop him. In the frenzy, his fangs sank into Irina's shoulder, latching onto her like a pit bull.

Ian had the vampire by the throat before my eyes could track his dash across the room. "If you ever touch her again," he growled, "I will destroy you."

After warning the others with a look that I wouldn't want to be on the receiving end of, Irina stepped up to Ian. "Let go of him."

Ian glared at the vampire a moment longer and then released him. "He's all yours."

As the vampire gripped his aching throat, Irina clocked him in the jaw so hard his head snapped back. He recovered from it, but a second blow almost knocked him off his feet. A third set of knuckles to the jaw sent blood spurting in every direction, his head slamming into the wall before he slid to the floor. She wedged her boot against his groin and gave his package a good press. "If you ever bite me again, *I'll* destroy you myself." Another firm shove of her boot had him groaning. "After I cut off your limp dick and shove it down your throat."

When I looked back at the Hollerwolf, it had shifted, leaving Beau standing naked in the corner, mesmerized by the pink-haired vampire who was now walking toward him.

Irina stopped within a foot of him and glanced down at his erection. Beau flinched, a slight gasp slipping from his gaping mouth, his eyes locking on hers as her fingers ran along the length of his growing cock with a featherlight touch. Her hand slid beneath it and cupped his scrotum. Then she pulled her hand and her gaze away, grabbing his clothes off the floor and pressing them to his chest. "Get dressed."

Clutching them, he swallowed hard and nodded, his eyes locking on hers until she finally let up and walked behind the bar to pour herself a drink.

"Well, that was awkward," I muttered as Ian came back over to me.

A hint of a smile appeared on his face. "For you, or him?"

"Hurry up," I said to Beau, ignoring the remark. "We're leaving." Then I turned to Ian. "Get the word out about the infected blood." On the way to the door I looked back at him. "If Ronan shows up here, call me."

I'd lit that fire. Ian had skin in the game now. But as

powerful as he was, I wasn't sure he was a match for that vampire. I wasn't sure any of us were.

TWENTY

We pulled out of Reaperstown so fast I thought my engine was going to blow. "What the hell happened back there?" I said to Beau, giving him the side-eye.

"What do you think? I told you not to leave me out there with all those degenerate vampires." He gazed out the window with a sigh. "They started sniffing around me like I was fresh meat. Then one of them ordered a beer and jumped over the bar while I was getting it for him."

"You actually worked the bar?" I thought Irina was just messing with him.

"Well, yeah. It was either that or tell a bunch of thirsty vampires they were shit out of luck."

"Irina was gone all of what? Five minutes?"

He snorted. "Five minutes my ass. I think she took a break, and then all hell broke loose after that first one tried to jump me. That's when I shifted."

I patted him on the shoulder. "Sorry I left you alone."

Samuel's name popped up when my phone rang. We were almost back to town, so I decided to let it go to voicemail because this was a conversation that needed to take place in person.

"Was that Samuel?" Beau said.

"How'd you guess? I'm sure he's wondering where I am by now."

Beau snickered. "I'm surprised he didn't track you down at the Beast."

It surprised me too. In fact, I'd noticed a lot of unusual things lately. Samuel not sensing me in Ian's office while he was pounding that woman on his desk was one of them. Something like that should have brought him running.

The Stag was packed when we got there. Samuel was sitting at the bar staring out the window, his eyes locking on mine the second we parked.

"He doesn't look happy," Beau said. "Good luck telling him where you've been tonight."

"Samuel doesn't own me, Beau. I don't need his permission to go to the Beast."

"Does he know that?"

I braced myself for an unpleasant conversation and got out. As soon as we walked inside, Samuel was on his feet. I couldn't tell if the look in his eyes was anger or relief. Whatever it was, it made me uneasy.

Beau headed for the men's room. "I need to take a leak. I'll jump behind the bar in a minute."

"Too much information, Beau. Just hurry it up."

Samuel's eyes were burning a hole in me when I met him at the bar. "Before you start with the questions, let's go to the back room."

Lucy set a drink down in front of a customer and went to the tap to pour a beer. "Can we get some help here? The place has been a madhouse since you two left."

To avoid the drama, I held my tongue. "Beau will be out in a minute."

"One minute or fifteen like he usually takes?"

Tucker came up behind Lucy, squirming like she had ants in her pants. "I need to run to the ladies' room. Can you hold down the bar for five minutes?"

Lucy swung around, nearly dropping the glass in her hand. "Hell no! I came in first, so I get a break next."

Mike was sitting a few stools down, snapping his fingers at her. "I'm still waiting for that beer."

Lucy tilted her head at me. "Maybe you need to get your customer a drink."

"Let's go have that talk," Samuel said, grabbing my arm.

"Nope." Lucy shook her head. "Charley needs to get behind this bar."

My head was starting to spin from everyone coming at me, and Lucy's voice was like fingernails on a chalkboard.

Dog stuck his head through the order window next. "Charley! A word?"

I closed my eyes when my breathing started to pick up. It grew more rapid, like my heart was about to pound out of my chest. My mouth had suddenly gone bone dry, and blood was rushing through my ears like a river. It felt like I was having a panic attack.

When my eyes popped back open, I looked at all the faces staring back at me. Their mouths were flapping, but their voices had blurred into a single high-pitched sound that assaulted my ears.

I pulled my arm out of Samuel's grip and stepped away as the room started to spin, the sound drilling deeper. When it got so intense that I thought my head would explode, I closed my eyes and covered my ears. "Will. You. All. Just. Stop!"

Everything went dead quiet. Other than my own heartbeat, I couldn't hear a thing. When I opened my eyes, the room was at a complete standstill. And I mean complete, with everyone in mid-motion, their mouths ajar as if words were still spilling out.

Even the TV on the wall was frozen like someone had paused it.

"What is happening to me?" I whispered, shaking my head as if it might wake me up from whatever dream this was. I realized I was gripping my amulet, terrified that I'd finally gone over the edge and those two spiders inside me were eating away at my mind.

"The spiders!" I let go of the amulet like it was red hot, squeezing my eyes shut again when a cloud of black filled my peripheral vision. I prayed for it to end.

"Charley?" Samuel placed his hand gently on my arm. "Are you all right?"

My eyes opened. The room was animated again. As if nothing had happened. I was definitely losing it.

He studied my face for a moment and then ushered me down the hallway, shutting the door when we reached the back room. "What just happened out there?"

I shook my head. "Nothing. I got dizzy when everyone started barking at me. I'm fine now."

His brow tightened as he examined my eyes. "No, you're not."

"I said, I'm fine." The words came out harshly.

He finally backed off and leaned against the desk. "All right. Where were you tonight?"

Beating around the bush would only prolong the questions. "At the Beast. I went there to talk to Ian," I quickly added when his eyes narrowed.

He laughed quietly. "Well, I certainly hope that's the reason you went down there and not for the crowd."

"I didn't tell you because I knew you'd insist on going with me. It would have been counterproductive if some of those vampires decided to start trouble." I shrugged. "Taking Dog would have been just as bad, so Beau went with me."

"Why did you need to talk to Ian?"

"I think Shane Ronan is handing out vampire blood contaminated with hepatitis C at those fights."

He cocked his head. "What makes you think that?"

"Because the co-op supply is contaminated, and I saw one of our donors at that fight the other night. One of the donors who tested positive."

Samuel didn't even try to suggest alternative explanations. He'd figured out what I had. I could see it in his eyes.

His expression turned bitter. "Even more reason to kill my old friend."

"I went to the Beast to warn Ian. It impacts his business, so now he's really motivated to help us find Ronan."

"Clever girl."

I laughed. "He can kiss his club good-bye if humans down there start getting sick." Ian had waited too long to get his hands on the Beast to lose it now. "He's probably already out there looking."

"He can look all he wants," Samuel said. "But like I said, Ronan won't be found until he wants to be. We need to be ready when he makes his next move."

There was a tap on the door. Dog stuck his head in the room and pointed at me. "I need to talk to you."

Samuel pushed away from the desk. "I was just leaving."

"I'll meet you in the kitchen in a minute," I said to Dog. After he left, I turned back to Samuel. "Can you stay? Have a drink?"

"No. I'd rather you came home with me," he said, running his hands up and down my arms. "But you have a business to run."

"I just want this to be over with, Samuel."

He lifted my chin to look in my eyes. "It will be soon. I promise."

"Just make sure you're the last one standing when it is."

The backs of his fingers brushed along my jaw and settled at the nape of my neck. "I'll never let you go, in life or death, and I have no intention of taking you with me to the grave." He leaned closer and kissed my cheek before whispering, "I will kill Ronan for even putting that thought in my head."

His words chilled me to the bone and excited me at the same time. Knowing he could end me with a slip of his fangs. That even before what had happened between us in that chamber, I'd always been at his mercy.

"I better go," he said, releasing me. "See you tonight?"

A smile flashed across my face. "Tonight."

When he was gone, I leaned against the wall to catch my breath, hoping the feeling never went away. The one I got every time he trained his intense blue eyes on mine.

After coming back down to earth, I went to the kitchen to see what Dog wanted.

He glanced up when I walked through the door. "Are you all right, Charley? You looked kind of shaky earlier."

I wasn't about to tell him I was losing my mind. That I'd hallucinated time stopping in the bar. "I'm fine. What did you want to talk to me about?" When he cleared his throat and started wiping down the cutting board without looking at me, I got nervous. "You aren't quitting on me, are you?"

He finally brought his eyes to mine. "What? Christ, Charley, why do you keep asking me that?"

I rubbed my stomach to calm the butterflies flapping around in there. "I don't know. Everything else is going to shit lately."

"I know it's short notice, but I need tomorrow night off."

I finally relaxed. "Of course you can have tomorrow off." I still needed to get him some help in the kitchen. "And I'll get that help wanted sign in the window tonight."

His forehead creased. "I'm rethinking that. I'm not sure I want some stranger messing around in my kitchen."

Well, it wouldn't be a stranger if they worked here.

"You work too much, Dog. You need some part-time help back here."

"Fine." He picked up the knife and pointed it at me. "But I get to sign off on who you hire."

I snorted. "Hundred percent."

"Good. And I appreciate the night off."

He had me curious, though. "You got plans with someone?"

"Yep." He grabbed an onion and offered nothing else.

Okay.

Then he gave me the side-eye. "Something else you want to talk about?"

I could take a hint. "Nope. I'm going to head over to the Cauldron for a few minutes, so call me if you need me."

"We've got three bartenders out there." He brought the knife down hard on the onion. "I think we can handle it."

I left the kitchen, feeling like I'd been dismissed, and stopped at the bar to let Beau know where I was going. Then I went to see the one person who might be able to explain the weird stuff that had been happening to me lately. I prayed Candy would tell me it was all normal for a blossoming witch whose powers were coming on like a freight train. That there wasn't some history of mental instability on the Wilderbrandt side that had me slowly descending into madness.

TWENTY-ONE

I'd called on the way over to let Candy know I was coming and why, but she wasn't up front when I walked into the Cauldron.

"I'm back here," she yelled when she heard the chimes on the front door.

I found her in the back room on her hands and knees doing something to the doorway leading to her infamous closet.

"What are you doing?" I asked, glancing at the pillow under her knees.

She straightened up and pushed her long red hair out of her eyes, pointing to the table. "Hand me that bottle of Florida water."

Florida what?

I grabbed the bottle and looked at the colorful label. "This one?"

"Do you see another bottle?' She snapped her fingers a few times. "My knees are about to give out, so open it and hand it to me."

I pulled the stopper out and took a whiff. It smelled pleasant. Like oranges or lemons mixed with some kind of herbs. "What are you doing?" I asked a second time.

"Making sure no one gets in here again."

Before he died, my father had broken in and stolen one of those dangerous objects she kept in that closet. A necromancer's charm. After that, we moved the worst ones to the Squad's house. Tossed them into a portal in the basement.

"The most dangerous ones aren't even in there anymore, so why bother?"

"I brought them back," she said as she sprinkled something on the floor.

I glanced at the shelf inside. Every one of those vessels we'd removed was back in its original spot. I'd know the one containing Atticus Devereaux anywhere. "Are you crazy?"

She smirked. "Just a touch."

"I'm serious, Candy. Why would you remove them from that portal?" *How* did she remove them from that portal?

A snicker came from under her breath. "You think I'd leave those vessels under the same roof as Desiree Dubois longer than I had to? That witch was probably planning to pluck them out herself and experiment with them, especially after she's had half a bottle of absinthe."

She poured some of the Florida water in her hands and rubbed them together, patting it on her face and arms. "That's better."

"What does that water do, and what's that stuff on the floor?" She'd finished sprinkling a line of rust-colored powder along the outside of the closet door.

"The water's for me. It's refreshing, especially after working on this floor. I think I'm starting to stink."

She did have a glisten to her skin.

"And that's red brick dust. Didn't Delia teach you anything?"

I'd heard of it before but not from my mother. It was used for protection in some cultures. "You don't really think that stuff will stop someone from going into that closet?"

She scoffed. "Of course not. You think I got this sweaty pouring a line of dust? It's a tripwire. If someone uninvited crosses that line, the wards I've been working on all day will come down on them like a hammer."

"What kind of wards?"

She flicked her devious eyes up to mine. "Ever witnessed someone getting struck by lightning?"

"No."

"They'll wish they had."

I took an involuntary step back. "Thanks for the warning."

"You're invited, so you don't have anything to worry about." She held her hand out to me. "Help me up." After I pulled her to her feet, she wiped her palms on her pants and blew a strand of hair out of her eyes. "Now, what's all this business about you losing your mind?"

Where to begin?

"A bunch of strange things have been happening to me this week."

"Such as?"

"It started a few days ago." My mind went back to the other afternoon when I had words with Lucy. When I threatened to shut her up and suddenly she was tongue-tied. I didn't think much of it at the time, but after what happened tonight, I wasn't so sure about writing it off as nothing. "You're going to tell me I'm imagining it, but I think I silenced Lucy the other day when she wouldn't keep her mouth shut."

"That's not crazy, honey. That's a gift to anyone who's ever had to listen to her." Her eyes narrowed. "Though I don't think anyone has ever made that girl shut up before."

"I'm serious, Candy."

"So am I. It's going to take more than that to convince me you're off your rocker, though."

"And then the other night when Ian Masterson showed up at my house and couldn't get back inside. What about that?"

A deep furrow formed between her eyes. "Now that was interesting."

"And now I think Samuel has lost his ability to sense me."

"Why do you think that?"

I wasn't looking forward to telling her where I'd been earlier that night. "Because I went to the Beast tonight. I expected Samuel to show up but he never did."

"Now why would you go do something stupid like that?"

I hadn't had the chance to tell her about the contaminated blood yet, but that discussion could wait until after we determined what was wrong with me. "Can we please focus on what's happening to me first? Samuel stopped by the Stag tonight and had no idea where I'd been. I'm telling you, he can't sense me anymore."

Candy tried to act casual about it, but I could see it had sparked her curiosity. "It's probably just your powers getting stronger. Being able to block vampires is a good thing. I wouldn't worry about it." She chuckled. "Unless you start reading minds or something just as impressive like manifesting thunderstorms or stopping time." When she saw my expression, her face went flat. "You're not reading my thoughts right now, are you?"

A funny little laugh slipped from my mouth. "Nope. Can't hear a word you're thinking. But that time-stopping thing? What exactly does that look like?"

She stared at me, probably waiting for me to laugh it off. "This isn't a joke, is it?"

I slowly shook my head again. "Something happened to me tonight in the middle of the bar, and I can't explain it. The only thing I know for sure is that for a few seconds, I was the only thing in the room moving."

She squinted at my eyes and tapped her fingers against her lips. Then she walked out of the room. "Let's go."

"Where?"

"Honey, this is witch business. Where do you think?"

TWENTY-TWO

The old Victorian was lit up like a Christmas tree when we arrived. The lights were on in half the rooms.

"Looks like they're having a party."

Candy glanced at me sideways as we walked up to the house. "They're night owls. You should see the place at three a.m."

The witching hour. I could only imagine what went on in that big house in the wee hours of the morning.

I'd filled Candy in on the hepatitis outbreak on the way over, but not all the details of my strange experience at the bar. The second I mentioned the room freezing like the frame of a movie reel, she told me to wait so I didn't have to repeat it when we arrived. Something about losing fine details with each retelling of a story.

Mia Winston opened the front door as we walked up the steps. She looked good for a woman who had been in a catatonic state only a week ago. My father had used a rather wicked spell on her. The same one he'd used to kill my mother. Now the witch would be a painful reminder every time I looked at her.

Her eyes lit up. "You're just in time."

"In time for what?" I said.

Mia's smile faded. "Dinner."

I glanced at Candy. "I... didn't know we were having dinner." My nerves were too shot to eat.

Candy nudged me through the door. "Neither did I."

Mia led us toward the back of the house. For a place that was so lit up, it seemed awfully empty and quiet. We came to the dining room at the end of the hallway. Like the rest of the house, the room was furnished with Victorian antiques. The members of the Squad were seated at a long mahogany table with quite a spread laid out: a platter with prime rib and another one with a whole roasted chicken. And there were enough sides to feed a small army. In the center of the table was a two-tiered cake with a single candle on top.

Katherine stood up when we walked in. "I hope you don't mind that we started without you."

"No," I said, giving Candy a questioning look.

She motioned to the vacant chairs on the other side of the table, and we walked around to seat ourselves, with me wondering how I was going to force down a polite amount of food. My mother always said, when someone takes the time to cook for you, you eat.

I grabbed one of the chairs and started to pull it out.

"Not that one!" Desiree snapped, shooting me a withering look. "It's occupied."

I looked down at the empty seat, my eyes wandering to the plateful of food in front of it. "I'm sorry. Is someone else joining us?" I wasn't about to air my secrets to a stranger, so that was going to be a problem.

Fay, who was sitting next to her sister, laughed quietly, but Desiree continued to throw daggers at me with her eyes. I didn't know why, but her animosity for me was off the chart.

"It's Victoria's birthday," Katherine said with a faint smile. "She's thrilled you're joining us."

I glanced at Candy for the tenth time, searching for any hint that I wasn't the only one in the dark.

"Just sit," she whispered.

When Candy and I were seated, Katherine passed a bottle of champagne across the table. "We were just about to toast Victoria."

Why not. I poured us both a glass and looked at the empty chair to my right. "Want me to top yours off?" I chuckled.

I set the bottle down when Candy kicked me under the table.

Katherine raised her glass. "To Victoria."

As I grabbed mine, I glanced at the one in front of our phantom guest, half expecting to see it rise up by some invisible hand. But this was nothing more than a commemoration dinner for the woman I'd recently found out was my great-great-grand-mother. It was creepy, though, the way they were all staring at the empty seat.

While the witches resumed their dinner, Candy plopped a drumstick and some green beans on my plate like I was a child. "Eat something," she muttered.

Reluctantly, I took a bite of a bean.

Desiree stuck a whole chicken wing in her mouth and pulled the bone out clean. After chewing and swallowing her mouthful, she picked her front teeth with her tongue and smacked her lips. "So..." Her eyes leveled on mine. "...What is this about strange things happening to you?"

Her tone couldn't have been more dismissive.

Katherine shot her a look. "Let our guest eat first."

"It's all right." I set my fork down, thankful for the interruption so I didn't have to force any more food into my nervous stomach. I'd tossed my lunch once before in their powder room near the front door and didn't want to become known as *that* guest. I figured I'd start with the strangest event and work my way to lesser ones if they were still interested. "Something happened to me at the Stag tonight."

"Out with it," Candy said when I hesitated.

I let out a sigh and got on with it. I was in a house with a portal in the basement, for God's sake. "I think I might have..." I glanced around the table as the words stuck in my throat because it was ridiculous. Preposterous. "...stopped time," I mumbled.

Desiree cocked her head. "What was that?"

"I said I think I stopped time," I blurted out.

She scoffed and got back to her chicken. "You think awfully highly of yourself."

I felt the floor shift under my feet, and the china on the table rattled. Either a rare earthquake had hit North Georgia or something very large had fallen somewhere in the house.

The fork slipped from Mia's hand as her eyes went blank. "You what?"

"Can you repeat that?" Katherine said, squinting at me.

"You heard her." Candy slid her eyes to mine. "Now, tell us exactly what happened at the bar tonight."

Desiree stood up, a saccharine smile plastered on her face. "I think this calls for a cocktail. Shall we adjourn to the living room?"

"For once," Candy muttered, "I agree with Desiree."

Fay gazed at the cake in the middle of the table, practically salivating. "But we haven't even cut the birthday cake yet."

Katherine's eyes never left mine as she stood up. "The cake can wait."

The rest of us got up, a tremor continuing to rumble under my feet as we followed her down the hallway. "What is that?" I finally said, looking at the floor.

A faint smile appeared on Katherine's face when she glanced back at me. "It's Victoria."

"Vic...?"

She looked away and led us into the living room. Desiree went straight to the bureau and grabbed a glass. "Absinthe, anyone?"

"Not in this lifetime," Candy muttered.

I shook my head when she jiggled the bottle at me.

She shrugged. "Suit yourselves."

"Go on," Katherine said. "Tell us what happened, and don't spare the slightest detail."

I changed my mind and decided to start with the small stuff and build up to the crazy shit. "It started earlier this week. I thought it was just my imagination, but I can't ignore it after what happened tonight. There've been a few instances where I've barked at people and they've..."

Desiree sat down with her green drink and groaned. "Just get on with it."

It was easier to give an example. "The other day when one of my bartenders was mouthing off. I got angry and warned her that if she didn't shut up, I'd do it for her. Next thing I knew, she was staring at me and clutching her throat like she was terrified. She went mute. Didn't say another word and ran into the bathroom."

Katherine shrugged. "I'd hardly call that strange. Maybe she took your warning seriously. You are her boss, right?"

Candy snickered. "You don't know Lucy Wyatt."

They clearly weren't convinced, so I decided to skip over what happened between me and Ian and get to the showstopper. "There've been a few other things, like Samuel no longer being able to sense me, but what happened tonight really shook me."

Desiree sipped her drink with a bored look in her eyes. "I certainly hope it's more interesting than your bartender needing to use the bathroom. We have a cake to cut."

I took a deep breath before continuing. "I'd already had a rough night when I got to the Stag, so I was on edge." I paused, trying to choose my words carefully so they wouldn't brush it off as my imagination. "When I got there, people were coming at me from every direction. My bartender was giving me attitude, Dog was shouting at me through the order window. And then Samuel grabbed my arm and was about to start lecturing me about where I'd been that night. A moment later, my head started to pound. I thought I was having a panic attack."

"And?" Katherine said when I stopped. They were all staring at me.

"And then the room started to spin." I shook my head briskly. "I snapped. I shut my eyes and yelled for everyone to stop." I shrugged, glancing around at the witches. "And then everything did. Everyone froze around me. Even the TV. It was like the world had been put on pause, and I was the only thing moving."

Candy's mouth was gaping when I looked at her. "Then what happened?"

"I realized I was gripping my amulet, thinking those spiders inside me were eating at my brain or something. Next thing I knew, Samuel was calling my name and asking me what was wrong. The world had just started up again."

The rumbling under my feet resumed. It was more of a vibration now. It traveled through the floor and into my legs, sending a strange sensation through me.

Katherine rested her hand on my forearm. "Is something wrong? You look like you've seen a ghost." Her eyes thinned as she continued to study my face, a sly smile appearing. "Have you?"

I met her gaze as the sensation faded. "Just tell me what's happening to me. Is it my father's spider?" His birthright was crawling around inside me, and I wondered if this was all payback for stealing it from him.

She pulled her hand away, but a trace of a smile remained on her face. "I think you might be right about Richard's spider, but my brother wasn't that talented. *This* was above his pay grade." She let out a quiet laugh. "It's above mine."

"*This* what?" I said, getting nervous from the way they were all looking at me.

"But not above..." The muscles in Desiree's face went slack, her mouth turning up into a frown. "It can't be true."

I looked back and forth between the two witches. "What are you talking about? What can't be true?"

"That's a good question," Candy said, eyeing Desiree. "Why don't you fill us both in?"

Katherine held Desiree's gaze for a moment as if speaking to her silently.

Desiree broke eye contact with her and scoffed. Then she downed her drink and plunked the glass on the coffee table. "It's preposterous."

Now I was really nervous about what the witches weren't telling me. At least those damn vibrations under my feet had settled.

Katherine looked at the portrait above the fireplace for a moment and then brought her eyes to mine. "I think Desiree is trying to say you might have gotten more than your father's magic when you inhaled his spider. Keep in mind, he stole most of his power." After letting that sink in, she continued with the revelations. "It appears you received Fawny's too."

Fawny Goodman. The conjure woman from the lake. My father murdered her and stole her magic to get to me.

"And now you're channeling some of her skills."

I cleared my throat. "Skills?"

"One of Fawny's most impressive. I believe you manifested the gift of time capture."

Candy gasped. "Well, fuck me."

The vibrations picked up again, and the walls were starting to shake. A picture fell, cracking the glass inside the frame when it hit the floor.

"Okay, I'm out of here." I got up and headed for the door. "I'll be waiting in the truck." When I grabbed the handle, it wouldn't budge. I tried it again but the house clearly didn't want me to leave.

Candy followed me into the foyer. "Come back to the living room, Charley. We're not done talking yet."

I hated when she looked at me like that. Like she was about to tell me something unpleasant that was supposedly for my own good. "Do I have a choice?"

When I walked back into the living room, the witches were staring at me. "What's wrong with this house?" I asked, still not sure if I wanted to stay or jump out of one of the windows.

Katherine glanced at the painting of Victoria Wilderbrandt again. "There's nothing wrong with it. Victoria is just giving her approval. Getting to know her great-great-granddaughter who will one day—"

"Nonsense!" Desiree stood up and stormed toward the hall-way, brushing past me on her way out.

"Did I do something?"

Katherine motioned to the sofa. "Have a seat."

"I'd prefer to stand."

"All right." Before continuing, she looked at Fay and Mia who seemed very eager to hear what she was about to say. "Why don't the two of you go check on Desiree. See that she hasn't broken open the bottle of mead in the kitchen."

Reluctantly, the sisters left the room to find the sullen witch.

When they were gone, Katherine continued. "Forgive Desiree for being so..."

"Rude?" I said. The woman made an art form out of it.

"Fair enough." She went to the bureau and poured a glass of amber liquid. Whiskey or bourbon. Then she came back over and offered it to me.

I shook my head. "No, thanks."

"You might need it."

"Just get on with it so I can leave."

She took a sip of the drink, her eyes fixed on mine. "You're a lot like her."

"My mother?"

A smile slid up Katherine's face. "Victoria."

I hadn't expected that. "Oh."

"You have the same fearless disregard for things that could bite you in the ass."

"I'll take that as a compliment," I said.

Katherine's eyes wandered around the room, and a slight laugh slipped from under her breath. "Victoria agrees."

I glanced at Candy, wondering if I was the only witch in the room thinking Katherine Belltower was even crazier than me. But Candy's face was unreadable.

"Why do you talk about Victoria Wilderbrandt like she's still here?" I asked Katherine.

"Because she is. She lives in these walls. Walks the halls at night. Has an eye on everything that happens in this house." Her chin lowered as she took a step closer to me. "Why do you think my brother tried to burn this house down?"

I looked to Candy for some clarity. "What is she talking about?"

Candy let out a steady groan. "Just tell her. She'll need to know eventually."

My brow tightened. "The two of you are creeping me out."

Katherine's intense gaze finally softened. "Victoria was buried in this house."

I pointed to the floor. "You mean down in that basement?" It wouldn't surprise me to find a body down there.

"In the walls."

I glanced sideways at Candy again, hoping for a sane voice to clarify what I thought Katherine had just said.

"It's true," Candy said. "Victoria's bones are in the walls."

Desiree was staring at me from the living room doorway when I turned to attempt another escape. If eyes were weapons, I'd be dead.

"I told you she'd never understand." Desiree seethed as she turned back toward the hallway, flailing her hand in the air as she stormed off again.

The whole house seemed to shake this time, and a sound caught my attention. The glass in the front door had broken, leaving a spiderweb of cracks along the pane. Seeing it ajar, I seized the opportunity to get out while I could.

"You have to understand, Charley," Katherine said as I hurried toward it. "About Desiree. This is her home, and you're a threat."

I stopped and turned to face her. "How am I a threat?" *To that crazy bitch*, I wanted to add.

"This house will be yours when I'm gone. Mia and Fay have accepted that, but Desiree worries about her future."

Candy had mentioned that, and it had also crossed my mind since I was her only living blood relative, other than Aunt Hester in Savannah who was a breath away from entering that forest permanently. "What if I don't want it?" I could barely keep up with my own house, let alone this mausoleum all the way out here in the woods.

Katherine's lips tightened. "A Wilderbrandt built this house over a century ago, and a Wilderbrandt has lived in it ever since. A great amount of responsibility comes with it. Make no mistake, Charley. This house will be yours someday."

The woman thought she could force this place on me?

She came closer and looked me dead in the eye. "I'll burn it to the ground myself before I see it fall into the hands of someone outside this family."

Candy stepped between us before I could say something I'd regret. "Settle down, Katherine. You're not going anywhere anytime soon." Then she grabbed my arm and pulled me toward the door. "Let's go."

When we got in the truck, I looked up at the turret on the top floor. Desiree was standing at the window staring down at us. At me. "Does Katherine really think I'd take that house? With a dead woman in the walls?" I let out a sarcastic laugh. "I'm pretty sure that's illegal, by the way."

"Not in this town," Candy muttered.

"And kick those women out of their home? What kind of person does she think I am?"

Candy sighed. "It's not Katherine you need to worry about." She followed my gaze as I looked back up at the witch standing at the window. "That's the one you need to watch out for. I'm assuming the house goes to the other three if you die before Katherine does."

And I assumed she was making a morbid joke, but as I started the truck and drove back toward town, I told myself that I needed to start sleeping with one eye open. Not for Shane Ronan, but for a witch who now had me in her crosshairs.

TWENTY-THREE

By the time I dropped Candy off and pulled up to the Stag, Dog was locking the front door.

"Sorry," I said to him as I got out of my truck. "I didn't think it would take so long." I'd called him on the way to the Squad's house to let him know I wouldn't be back for a while, and a while turned into most of the night. "Anything happen while I was gone?"

He glanced back at the bar. "The usual Saturday night. The place is still standing."

The Stag had been doing just fine without me lately. Not sure how I felt about that.

"Everything okay?" he asked, glancing at his truck like he was eager to leave.

Everything was not okay, but it was too late to get into a conversation that would require more than a few minutes standing on the sidewalk. "Are you sure *you're* okay?" I said as he walked past me to his truck and got in.

"Why wouldn't I be?"

I shrugged. "Just asking."

He gave me a brief smile as he backed into the street. "Try not to burn the kitchen down while I'm gone."

"No promises," I yelled as he started to drive away. "Enjoy your night off." He didn't even look back at me through the side mirror.

I thought about going inside and maybe getting a few things done. But I'd had enough for one night.

After double-checking the front door, and of course finding it locked, I got back in my truck and drove to Samuel's house. He was sitting in the living room with a book in his hands when I walked in.

I leaned over the back of the sofa and wrapped my arms around him. "What are you reading?"

"Is this the book Candy wants to borrow?"

I folded the cover over and looked at the strange symbol on the front. "That's it."

He closed the book. "I found it on the table in the study and thought I'd have a look. See what she found so interesting."

"It's the Squad who wants to borrow it. Candy and I should have swung by earlier to grab it. We just got back from their house."

"You were at the Squad's house?"

I really wasn't in the mood to discuss my new emerging skills, at least not until I figured them out myself. "Looks like I'm next in line to inherit that old house." It was a good enough explanation for now.

"It shouldn't surprise you. You're Katherine Belltower's niece. It makes sense."

I chuckled. "Tell that to Desiree Dubois." I came around the sofa and sat down next to him, changing the subject as quick as possible to avoid the memory of her hateful eyes staring down at me from the turret. "So, is there anything interesting in that book?"

Samuel opened it up again and flipped through the pages.

"Looks like some sort of record, although why Pullman would keep it in the library is a mystery."

"Well, it is a book so..."

"But something like this is usually kept under lock and key."

I glanced at the book again. "The man was a vampire. I'm sure he wasn't concerned about someone coming in his house and plundering his library. It was also kind of hidden at the top of the bookcase. Candy noticed it pushed against the wall and used the ladder to reach it." And Clifford Pullman did die suddenly. Maybe he'd been reading it the night he went out and didn't expect to never make it home again to put it back in its proper place.

Samuel continued to study the pages. "Still, it was sloppy to leave it out. His fellow members would have ex-communicated him for exposing their secrets. Or worse."

"What do you mean by 'members'?"

He snapped the book shut and handed it to me. "Cliff Pullman was a member of a secret society."

The laugh coming from my mouth was cut short when I realized he was serious. "Really?" I ran my hand over the symbol on the cover, Candy's comments making perfect sense now. "Maybe we should look through that library for more juicy stuff."

"Right." Samuel stood up. "First, though, I think you need some food. I'm sure you haven't bothered to eat tonight."

He knew me very well, but my appetite wasn't any stronger now than it had been at the Squad's house. "Maybe a bite," I said, more to satisfy Samuel than me.

As I got up to follow him, something loud struck in the distance. "What the hell was that?"

It was enough to shake the house. I would have guessed thunder, but the weather was fine a few minutes ago. The night sky had been clear as a bell.

He froze, his hyper-sensitive ears picking up on something. "*That* was an explosion."

We went outside and looked up. The sky was aglow with orange light, and it was coming from the direction of the town square.

My breath caught as adrenaline raced through me. "The Stag!"

We climbed into my truck and followed the kaleidoscope of fiery colors billowing into the sky, my heart dropping into my stomach as we rounded the corner near the bar. A Crimson PD patrol car had the street blocked off, so we parked and headed toward the Stag on foot. I nearly dropped to my knees when I saw flames exploding from what remained of the restaurant across the street, pieces of the rubble exploding like fireworks into the sky.

When I pulled my eyes away from the destruction to see if any other buildings were impacted, I saw Tom Murphy walking toward us. For once, I was glad to see him.

"The Stag is fine," Murphy said when he reached me. "Looks like someone got tired of looking at that heap of a restaurant across the street, though." He glanced back at the burning remnants of Morceau. "I guess the taxpayers won't be paying for the demolition after all. Someone blew the place up."

"It was a bomb?" Samuel said.

Murphy nodded once. "Got an eyewitness who saw a couple of men running from the place. A minute later... boom." He scanned the growing crowd before bringing his eyes back to mine. "Where's Dog?"

"Dog? Why?"

He came closer and pinned me with a cold stare. "Because my witness said those men dropped down on all fours before taking off into the woods."

I backed away from him. "You think Dog and the pack did this? Why the hell would they do that?"

He shrugged. "Why would anyone blow up a building that was half gone anyway? All I know for sure is I've got a credible eyewitness who saw wolves running from the place a minute before it blew, so I need to have a talk with your cook."

Samuel eased me back when I started to inch closer to Murphy again. He was right to do so because I was a second away from finding myself in the back of that patrol car blocking the street.

"Let's get out of here," I said to Samuel without taking my harsh gaze off the cop.

"If you find Dog before I do," Murphy said as we headed back toward my truck, "tell him I'm looking for him."

I gave him a middle finger salute without looking back. To hell with his witness. Murphy could fuck off for even suggesting that the pack had anything to do with it.

As we approached the truck, I slowed down and came to a halt as other suspects entered my mind. Suspects that brought trouble every time they came to town. "Damn it," I muttered as I reached for my phone.

"Who are you calling?" Samuel asked.

"Dog." I dialed his number, but it just kept ringing and finally went to voicemail. I tried again with no luck. "He's not answering. Let's go before Murphy decides he wants to have another chat."

"Go where?"

"To the pack's compound. I need to get to Dog before Murphy does."

* * *

"Wait in the truck," I said to Samuel as two sets of glowing eyes appeared in the headlights. It was never a good idea to show up at the compound uninvited, but Dog had left us no choice. I could talk my way in, but the pack wouldn't be so welcoming to a vampire. I needed to smooth things out and explain why we were here before Samuel got out of the truck.

Careful not to get too close because I didn't have a clue about which wolves I was dealing with, I got out and approached them. Most of the pack knew me, but there were some who rarely, if ever, came into town. The younger ones. Their amber eyes and glistening fangs gave away nothing about who these particular wolves were.

"It's Charley Underwood. I'm here to see Dog."

One of the wolves looked back at the truck, its snout lifting with its fangs bared, as it caught a whiff of Samuel.

"That's Samuel Cain. He's a friend of Dog's too. This is kind of an emergency, so if we could speed the introductions along."

When the wolves started to advance, I backed up toward the truck, wondering how fast I could dart inside if they charged. Just in case, I worked up some energy in my palm, hoping I wouldn't have to use it.

Samuel was out of the truck before I even saw his door crack open. "Over here," he said, whistling.

When one of them lunged, a third wolf appeared from the bushes. It was Loki. He shifted a second later. "Back off!" he ordered. The two wolves immediately stopped and cowered at his voice. "Get back to work," he growled at them.

The energy in my hand dissipated as the wolves took off into the woods. "Who the hell were they?" I asked Loki. I may not have personally met the entire pack, but most of them at least knew my name, seeing as how their pack leader worked at my bar.

"Pups," he said. "Young and still stupid as hell. Sorry about that, but you know better than to come out here unannounced." He glanced at Samuel standing on the other side of the truck, his eyes filled with suspicion. "Especially with a vampire. What are you doing out here this late?"

"I need to talk to Dog." I glanced over his shoulder, trying to get a view of the clearing through the trees. We were almost to the edge of it when those guards stopped us. "I tried to call but he isn't answering his phone, and this can't wait until tomorrow. Is he here?"

Loki's eyes darted in the direction of Dog's cabin before coming back to me. "I can relay a message to him if you want."

Relay a message?

"I'm not fucking around, Loki. This is important."

He let out a long breath. "Neither am I. Dog's busy right now."

"To hell with it," I said, walking around him toward the house.

When Loki tried to stop me, Samuel grabbed his arm. "Don't even think about it."

Loki dropped down on all fours and slipped from Samuel's grip. He gave a warning growl and then took off past me, shifting again a few yards away from Dog's front door. By the time I caught up to him, half the pack had shown up in the clearing and had their eyes on us.

"Are you really going to stop me from knocking on that door?" I said to Loki. I didn't know what was going on, but I intended to find Dog, even if I had to use my magic to get through every one of those wolves.

"Jesus, Charley!" Loki glowered at me. "You've got a fucking stubborn streak worse than your mother's. Get back in your truck and go home."

Lux stepped out from the others and came up beside Loki. "He's right. You should leave."

There wasn't a chance in hell I was going anywhere until I saw Dog with my own two eyes. "Did something happen to him?" My heart started to thump as my imagination ran wild. "Dog!" I yelled. "If you're in there, I need to talk to you!"

Just as I was starting to panic, the front door swung open.

Dog was standing in the doorway wearing nothing but a pair of jeans. His braid was undone, and his long black hair cascaded down his chest. I couldn't put my finger on it but there was something in his eyes that alarmed me.

He leaned against the doorframe and crossed his arms. "Let her through."

I glanced down at his bare feet and brought my eyes back up to his. "Are you sick?"

After pushing away from the door, he rubbed both hands over his face and let out a wheezing laugh. But there was nothing funny about the way it sounded. He looked exhausted.

"He's sick all right," Lux muttered as she walked toward the others in the clearing.

I glanced back at Samuel who was keeping his distance and then walked past Loki toward the cabin. When I got to the door, I saw someone standing behind Dog. A tall woman with dark hair and memorable green eyes was staring at me over his shoulder. But it was the tattoo running down her neck that jogged my memory.

"Oh, you have got to be kidding me." I shook my head, muttering some choice words as I turned around and walked toward the truck. "Let's get the hell out of here," I said to Samuel.

He grabbed my arm when I blew past him. "Hold it. Who's there with Dog?"

I pulled my arm free and glanced back at the house. At Dog who was standing on the porch now. "A woman, and she's the reason that restaurant was blown to smithereens tonight. It was a message from the northern pack, and the Stag will be next."

TWENTY-FOUR

When Dog yelled for me to come back, it took everything I had to keep from continuing to the truck and driving out of those woods. But the situation was what it was, and running away from it wasn't going to make it any better. Dog was harboring Zane's *woman*, and I needed to find out why. Then I needed to figure out how to hand her back without getting my ass chewed off.

"You need to hear him out," Samuel said.

"Why are you always the voice of reason?" I sighed and headed back toward the house, avoiding eye contact with Dog as I walked past him to go inside. Tempest caught a wicked glare from me, though. That wolf was causing me nothing but trouble, and I'd had enough of it at that moment.

"Let's just get this over with," I said when Samuel and Dog followed me in. "What is she doing here?" She was wearing one of Dog's T-shirts. It barely covered her ass, and I doubted there was anything under it. "Never mind. It's kinda obvious." I finally gave Dog my full attention. "Jesus, Dog. Sleeping with the enemy? You couldn't find a local to pass the time with?"

Tempest lived up to her name and had me backed against

the wall before I saw her coming, her wolf morphing in and out as her golden eyes bored into mine. "Watch your mouth."

I rammed my palm into her, a crackle of energy spreading across her chest. She flew backward, her wolf fully emerging as she slammed into the opposite wall of the small living room.

Dog stepped between us when the wolf shook off the magic and started to charge. "Enough!" She submitted under his warning gaze. Then he pointed his finger at me. "You, settle the fuck down."

Samuel was leaning against the door with his arms folded. He just stared back at me with the same look Dog was giving me.

When I turned back to Dog, he was bent down next to the wolf, whispering something I couldn't make out. Tempest shifted and grabbed the T-shirt off the floor, confirming that there was indeed nothing under it. I noticed a mark in the center of her back as she skedaddled to the bedroom.

While she was gone, I took the opportunity. "What the fuck, Dog?"

"If you settle your ass down, I'll explain."

"What's to explain? You're sleeping with her."

Tempest came back into the living room wearing a pair of jeans and a tight tank top, her pack tattoos spilling out from under it like warning signs. "Sorry about that, Charley, but you pushed the wrong button." Her voice was smooth with a bit of a rasp.

"And your pack blew up a building in town tonight." At least I was ninety-nine percent sure it was them. Who else would it be?

Dog's face turned to stone. "What?"

"Morceau. Atticus Devereaux's restaurant. Someone blew it up tonight, and Murphy has an eyewitness who saw wolves running out of the place just before it went up. He thinks it was you and your pack, so he'll probably try to haul you in for questioning."

A growl snaked up his throat. "Son of a bitch."

I threw Tempest a glance. "Her pack knows she's been in my bar, so that message was meant for me."

Dog's jaw tightened. "I'll make it right."

"It'll be the Stag next if we don't hand her over." I turned my eyes to Tempest again. "Better yet. Now that she's had some fun, maybe it's time for her to run along home and fix this shit."

When the wolf's eyes started to heat up again, Dog took a step back. "You two want to go at it again? Knock yourselves out."

"I just want this mess to go away," I said. "We need to put our energy into finding Shane Ronan, but it's hard to focus on that when I'm worried about a Molotov cocktail flying through the front window of my bar."

Dog rubbed his forehead like he had a headache coming on. "You don't know the whole story, Charley. Tempest didn't just wander into town looking for some *fun*. She's running."

"And she just happened to run straight to you?"

"That's right. She did. We go back a long way, and I'm going to do whatever it takes to make sure that son of a bitch never gets his hands on her again."

"You mean her fiancé, Zane?" Tempest visibly flinched when I said his name, and it struck me that maybe Dog was right. "Did he do something to her?"

Dog held my gaze but refused to speak. Then his eyes went to Tempest.

She hesitated but then turned around and lifted her shirt halfway up to her shoulders. "He gave me this." It was that mark I'd noticed earlier in the middle of her back. It matched the tattoo on her wrist. After dropping her shirt, she turned around and looked at me with a dull expression. "He used a knife."

"She was given to Zane by her own father," Dog said. "Like fucking chattel."

I just stood there looking at her, horrified. "He cut that symbol into you?"

"He dipped the blade in colloidal silver first."

That was the stuff Samuel had mentioned. It was used in that weapon against vampires, but I had no idea how it affected wolves. I glanced at Dog for clarification.

"It keeps our skin from healing smoothly," he said. "Forms scar tissue."

Tempest wiped her nose with the back of her hand and averted her eyes from mine. "Yeah, and someday I'm going to castrate the bastard for it."

Another growl came from Dog's mouth. "If I don't do it first."

They weren't telling me everything, though. Dog wasn't just helping out an old friend. There was clearly something else between them. "You said you've known each other for a while?"

Dog locked eyes with Tempest, carrying on a silent conversation with her. "Since we were pups. We were born into the same pack." His eyes went dark. "All three of us."

"You, her, and Zane?" I knew Dog had come to Crimson not long after I was born as a much younger wolf. He never talked about where he was from, though, and I never asked because my mother advised me not to. But we were about to finally have that conversation.

He pulled his eyes away from Tempest to look at me. "Zane and I were pretty tight growing up. Thick as thieves. Until that first rut."

"Rut?" The word didn't register right away because you didn't associate your friends with mating cycles—unless they were wolves. Seeing Samuel raise a brow from across the room sped it up for me, though. "Oh..."

"Zane went after Tempest. She was way too young, but he

didn't give a shit." Dog locked eyes with her again. "He wasn't the wolf she was interested in anyway. After that, things got rough between me and Zane and we both got kicked out of our pack. A few years later, he started his own pack up in the mountains and I came to Crimson."

"And Tempest?"

She answered for herself. "After my mother died, my father promised me to Zane. I told him I was too old to be promised to anyone, but it didn't stop him. He thought he was doing me a favor by binding me to the leader of the northern pack."

Tempest looked younger than Dog. Maybe by five or six years. I couldn't imagine trying to *bind* a thirtysomething-year-old woman to another wolf against her will.

Dog scoffed. "Doing you a favor, my ass. It was a political move. Sold his own daughter to earn favor with the northern pack."

I didn't know the woman, but I could see Dog's brazen comments were making her uneasy. "You want to take it down a notch, Dog."

Tempest shook her head. "He's right, though. It's amazing how you can convince yourself you're doing something noble when you're really just serving your own interest. He was shit for a father anyway."

Dog's eyes were seething again. "That son of a bitch, Zane, will have been waiting all these years to make you pay. He'll have to go through me first."

I understood now. Dog was as loyal as they came, and Tempest was an old friend. Although it looked like they'd taken that friendship to the next level, which made him harboring her even more dangerous.

"The binding ceremony is coming up," she continued. "Once that happens, it's over for me. I'm dead if I try to leave after I'm officially the pack leader's property, so I ran while I still could."

"Jesus, Dog." I wasn't sure I wanted to ask the next question. "You're a pack leader. Is it the same with you?" I couldn't imagine him forcing a woman to do anything, let alone serve as his mate.

His brow furrowed. "Hell, no! I can't believe you'd even ask me that."

"You're right. I'm sorry." But I was relieved by his response.

Awkward quiet filled the room. "So what do we do now?" I said.

Dog looked at Tempest and then back to me. "*We* don't do anything. Go home, Charley. Better yet, go to Samuel's house."

Samuel finally broke his silence. "Dog's right. There's nothing we can do tonight, and we have a bigger problem to deal with." He opened the door. "We should go."

"I'll meet you at the truck in a minute." After he walked out, I gave Tempest a commiserative smile. "Sorry about the misunderstanding earlier."

"Don't be. If I'd caught you in here with Dog wearing nothing but a T-shirt, I would have thought the same thing. That you were just looking for a quick fuck."

That image needed to take itself right out of my head.

"And I'm sorry for dragging you into this mess," she added. "I shouldn't have met Dog at the Stag the other afternoon. It was even more careless to show up at the bar again that night."

That particular afternoon suddenly came back to me. That musky scent in the kitchen, and Dog being so jumpy all day.

Dog averted his eyes when I looked at him. "Yeah, that was probably not the best idea." He'd maintained a stellar poker face when he'd glanced at her through the order window that night. It was time to leave before I found out what they'd been doing in that kitchen. "Will you walk me out?" I said to him.

When we were in the clearing and out of earshot, I stopped to face him. "This is bad, Dog. Really bad."

"I'll take care of it."

"Zane isn't going to stop looking for her. You know that."

"He's already tracked her here, but I never thought he'd have the guts to show up at the Stag. After the other night, I figured he'd move on and focus on trying to breach the compound. I'm sorry, Charley. I never meant to drag you into this."

I didn't know whether to laugh or cry. "Well, you did, so now you need to get her out of town. Hell, get her out of the state. Take her somewhere far away from here and leave a trail for those wolves to follow."

He took a deep breath. "Why do you think I asked for tomorrow night off? I've got friends south of Atlanta who owe me. We'll head north tonight across the state line. Then we'll backtrack south. Let Zane's pack sniff around Tennessee for a few weeks while the trail goes cold."

"Good. Call me when you get back."

I closed my eyes for a second as I walked away, taking a deep breath of my own as I prepared to drive back to town to find Shane Ronan. The Tempest problem wasn't over yet, but at least for now it was contained. And I doubted those wolves would be stupid enough to show up again tonight with the crime scene being investigated and the fire department dealing with that explosion.

Samuel was waiting outside the truck with those two wolves keeping him company. "They really don't trust vampires, do they?" he said as I walked up.

"They'll get used to you eventually."

He climbed into the passenger seat, saluting the wolves as he shut the door. "That would require me coming back here, and I'd prefer not to."

I started the truck, glancing in the direction of Dog's cabin before heading back to town. "Let's hope no one gives us a reason to."

* * *

There was a lot of activity in town when we arrived. The flames were out across the street from the bar, but the fire department was still there making sure all the embers were extinguished. The air was thick with smoke, and we'd all be choking on it for the next week. At least that daily reminder of Atticus Devereaux was gone for good.

Murphy's patrol car was parked in the same spot, blocking off the street, so I turned left and took the back way around town before he spotted my truck and flagged me down to ask more questions about the pack.

Samuel nodded in the opposite direction. "My house is that way. Where are we going?"

"To the Cauldron. I need to tell Candy what's going on and let her know I'm okay." I was surprised she hadn't been blowing up my phone by now.

We bypassed everything and pulled up to the shop from the opposite end of the street. The lights were out, which didn't seem right. We'd heard and felt that explosion all the way out at Samuel's house, so it must have rocked every building in town, including the Cauldron. There was no way Candy had closed up for the night and gone to bed. Not without talking to me first.

I turned off the engine and looked through the window of the shop. "Something's wrong."

"Maybe she's over at the square watching the commotion." Samuel nodded down the street where a crowd was still gathered.

I prayed he was right, but it didn't explain why she hadn't called me.

We got out and walked up to the entrance. As I was about to dial her number to let her know we were coming in, I noticed the door was cracked. Samuel pushed it open and walked inside, listening with his finely tuned ears. I followed him in and immediately went to the door leading to her coveted back room. It was wide open.

"She would never leave this open," I said before taking the stairs two at a time to the second floor. Samuel was right behind me as I went down the hallway to her bedroom. "Candy?" There was no answer, so I reached for the knob, my heart in my throat as I pushed the door open.

Odin brushed past my legs, growling as he ran down the stairs to the shop. We followed him, stopping when he jumped on the counter and looked down at the glass case underneath him. His tail kept swishing back and forth as he continued to stare at something.

I flipped the lights on and went over to see for myself, barely able to breathe as I looked at the top shelf. It was Candy's amulet, with the chain curled up on top of a piece of paper.

My shoulders sagged with relief when I didn't see a body part in there. It wouldn't have been the first time. "Thank God."

Samuel wasn't quite as relieved. "It's her amulet, Charley. Would she take it off and leave it in there?"

But it wasn't really a question. "Of course not."

He went around and reached inside for the piece of paper. There were two words written on it.

FIGHT CLUB

TWENTY-FIVE

The last person who separated Candy from that sapphire amulet around her neck was my dead father, and only by way of a powerful spell. But Shane Ronan was no witch, and I couldn't even imagine how he'd gotten into the Cauldron without an invitation. The shop doubled as Candy's home, so that vampire wasn't at liberty to just stroll inside. Somehow he'd gotten in and compelled her to part with her most precious possession, her power, and I refused to even consider the worst possibility.

It was an ungodly hour to drive out to the Squad's house, but Katherine Belltower suggested we meet there because the center of town was still a crime scene. Having Tom Murphy or Rick Carter pull up to the Cauldron while we were meeting inside would be a disaster, especially if we couldn't produce Candy and had to explain her whereabouts.

Ian Masterson was standing in the middle of the dirt road leading up to the old Victorian. I nearly ran him over before hitting my brakes when I caught him in my headlights.

"Remind me again why he's here?" Samuel said, glancing at the vampire as I swerved around him and continued up to the house.

"Because we need all the help we can get." The pack was busy smuggling their contraband across the state line, so they weren't available at the moment. That left Ian and his vampires as our only other option. Since Ian had plenty riding on Ronan's demise, he was more than happy to oblige when I called him to tell him we were going in for the kill.

Ian walked up to the truck as I was getting out. "Could have offered me a ride up to the house."

"And you could have stepped out of the road so I didn't almost wreck my truck." I continued past him up to the house and knocked.

"Come in," I heard Katherine say from inside. I opened the door and walked in, but Ian hit a wall when he tried to follow behind Samuel.

He cleared his throat loudly. "You're forgetting something."

I glanced back at him, taking great pleasure in seeing him stuck on the other side of the threshold. "You need to invite him in," I said to Katherine as she met us at the living room entrance.

She let out a long sigh. "Must I?"

"I'm afraid you must." We needed that vampire.

Katherine stepped into the hallway. "Mr. Masterson, won't you please come inside."

"Yes, I think I will." He stepped through the door and lowered his chin, grinning at the witch as he approached her.

"This is a one-time invitation, so don't get any ideas about strolling in here whenever you like."

Ian's grin flattened, but his steady gaze remained glued to hers. "Charming as usual."

He followed her into the living room and glanced at the witches. "Ladies." Then he looked at the painting of Victoria Wilderbrandt hanging on the wall. "I remember that one. From her younger days," he muttered under his breath, a roguish grin spreading across his face.

Katherine's eyes narrowed. "Careful, Mr. Masterson."

Desiree recoiled in her chair when he came closer, like he had a communicable disease.

"See something you like?" he said as his eyes shifted to hers.

Her upper lip curled. "I should string you up by your fangs for that."

Ian's lips parted, giving her a good look at them. "Bring it."

I'd had enough of the pleasantries. "If you two are done with the foreplay, we need to get down to business." Ronan had finally made his move. He'd taken Candy, so we needed to come up with a plan fast. "He's holding her at that old warehouse outside of town." That place was becoming ground zero, and we needed to burn it down once we got Candy out of there.

Desiree pulled her menacing gaze away from Ian. "How do you know that?"

I tossed the piece of paper on the coffee table. "Like I told Katherine on the phone, we found her amulet at the Cauldron. It was on top of that note."

Katherine picked it up. "This vampire has given you instructions." She dropped the paper back on the table. "So it's a trap."

"Of course it is, but Candy's in there."

"It's a trap for me," Samuel said.

My chest swelled with anger. "He's not getting his hands on you. We're going to get Candy out of there and send Shane Ronan to hell where he belongs."

A smile played across Ian's face. "You're quite the savage these days, Charley."

It had become so easy for me to talk about killing, but every death I'd had a hand in was well deserved. Necessary. Even my father's.

I shifted my eyes to his. "You're right, and anyone who threatens the people I love will meet the savage Charley. Anyone."

After holding my gaze for a moment, he turned to Samuel.

"I say the two of us go in there and take him out quickly. Sever the bastard's head so we can all get back to business."

"And if he has a horde of vampires waiting for you like he did at the fight the other night?" I may not have known Ronan as well as Samuel, but I did know that vampire wasn't stupid. "We've got a room full of witches here, for God's sake. Surely we can come up with a better plan than rushing in there and gambling on him being alone in that warehouse."

Mia Winston leaned forward in her chair. "Have you considered walking in and having a conversation with this vampire? To find out what he wants?"

The witch clearly hadn't been fully informed. "He wants to kill Samuel."

"Are you sure?"

I turned to Samuel. "You want to answer that?"

"He wants revenge for me killing his maker," Samuel explained. "Victor Steele. So yes, I'm fairly sure he wants me dead."

Her brow pulled tighter. "Yes, but Victor Steele was your maker too. That would make you and this vampire siblings?"

Samuel's jaw tightened. "Technically, yes. But there's no bond between us. Not anymore."

"Are you sure?" Katherine asked.

Anger started to build in his eyes. "Very."

I understood what the witches were getting at. Samuel had told me himself that Shane Ronan wanted to make his revenge as painful as possible. Maximize Samuel's suffering before his demise. But they did have a connection. A past. Mia's comments were worth exploring.

"Maybe Mia's right," I said. "And if we rush in there, he could kill Candy."

Desiree's eyes flicked to mine. "If he hasn't already."

I wanted to knock the smirk off the witch's face, but I reined in my anger and continued with my idea. "I think you and I should go in there alone and ask him point blank what it'll take to make him go away. Bargain for Candy's life. You said yourself he's a hustler. Maybe there is something more important to him than revenge."

Ian had to give his own two cents. "And if he does have an army of vampires waiting inside?"

"Then we signal to our own army of *your* vampires waiting outside. In the woods next to that warehouse."

Ian snickered. "I knew there was a reason I was invited to this shit show."

"You're putting a lot of faith in this," Samuel said to me. "That Ronan has an ounce of decency in his black soul."

"Oh, I don't think he has a shred of it. But I do think he's motivated by greed, so let's see what he wants." I glanced at Ian. "Get your vampires ready."

"Yes, ma'am." He pulled his phone out and walked into the hallway.

Samuel studied me for a moment. "You really believe this will work."

I could see that he didn't. That he'd call in Ian's army the moment it went south. But I'd do whatever it took to up the odds of getting Candy out alive, so we were going to try it my way first. "It has to," I said. "For Candy's sake."

* * *

The warehouse was completely dark when we drove up. Other than Samuel, there wasn't a vampire in sight. I couldn't see any movement through the windows either.

"Maybe he is alone in there." I reached for the door handle to get out, reminding myself that we had backup a stone's throw away in those woods.

Samuel eyed the building. "Don't be fooled. Vampires are good at blending into the darkness."

They didn't call them creatures of the night for nothing. And I wasn't foolish enough to really think Shane Ronan didn't have his own backup. I just prayed we could get Candy out of there before he called them in. Have Samuel appeal to the vampire's sense of loyalty, if he was capable of it to anyone but his maker. But I was really counting on Ronan's greed. Hoping there was something more compelling than revenge to make him go away for good.

"Just keep your head on straight," Samuel said. "Follow my lead if it gets dicey in there."

Yeah, right. I pumped my fists as nervous energy shot through me like a bolt of electricity, glancing at the woods on our way to the building. "They better be out there." If things got *dicey*, one of us was to smash a window, signaling to Ian and his vampires to converge on the building. From what I remembered of the other night, there was plenty of debris all over the place to do so. And if not, I wasn't above throwing myself through one of those glass panes to signal the troops. If I could reach one.

"Masterson wants to get his hands on Ronan almost as much as we do," Samuel reminded me. "They're out there."

My nerves erupted as we approached the entrance, the door creaking as we pulled it open. It must have announced us to any vampire in the place. But I couldn't hear a sound as we stepped inside. At least the warehouse was brighter than it had looked as we drove up, the light from the moon illuminating it enough to see shapes and outlines of old equipment in the corner of the room. Equipment large enough to conceal lurking vampires.

My eyes darted around the expansive space as they played tricks on me, flickers of shadows caught in my periphery. But there was nothing there. We'd just walked in, and I was already getting inside my own head. It needed to fucking stop.

Hearing a slight gasp slip from my mouth, Samuel gripped me and pressed his lips to my ear. "Get it together, Charley."

I was literally vibrating. Fighting the chaotic energy threatening to ignite in my palms. After a few deep breaths, it settled. "I'm okay."

Samuel nodded toward the other side of the warehouse. To the rooms where Ronan had kept him captive days earlier. There was light coming from under the door of the one closest to us. If Candy was here, she was probably in that one, and Ronan was making sure we knew it.

When I picked up the pace, practically running ahead of Samuel, he grabbed my arm. "What?" I said, turning to look at him.

"Slow the hell down."

He was right. I wasn't using my head. "Let's just get to that room."

His stern look suddenly faded as he cocked his head. "Do you hear that?"

All I could hear was the sound of cicadas buzzing in the surrounding woods. "Bugs?"

"Listen," he said.

This time I heard it. The sound of muffled voices so faint I could barely hear them. It must have been amplified by Samuel's acute hearing. "Where is it coming from?"

He nodded to the room with the light coming from under the door. "In there."

We quickly made it to the room, but Samuel stopped me when I reached for the doorknob. Then he moved me out of the way and pulled a dagger from his boot. He gripped the knob firmly. Without hesitating, he twisted it and shoved the door open.

There was a small folding table in the middle of the room. Candy was sitting on one side and Shane Ronan was seated opposite her. She was holding cards in one hand and a stack of poker chips in the other. Both of them turned as we burst inside.

"You're just in time for a new game," Ronan said, his eyes shifting from me to Samuel. "Care to gamble?"

TWENTY-SIX

I was looking at the real Shane Ronan, his facade stripped away to reveal the vampire I'd seen the other night. The dark vampire with sapphire eyes eerily similar to Samuel's.

"Are you okay?" I said to Candy.

She tossed her chips in the middle of the table. "Right as rain, honey. Mr. Ronan and I are just playing a friendly game of poker."

She was acting too calm. "Did he do something to you?"

"He hasn't touched me. In fact, he's been quite the gentleman." She laid her cards down, revealing a straight flush before looking up at the vampire. "Unless you've got a royal flush in your hand, I win."

His lips spread into a smile. "Care for another game?"

"I think I'm all played out for the night."

"And I was just getting to know the lovely Candy Cane."

"My friends get to call me Ms. Cane." Her eyes leveled on his. "It's Candy Palmer to you."

I cringed inside when I saw the look rolling over Ronan's face. Candy had just pushed one of his buttons. Offended him. And she was in no position to do that at the moment.

He stared at her as his face tensed tighter. "And here I thought we were becoming friends."

"Friends?" Candy scoffed. "You hijacked Charley's body and walked into my shop." Her calm demeanor turned to anger. "Then you took advantage of me."

My breath caught. "He did what?"

"The bastard grabbed my amulet and yanked it from my neck while my guard was down." She glared at Ronan. "Then he dropped the charade and showed me his real face. Said he'd kill you if I didn't come with him."

"But how did he get inside the Cauldron? He's a vampire. He still needs an invitation."

Ronan seemed to be taking great pleasure from my confusion. "I don't need an invitation when borrowing a human." His grin grew wider. "I can day walk too."

"I told you this was all a game," Samuel said to me with his eyes trained on the vampire.

All this time I thought I was safe in my own house, but Shane Ronan could have gotten in simply by *borrowing* someone. Beau or Lucy, or even Candy again. But Ronan had other plans for how his game would play out. How it was about to play out.

Candy let out a deep sigh. "I wish you wouldn't have come here, Charley."

As if that were possible.

With that dagger still gripped firmly in his hand, Samuel was laser focused on Ronan.

"Can you move, Candy?"

"Of course I can move."

"Then get up and back away from the table." He gripped the knife tighter, the tension in the room so thick it was palpable.

Ronan grinned across the table at her. "Still feeling lucky, Ms. Palmer?"

As Samuel was about to make a move, Candy held her hand up to stop him. "Stay right where you are, Samuel."

I noticed Ronan's other hand was under the table. "I think he has a gun." I couldn't actually see it, but it had to be a weapon keeping her from jumping out of her seat, and a knife was no guarantee of killing her before Samuel reached him.

Ronan's hidden hand suddenly snapped up, knocking the table over and sending cards and chips flying in the air.

It was a gun all right. A large revolver that could blow a hole clean through Candy's chest. I had zero doubt he'd use it the second Samuel lunged or if I tried to hurl a ball of magic at him.

The vampire raised the gun and aimed it at Candy's face, shifting his eyes to Samuel. "What are the odds of you severing my head before I take hers off? Care to wager on it?"

Samuel backed up toward the door. "No more games. What will it take to make you leave? Money?"

The vampire stood up. "I don't want your money, Samuel." His lips curled into a snarl as he turned his gaze to me. "I want you to take that knife in your hand and slowly insert it into Charley's heart. Then give it a good twist."

Samuel's jaw tightened. "Why would I do that?"

The muzzle of the gun was inches from my forehead before I could react. "Because you killed my maker, and I want you to *suffer* before I kill you." The word was like venom on his lips.

Candy was on her feet instantly. "You so much as leave a mark on her head, I'll hunt you down and kill you myself." She was powerless without her amulet, and if she didn't keep quiet, he'd turn the gun on her next.

"I'd like to take you up on that game, Ms.... Cane."

She wisely held her tongue.

For the first time... ever, I saw real fear in Samuel's eyes. I think Ronan noticed it too because his smile returned.

"He was my maker too," Samuel said, "and he betrayed me. It was me or him."

Ronan laughed. "You were nothing but payback for your father's sins. An accident."

Samuel cocked his brows. "We share Victor Steele's blood. That means nothing to you?"

"It makes me sick!" Ronan's eyes were filled with loathing. "I will relish driving a stake through your heart."

"But you won't get the chance to kill me. You had it the other night, but you blew it. How about if I give you another chance now?"

Ronan pressed the gun firmly to my forehead. "I'm listening."

"Let them go, and I'm all yours."

"Samuel!" I doubted Ronan intended to let any of us out of here alive. Our best chance was to get out of this room and find a window to break. To signal Ian and his vampires.

To my surprise, Ronan pulled the gun away and flicked his head toward the door. "Get out."

When I refused to move, he pulled a second gun from his jacket and pointed it at Samuel. "I said, get out!"

"Do as he says, Charley."

"Yes, Charley. Do as I say, or I'll incinerate your boyfriend right here."

The look on Samuel's face conveyed a thousand words. "Sunlight bullets," I whispered as he glanced at me one last time and then disappeared with Shane Ronan through the rear door of the room.

Candy grabbed my arm when I tried to go after them. "We have to leave."

After getting it through my thick head that they were gone, I followed her out. As we ran for the truck, I looked back, stunned that Ronan had gotten his hands on sunlight bullets. Samuel was wrong. There were more of them.

As we were about to get in, Ian appeared next to the truck.

He narrowed his eyes at me. "Where's Samuel?"

"He's gone. Ronan took him."

"Why didn't you break a window?"

All I could do was shake my head. I felt numb. Useless.

Candy came around to the driver's side. "I'm driving." Then she looked at Ian. "We're going to need you too, so get in."

"And make sure your vampires are on standby," I added, finally snapping out of my shock.

He looked back at the woods and gave a signal to his vampires. Then he walked around to the passenger side and climbed in ahead of me. "Are you coming?" he said when I stood there staring at him.

"Why don't you meet us there." I wasn't interested in riding back to town with him squeezed in the cab between us. "Or you can get in the back."

After glancing at the bed of the truck through the rear window, he brought his gaze back to mine. "I don't think so." He patted his thigh. "You can sit on my lap if you'd like."

Candy started the engine. "Just get in, Charley. We don't have time for this."

I shoved him over and climbed in, practically hugging the door to get away from his overpowering scent. "What is that smell?"

His face was inches from mine when he turned and smiled down his nose at me. "Pheromones."

I was sorry I asked and stared out the window as we drove down the dirt drive, flashes of movement catching my eye as Ian's vampires dispersed through the trees.

"I'll ask again," Ian said when we were back on the main road. "Why didn't you signal us?"

"Because he outsmarted us all." I couldn't get that look on Samuel's face out of my mind. "Ronan got his hands on sunlight bullets. He threatened to use one on Samuel and took him out through a back door. Right past your vampires, by the way."

Ian's snide expression softened. "Fuck. Are you sure?"

I nodded. "Let's just figure this out. Where else would he take Samuel?" I looked out the window again at the vast stretch of forest. They could have been anywhere in there. "You're a vampire. Where would you lurk?"

"I don't *lurk*."

"We have to wait," Candy said.

I stretched my neck to look at her. "We don't have time to wait. Samuel's as good as dead if we don't find them fast."

"Candy's right," Ian said. "Ronan will be in touch very soon."

"For what?"

"For the grand finale."

What was he talking about? "Would you please get to the point? Quickly."

For once he didn't go out of his way to annoy me. He got straight to the brutal reality. "Fuck with a vampire's maker and feel their wrath. Shane Ronan won't just kill Samuel, he'll execute him. Publicly. And I'm sure he intends for you to have a front-row seat for it."

He'd tried to do that the first time, until Samuel turned the tables on him. Or did he? I was starting to wonder if his first attempt to kill Samuel had all been a part of his game. If everything was leading up to this moment. The grand finale, as Ian called it.

I turned toward the window and closed my eyes, haunted by the word *execution*. But if Ian was right, we still had a chance. A final opportunity to save Samuel and kill that vampire.

When we pulled into town, the commotion in the square had died down, and the fire truck was gone, leaving yellow tape cordoning off the crime scene. Murphy was probably around somewhere, though. I couldn't bear the thought of dealing with him, so we took the back way to the Cauldron.

"Are we done here?" Ian asked as we got out of the truck.

Candy unlocked the front door. "We are for the night."

I couldn't even imagine being done, let alone sleeping, but there was nothing else we could do for now.

"Are you staying here tonight?" Candy asked me.

I shook my head. "I want to sleep in my own bed." I'd probably stay up for what was left of the night and run gut-wrenching scenarios through my mind every minute. "I need to check on Rex anyway." I was surprised he hadn't shown up with his buddies at that warehouse tonight like he did the last time we were there.

"You be careful," she said.

I wasn't worried about Ronan showing up at my house. That vampire had other plans.

Ian looked back at me as he walked toward the corner of the building to do his disappearing act. "Call me when you get that invitation."

As I was about to get back in my truck, I got a text message. I froze when I saw Samuel's name appear above it. "I think I just did."

TWENTY-SEVEN

The text I'd received the night before had simply said to keep my phone handy. No date. No time. Just a message telling me to stand by. That vampire was taunting me. He was taunting all of us.

The wait had been torture. After scrubbing my house all day to try to take my mind off it, I went to the Stag early to get some things done there. Maybe take inventory and place some orders. But all I did was stare out the window at what remained of the restaurant across the street and wait for Shane Ronan to make a move. I was useless.

"You okay, Charley?"

I snapped out of it and glanced at Lucy. "Yeah, I'm fine. Why wouldn't I be?"

Her eyes narrowed. "You don't look fine, and you're making a mess that someone's going to have to clean up." She looked at the napkin I was gripping for dear life. I'd mutilated it with one hand and dropped the shreds on the floor. "You look like you've been ridden hard."

"Thanks, Lucy. I love you too." She was right, though.

When I looked in the mirror behind the bar, I noticed bags forming under my eyes from all the stress lately.

Bags.

"Why don't you just go home? Beau and I can handle the bar tonight."

She just wanted to get rid of me so she'd have the run of the place. Drink with the customers. "Not a chance." Although I'd have to make a decision about that if that message came through. "Where is Beau anyway?"

"How should I know?"

He came through the door a moment later looking like he'd gotten some sun, and his hair was tousled like he hadn't spent his usual hour coiffing it to perfection.

"You're late." We didn't open for another half hour, but he was supposed to be here before Lucy.

"Sorry. I went for a hike with Diablo and lost track of time." He shook his head. "That hound gives me a workout."

He glanced toward the kitchen. "I forgot. Dog's off tonight."

"Yeah. He's taking care of some personal business." Business that would be far from over even after Tempest was gone.

Beau went to the window and looked at the rubble across the street. "That's some messed-up shit over there. Who do you think did it?"

"Who knows?" I wasn't about to implicate the northern wolves and then have to explain how Dog was sleeping with their pack leader's *intended.* That was his business to tell. "That restaurant caused a lot of grief in this town. I can name a dozen people who could have struck a match to it."

Beau shook his head. "A match didn't do all that damage."

And now we'd all be choking on it until the air cleared.

"By the way," I said, "if those northern wolves show up here again, tell them to leave."

Lucy scoffed. "And if they don't want to leave?"

"Then find me and I'll tell them." She was right, though.

Those wolves wouldn't just walk out after being told they weren't welcome in the bar. It was another train wreck waiting to happen.

I looked at my phone for the hundredth time, checking to make sure it wasn't on silent mode. I had no idea if those instructions would come tonight, tomorrow, or the next day, but the wait was killing me.

The front door opened as I was fiddling with the volume. "We're not open yet." When I shoved the phone in my pocket and looked up, Mabel Gentry was walking in.

She frowned and turned to leave. "I'm sorry. I can come back later."

"No, it's fine. Is everything okay?" She'd cancelled her order with the co-op because of the outbreak, so I couldn't imagine why she was here. She wasn't a drinker, so it certainly wasn't for that. Unless she'd gotten desperate for blood and changed her mind. Not that I had any to give her.

"I just wanted to stop by to thank you."

"Thank me for what?"

Her smile returned as she walked up to the bar. "For sending that nice donor over to my house."

My mind scrambled. "What are you talking about, Mabel?"

"Mr. Stephens." Her smile started to fade as confusion rolled over her face. "That nice vampire you and Patrick sent me."

Vampire? I had no idea what she was talking about.

"Will you excuse me for a second?" I said to her. "I have to check on something, but I'll be right back." I leaned into Beau on my way to the hallway. "Get her whatever she wants on the house, and don't let her leave."

I ducked into the kitchen to call Patrick.

"This better be important," he said without a greeting. "I had a late night."

"Why is Mabel Gentry in my bar thanking me for sending a vampire over to her house?"

He went quiet for a moment before answering. "It's our new model. I was going to tell you about it tonight."

I pulled the phone away and stared at it for a second before pressing it back to my ear. "What are you talking about? Who is this Mr. Stephens?"

"Folk still need their blood, so I sent Mabel her own personal supply."

"Have you lost your mind?" I was ready to drive over there to have a come-to-Jesus with him, but I had other things to deal with, like waiting for that text message to come through. "We just shut the co-op down because of a hepatitis outbreak, and you sent a vampire to Mabel Gentry's house? What if he's infected?"

"Calm down, woman. He's clean. I recruited a bunch of vampires who practice exclusivity, and they're all looking for exclusive human donors. That's how everyone stays clean."

"You mean..."

"A reciprocal relationship. Marty Stephens feeds Mabel Gentry. In return, she feeds him." He chuckled. "And I mean straight from the vein."

"Marty Stephens from the bakery?" His bakery supplied restaurants and grocery stores in Crimson and Adlersville with bread. It was the perfect business for a vampire, baking through the night and making deliveries before dawn.

"Yep. And it ain't just Mabel. I hooked up Hank and Mary with a couple of donors too."

I nearly dropped the phone visualizing Mabel Gentry feeding from a vampire and then letting him bite her. "Wow."

"Are we done?" Patrick said. "Because I need to get me some sleep."

"For now, but we'll continue this discussion later."

After hanging up, I stared at the wall for a moment. I guess it was a solution to our problem, at least temporarily, but I couldn't imagine all the co-op members agreeing to such a drastic alternative. There was nothing wrong with two consenting adults feeding from each other, but not every human was cut out for it. I still vividly remembered the first time I let Samuel drink from me. It was such an intimate act, and it led to our first night together.

I shook off the image of Mabel and Marty feeding from each other and went back out to the bar with a forced smile on my face. Mabel was enjoying a glass of something with a wedge of lemon in it, and I couldn't deny how vibrant she seemed. She hadn't looked that good in a while.

"There you are." She took another sip of her drink and smiled. "How much do I owe you for the seltzer?"

"It's on the house." Her eyes were practically sparkling. "You look fantastic, Mabel."

"I *feel* fantastic." She set her glass down and leaned closer, her fingers grazing two fading marks on her wrist. "I never thought I could let a vampire bite me, but it was barely a pinch." She laughed quietly. "And then it felt good. Who would have thought?"

"People make a bigger deal out of it than they should," I said. "As long as it's consensual, it's perfectly fine." I watched as her smile grew wider. "You like this Mr. Stephens?"

"Oh yes. He's very respectful. We'll be meeting once a week to... you know... exchange. But only with each other. That's the arrangement."

It seemed like the perfect solution, and I was starting to think it might be a long-term one. After all, the co-op had been formed to fill a need in the community. And there were more than enough vampires in Crimson to fill that need. If it could be done in a safer, more convenient way for everyone, I was all for it. And the best part was it was free. But Patrick and I still needed to have a long talk about it. Make sure all the members were on board. Perhaps educate those with fear or other reservations.

Mabel finished her drink and stood up. "I better get going. I just wanted to stop by to thank you."

She should thank Patrick.

"Well, I'm glad it's working for you."

As she walked out the door, Beau leaned over the bar and lowered his voice. "Is Mabel Gentry hooking up with a vampire? At her age?"

"She's in her fifties, Beau. She's not dead. And no, she's not *hooking up* with a vampire." Then again, would that be so bad? The woman was a widow. "They're in a feeding relationship because of the co-op situation. And it might last for a while," I added since he was helping out with the co-op these days.

His eyes grew wider. "You mean the co-op might shut down permanently?"

I didn't have an answer for him. "Ask me in a few days." I checked my phone again. Why wasn't Ronan contacting me? My heart began to race when horrible thoughts started going through my mind again. What if I never got that message because Samuel was already dead, and the real torture was never knowing? What if Ronan took him far from here and intended for me to spend the rest of my life searching and wondering?

The familiar ping of a notification sounded just as I was about to start hyperventilating. A text message had arrived, and I nearly dropped my phone trying to pull it out of my pocket with a shaking hand.

Candy came through the front door as I was reading it. "Charley?" she said when she saw the look on my face. "Is that...?"

"Yes." I looked at the time and stuffed my phone back in my pocket, debating whether to close the bar for the night since

Dog was off. I finally decided to take a leap of faith and looked at Beau. "Can I trust you to run this place without me tonight?"

He hooked his thumb toward Lucy. "You're leaving me here with that?"

"I have some business to take care of tonight, so yes." I patted him on the shoulder. "I'm trusting you, Beau, so don't mess this up."

"Where is this business?" Candy said.

I held my phone up to show her the text message.

FIGHT CLUB

MAIN EVENT

TONIGHT

TWENTY-EIGHT

I was wearing out the floor in the back room when I heard a commotion in the bar. "That damn vampire doesn't listen," I said to Candy as I headed for the door.

She followed me into the hallway. "They never do."

When we got up front, Ian was leaning over the bar. "Are you deaf?" he said to Lucy who was backed up against the wall of liquor bottles. If she pressed any harder, I'd have an expensive mess on my hands when they came crashing down around her.

"Back off, Ian." I'd called him to let him know about tonight. I'd also told him to come in through the alley to avoid this very thing.

He glanced over his shoulder at me. "Why? I ordered a drink, but your bartender is having trouble doing her job."

I noticed that the stools on either side of him were vacant. Everyone had congregated at the far end of the bar. The only reason I still had customers in the place was because his chief thug, Marcus, and Irina were blocking the exit.

"Get him a drink," I said to Lucy.

Irina joined Ian at the bar, her eyes wandering over to Beau standing near the order window. He swallowed hard, anxiety creeping over his face as she eyed him intently.

Candy grinned. "I think that boy has met his match."

"You're right about that. Should have seen her flirting with him at the Beast last night."

"Flirting?"

"Well, it was more like foreplay."

She shook her head. "God help him if that one takes a liking to him. I guess we better do something before he pisses his pants or she eats him." She walked around the bar and stepped between them, looking at Irina. "What can I get you?"

While she rescued Beau, I glared at Marcus. He'd been staring at me since I walked into the bar. Not a single positive thing had ever come from the two of us being in the same room together. But we were on the same side tonight, so he needed to direct his beady eyes elsewhere.

Lucy set a drink down in front of Ian, but when she opened her mouth to ask him to pay for it, I shook my head.

"Let's talk in the back," I said to him. My customers were getting antsy.

Candy came back around the bar, and Ian downed his drink, motioning for Irina and Marcus to follow us.

Irina's eyes lingered on Beau a moment longer before falling in line.

Beau's jaw went slack as he gave her a limp wave.

"Way to go, asshole," Lucy said as he dropped his hand. "You just gave that vampire ideas."

When we got to the back room, I turned to Ian. "I told you to come in through the alley."

"I don't enter through alleys."

Candy huffed. "Oh, that's right. You prefer to enter uninvited through the front door." She smiled at him. "But not anymore, I hear."

"Watch your mouth," Marcus said.

She gave the vampire a sharp look. "Watch your back."

Irina chuckled and leaned against the wall. "I like this woman."

Ian threw his hand up when his henchman growled. "The two of you can play another time. Right now, we need to focus on killing a vampire."

"We need to focus on getting Samuel out of that warehouse in one piece," I clarified. "Killing Ronan is just a bonus. Samuel comes first. Got it?"

"Yes, captain."

I took a deep breath and nodded once. "Good. Let's go."

"Does that mean you have a plan?" he asked.

"I don't have a clue, but time is ticking. We'll figure something out on the way to the warehouse." Ian held my gaze for a moment, and I thought I saw a glimmer of compassion in his eyes.

"All right then," he said. "Lead the way."

The truth was, I was terrified. If ever I needed Dog, it was at that moment. But I was on my own, except for a bunch of vampires backing me up, and one way or another it ended tonight. Come hell or high water, I was walking out of there with Samuel alive. That was non-negotiable.

* * *

Candy had wanted to come with us, but I put my foot down, reminding her that she'd just be more ammunition for Ronan if things went south. Knowing how important she was to me, he'd try to use her against me like he had before. That meant I had to suffer alone on the drive out there with Ian sitting next to me.

After turning off the main road, we parked at the edge of the woods away from the warehouse.

"I wish Dog was here." I'd thought about calling him to see

if any of his wolves were available, but he probably would have nixed his plans to get Tempest out of North Georgia and come back. I wasn't going to let that happen because we needed that wolf gone.

"Why call a wolf when you have me?" Ian's eyes slid to mine. "You don't take a dog to a cat fight."

"Are you comparing yourself to a cat?"

He ignored the comment and opened the door. "Let's just get this over with."

As soon as we got out of the truck, I heard a ruckus coming from the warehouse. Like a lot of people had shown up for a fight.

Ian glanced at the trees that buffered the building from the road. "Sounds like the show has started."

"What is that bastard up to?" I said as I started walking up the dirt road.

Marcus stepped out from the trees and blocked my path. When I tried to go around him, he blocked me again. What was this guy's problem?

I looked back at Ian. "Tell your vampire to get out of my way." My palm was itching to make him move myself, but it would have been counterproductive to waste my energy before we even made it inside.

"Patience, Charley." Ian gave Marcus a questioning look. "Well?"

"The place is packed," Marcus said. "A couple of humans are beating the shit out of each other in there right now."

Ian glanced at the woods. "Get Irina and meet us at the entrance."

I studied Ian for a moment trying to gauge what he was up to. "We're all just going to stroll in there?"

"Why not? We've been summoned."

"Then let's go." I gave Marcus a warning look to get the hell out of my way. This time he wisely stepped aside and disappeared back into the woods while Ian and I continued up the road. The warehouse was lit up when we came around the bend, and the parking lot was packed with cars. Irina and Marcus were waiting for us near the entrance.

"So the plan is still to go in there and wing it?" I said as we approached them. With Ian's crew as backup, we figured at worst it would be an even fight.

"Unless you've come up with a better one in the past five minutes. I say we go in there and slaughter our way from one end to the other."

Yeah, that was a smart idea.

"I'm not getting Samuel killed because you and your vampires are in the mood to burn off some steam."

Ian shrugged. "Technically he's already dead."

I held his cocky gaze for a moment and opened the door. There was no bouncer collecting money tonight—which was good because I didn't bring cash—so I continued inside and pushed through the crowd to get a look at the ring. Like Marcus said, there were two men in the center throwing punches, a sight that had my fellow citizens riled into a frenzy. I wondered if their thirst for blood would lessen once we buried Shane Ronan and shut this place down, or if they were ruined for life and Crimson would be dealing with a new wave of derelicts.

When I looked closer at the two men, I spotted a set of fangs protruding from the mouth of one of them. They'd moved on to the second round—vampire against human.

The crowd grew denser. The fight taking place in the center of the room started to disappear from view as I was blocked by figures standing in front of me. I looked at the side of the ring for that chair Ronan had been sitting in the other night. His throne where he got off on the bloodlust. It was empty.

A gap opened in front of me as the crowd roared, giving me

a view of the ring again. The fight was over, and the vampire was on his knees digging his fangs into the human who was sprawled on the floor next to him. I couldn't take it anymore and looked away, coming face-to-face with Shane Ronan standing just feet away from me.

A grin slowly spread across his face. "It's good to see you again, Charley." Then his smile went flat. "Let's play."

The crowd shifted, and I was sucked into the mob of spectators. I clawed my way back toward Ronan, but when I got there he was gone.

A whistle came from behind me. It was Ian. He pointed to Ronan across the room to my right. I shoved my way through the thick crowd, but by the time I made it there, Ronan was gone and Ian was standing in his place.

"Where is he?" I said.

Ian's face twisted into a snarl as he looked toward the exit where we'd left Irina. Ronan was gripping her tightly with a knife at her throat. "I will slaughter that vampire if he draws a drop of her blood!"

I grabbed his arm before he could do something stupid. "He'll do more than that if you rush him." Ian was fast, but so was Ronan. And seeing Irina's head roll would destroy our mission.

He pulled his arm free and scowled at me. When he looked back at Irina, Ronan was gone and she was spinning in circles looking for her assailant.

"That slippery fucker!" he spat.

"He's enjoying making us look like fools." That vampire had us running in circles.

I nodded toward the infamous rooms at the other end of the warehouse. "Samuel has to be in one of them."

He followed my gaze. "Then let's get your boyfriend out of there and burn this place to the ground."

"You're not serious?"

He turned his dark eyes back to mine, giving me a glimpse of the old Ian. The ruthless vampire I'd encountered in Reaperstown all those months ago. "You're lucky I don't do it right now."

"There are innocent people in here, Ian."

"Innocent?" A wicked laugh slipped from his mouth. "You're looking at the sewage of Crimson." Then he took off toward those rooms.

As I went after him, the crowd went up in a roar again. I stopped and turned, seeing Ronan standing in the middle of the ring. His eyes locked on mine, their color flashing ruby-red before going completely black, taunting me with a decision as he held his hands out. There was something in them. Vials of blood, and I had no doubt every one of them was tainted.

I glanced at Ian moving across the room. "Fuck," I growled, choosing to run back to the ring when Ronan tossed the blood into the air, showering the crowd with tiny red vials. He pulled more from his pocket and threw them as well.

"It's contaminated!" I yelled, but my voice was a muffle under the squeals of excitement. The frenzy as humans grabbed for the vials. Fighting their own neighbors for blood that would cause them so much grief in the weeks to follow.

Ian suddenly appeared behind me and reached for my arm. "They're lost, Charley. You can't save them from themselves. Now, let's get Samuel out of here."

After pulling my arm free, I looked back at the chaos. "Fucking animals." Then I followed him toward the rooms. We'd get Samuel out, and then I'd make Ian see reason. Spare those idiots.

When we checked the first room, the only things we found inside were that card table and the two folding chairs from last night. The second room came up empty too. "Where is he?" I said, running back to the first one to look again, as if I'd somehow overlooked him in there.

Marcus appeared in the doorway as I stared at the empty room. "You two need to see this."

Ian and I followed him out. Halfway across the warehouse, I came to a stop. Even from a distance and through the crowd, I could see him. Samuel was sitting in a chair in the middle of the ring. There was a second chair positioned opposite him.

Ian looked back at me. "Found him."

I ran toward the ring, but the wall of spectators blocked my view again. As I tried to shove through the mob, I heard Ronan's voice.

"Where are your manners?" he said to the crowd. "Let her through."

Every head in the place turned. The sea of people parted, giving me a clear view of Samuel. There was a thin wire wrapped around his torso. It led to the opposite chair where a gun was secured to the top rail with its barrel pointed at Samuel's head. The taut wire stretched across the seat and snaked up the back of the chair where it was tied around the trigger.

I took a step toward the ring.

Samuel's eyes remained fixed straight ahead. "Don't come any closer, Charley."

"Yes," Ronan said. "I wouldn't get any closer if I were you." He was standing behind the rigged chair, precariously moving his hand toward the wire running up the back. "Wouldn't want to discharge a precious sunlight bullet prematurely."

Ian appeared at my side. "Easy, Charley," he whispered. "Unless you'd like to see Samuel burn from the inside out." His eyes wandered to his vampires positioned around the warehouse. The ones from the surrounding woods. He must have called them in. "Play his game while we wait for the right moment."

"I don't know if I can do that," I whispered back.

"You have no choice."

The crowd shifted, tightening around the ring, the crush of bodies pressing me into Ian. People were getting restless.

"Give us more blood!" one of them yelled.

Others in the back joined in. "Throw some of those vials back here for the rest of us!"

A chorus of gasps filled the warehouse when Ronan hopped up on the rigged chair, straddling the wire with his feet planted on the arms, his legs wide enough for the gun to stay trained on Samuel. He let out an ear-piercing whistle. "Quiet! You're here for more than blood and entertainment. You're here to serve as a jury!"

My eyes shot to Ian's. "Jury? What is that bastard doing?"

"We're about to find out."

Ronan continued with his game. "The defendant, Samuel Cain, has been charged with murdering his maker!"

The crowd roared, their fists pumping the air.

Ronan leveled his eyes on Samuel. "How do you plead?"

Samuel didn't move. Didn't make a sound.

"No defense?" He sneered. "Then I declare you guilty."

A painful rush of air filled my lungs when the vampire's foot swung toward the wire. Ian caught me when I lunged forward.

Ronan's foot cleared the wire as he jumped back down to the floor. "I sentence you to death!"

My hand burned from the energy building in my palm. "I'll hunt you down and kill you myself," I said to Ronan when his eyes found mine, to feed off my pain. But I couldn't use my magic. Couldn't risk him tripping that wire just inches away.

Samuel barely turned his head to look at me. There was something final in his eyes, and it *nearly fucking broke me.*

Another roar came from the crowd. Half of them were hopped up on vampire blood, and the other half were begging for it. I ran my eyes over them, burning every one of their faces into my memory. For payback.

I looked back at the ring when Shane Ronan turned to us, my stomach sinking from the hardening of his face. The hate in his eyes as he scanned the crowd.

"You're in for a treat tonight," he said, his voice dropping several octaves, settling into something so dark it sent a shiver racing up my spine. "Buckle up. It's time for an execution."

TWENTY-NINE

The sound in the room began to fade. I felt lightheaded and the world seemed almost like a scene from a movie. A scene from someone else's life.

Ian turned me around, forcing me to face him, his eyes revealing the gravity of what was about to happen in that ring.

"Focus on me, Charley."

I pulled my arm free. "Do something!" I looked back at the ring. If Samuel died tonight, I wasn't going to turn my back on him while it happened. There had to be a way to get to that gun before Ronan tripped the wire.

As my eyes darted around the warehouse looking for a vantage point where Ronan wouldn't see me coming, I caught a glimpse of his fangs descending. He brought his face to Samuel's and then continued lower, grazing Samuel's neck with the tips while his fingers danced within millimeters of that wire. One flick of his hand, and Samuel was gone.

And then Ronan struck, piercing Samuel's flesh. But Samuel didn't flinch. He kept completely still as the vampire tore at his flesh.

A smile spread across Ronan's face as he raised his head, his fangs glistening red, and looked at the frenzied crowd. "You want blood? Then feast!"

Ian caught me when my knees buckled.

While most of the humans seemed confused by Ronan's offer—or maybe their sense of decency had finally kicked in—a few wasted no time.

"*Stop!*" I screamed when they converged on Samuel. But it was too late. The chair slid back when they slammed into him, the wire engaging the trigger. A flash came from the gun as the hammer released and propelled the bullet down the barrel.

The world slowed as a strange ringing sound filled my ears, adrenaline assaulting my heart. It raced through me, leaving a metallic taste in my mouth as I watched the surreal scene unfold around me. People froze in their tracks, the buzz of the cicadas in the woods falling silent outside. Every sound faded, and I felt like the only living thing on earth at that moment.

The ringing in my ears abruptly stopped, and I was staring at something suspended in the air, surrounded by a plume of smoke captured like a photograph in front of me. The bullet, trapped in motion except for the burst of sunlight radiating from its core.

I believe you manifested the gift of time capture.

"Fuck!"

Ian stood motionless next to me, along with every other frozen human and vampire in the place. But when I glanced behind the rigged chair where Ronan had been standing, he was gone. I didn't have time to worry about Ronan, though. The spell wouldn't last for long. I needed to do something fast because that bullet would be back on course soon.

I started by prying those heathens off Samuel, their bodies falling to the floor like stiff mannequins. I kept glancing at that bullet suspended behind me, wondering how long it would take for the world to wake up again.

"Samuel!" I grabbed his face with both hands and shook him. "Snap out of it!"

A rustle came from behind me. I flinched when I heard it again and reached for the dagger in Samuel's boot. When I turned around, I almost dropped it. I was staring at myself.

"You almost had me, Charley." The face and body were mine, but the voice was Ronan's. "But you can't use your magic on yourself."

I gripped the knife tighter, reminding myself that it was Ronan standing in front of me. I lashed out, leaving a deep gash in his... or... my arm. Then the facade faded away, and the vampire was suddenly staring back at me. When he looked down at the wound, I jabbed the knife into his chest.

He grabbed my wrist as his lips curved into a wicked smile, driving the blade deeper into his own ribs before twisting my hand. "Now, that's how you stab someone." His eyes roamed around the room. "That's quite a trick." A second later, he was holding my hand up in front of me, the bloody dagger still firmly gripped between my fingers. "Now I'm going to teach you how to properly kill a vampire. Samuel can help with the demonstration."

As Ronan dragged me by my wrist toward Samuel, my palm began to glow. The knife dropped, and the energy started to travel into his hand.

He let out a strangled growl and shoved me so hard I hit the floor. "You'll pay for that, witch!"

My head took the brunt of it as I slammed against the concrete. I struggled to sit up as that strange ringing in my ears returned. When my vision started to clear, I saw something move. A twitch of a foot next to me. The world was coming back to life.

As Ronan turned toward Samuel to finish the deed, a blaze of ruby shimmered in Samuel's eyes. He was waking up, and so was that bullet.

Samuel jumped to his feet as the bullet started back on its trajectory. With his bare hand, he snatched it out of the air, wincing as the light radiating from its core blazed in his fist.

Shock rolled over Ronan's face when he saw the brilliant light coming from Samuel's hand. "No!" he growled, lunging forward.

Samuel hurled the bullet at Ronan, hitting the vampire square in the chest. Stunned, Ronan came to an abrupt stop as a glow began to emit from every orifice of his body. The light continued to build inside him, creating an inferno that consumed his torso and then spread to his arms and legs, seeping from his pores.

Knowing what was coming next, I turned and covered my face, cringing when the vampire exploded. Bits and pieces of him sprayed the crowd as the spell broke completely, and everyone scrambled toward the exit.

Samuel came over to help me up. "Are you okay?"

I rubbed the back of my head and wiped some gore from my face, looking at the middle of the ring. Shane Ronan was nothing but a puddle of slime that would soon turn to ash. "I'm super."

Ian was standing behind me when I turned around. "You missed some." He brushed some entrails from my shoulder.

"So did you," I said, looking at the blood spattered on his face.

He grinned. "I'm used to it."

"That's gross, Ian."

Both of them were suddenly staring at me. "What?"

"I'm not sure what happened here tonight," Samuel said, "but I think you have some explaining to do."

Ian raised his brows. "Yes. I think she's been holding out on us."

"Holding out?" I snorted. "I don't know what you're talking about." I hadn't decided yet if I wanted to let Ian Masterson know about my new powers. It couldn't hurt to hold some of my cards close.

"We can talk about it later," Samuel said. "Right now, I need a shower and some rest."

And he needed to feed. Ronan must have denied him blood to keep him weak. But not weak enough, apparently.

Ian's eyes were still filled with suspicion. "Fine. We'll regroup tomorrow."

"What about all this?" The warehouse was a crime scene, with blood spattered everywhere.

Ian pulled out his phone and sent a text. "Always be prepared to cover your tracks." A minute later, Irina and Marcus came through the door carrying cans of gasoline. "It's time to burn this place to the ground."

Samuel nodded. "Excellent idea."

"Why, thank you."

They got to work spreading the accelerant around the perimeter of the warehouse, shaking the last of the cans' contents on top of Ronan's remains.

Ian pulled a book of matches from his pocket but stopped short of lighting it. "Would one of you like to do the honors?"

"Another excellent idea," Samuel said, looking at me. "Charley?"

"I'd love to." I was looking forward to lighting up what was left of that asshole because I didn't trust him to stay dead. But nothing would rise from the ashes of an incinerated warehouse. "Save your matches," I said when Ian held them out to me. I had a better idea. One that would release all that pent-up energy coursing through me. "You both might want to stand back for this."

"Wait a minute." Samuel walked over to the rigged chair and untied the gun. "Well, look what we have here." He emptied the chamber, and two more bullets fell into his hand.

Ian stretched his neck to see. "Are those...?"

"Spare sunlight bullets. These will come in handy someday."

"Feel like sharing?"

Samuel gave him a dull look. "No." Then he nodded for me to proceed.

When they were safely behind me, I conjured an image of Ronan's face and all the misery he'd caused, manifesting a sphere of energy in my palm. Gave it a minute to build. When it was good and hot, I hurled it at his remains and watched the flames ignite with great satisfaction.

When the fire quickly spread along the trail of accelerant, we headed for the exit. On my way out, I looked back and finally believed it was over.

The parking lot was a ghost town when we walked outside. Not a single person had lingered to see how it ended. They were all probably thankful to survive the night, but I had a feeling there'd be some cleanup later. Loose lips around town we'd have to deal with.

Halfway to the truck, we stopped to watch the fire do its job. The flames engulfed the back and side walls and quickly circled around to the front of the building. The ceiling caved in a minute later, reducing the Stokes Tractor warehouse to a giant bonfire.

I looked up when I caught sight of a flock of birds rising from the trees. A sea of black wings.

"You seem to attract those flying rats," Ian said as he followed my gaze.

"Yes, I do." Rex had become my shadow, but I didn't need his help tonight. He must have sensed that.

We left the place and continued down the road toward the truck, leaving behind nothing of Shane Ronan but his ashes to be blown away on the wind by morning and his black soul to rest in the bowels of hell.

THIRTY

As Samuel entered the Stag, Murphy was exiting. The cop glowered and grazed him on his way out the door.

Samuel came up to me and looked out the window as Murphy climbed into his patrol car. He backed out so fast he nearly slammed into another vehicle. "What's his problem?"

I let out a deep sigh. "He's looking for Dog."

"Isn't Dog here?" he said, glancing toward the kitchen.

"If he was, he'd be in the back of that patrol car right now. Murphy is still convinced Dog's pack was responsible for the building explosion across the street. He was also asking me if I knew anything about the warehouse we incinerated last night. He's got it in his head that the explosions are connected." Murphy was way off about that.

"Dog didn't show up tonight?"

"No," Lucy said as she poured a beer from the tap behind me. "Easy to see who your favorites are. If I didn't show up for work, I'd be standing in the unemployment line."

"You still could be if you don't mind your own business. Dog texted me and said he needed another night off."

Samuel stared at me for a moment. "You don't think that's odd?"

Odd was putting it mildly. "Just the fact that he texted me instead of calling is odd." I'd had to practically force him to take the weekend off, and that was only because he had something critical to do. But for Dog to text me?

"I'll call him in a few minutes and see what's up." And to warn him that Murphy was still gunning for him and the pack.

"I brought you this." Samuel handed me the book he was holding. It was the one Candy said Katherine wanted to borrow. "Tell Katherine she can keep it. I doubt I'll be reading it."

"Thanks. I'm sure she'll appreciate that." I flipped the book open and skimmed some of the pages. "I'm real curious about what's so interesting in this book." Then I closed it again and ran my fingers over the symbol on the cover. "Maybe I should read it first." Like I had time to read anything these days.

As I walked around the bar and tucked the book under the counter, I could have sworn I caught a shimmer of magic coming from that symbol. Probably my eyes playing tricks on me. Or maybe it was the reflection from the headlights of Patrick's car pulling up to the bar.

He came inside and grabbed a stool across from me, placing his sunglasses on top of his head. "Look at you," he said.

"What about me?"

"You're still alive."

He'd texted me that afternoon, but I'd gotten distracted and never replied. "Sorry. I had my hands full and forgot to call you back."

"Never mind." He nodded to the bottle of gin behind me. "Give me a G & T."

Taking his cue, Samuel pushed away from the bar. "I'll let you two talk. I'll see you later tonight."

After he left, I poured Patrick a drink and came around the bar to sit next to him. We needed to have a serious conversation before it got too crowded to talk. "What are we going to do about the co-op?"

He stirred his drink and took a sip. "We're going to continue playing matchmaker for now."

"You mean finding personal donors? I'm not so sure everyone will be on board with that." While it was a solid solution, I knew we'd get pushback from members who were on the conservative side. It was like eating meat. People enjoyed a good steak, as long as they didn't have to kill the cow themselves.

A playful smile briefly crossed his face. "Then I guess you don't know people around here as well as you think you do."

I squinted at him. "What are you talking about?"

"I facilitated a little meet and greet last night for some of the members and prospective donors. The ones most likely to have a stick up their ass." He chuckled. "Should have seen how fast those sticks got pulled out after getting a taste of blood straight from the vein."

Patrick never ceased to surprise me.

"Did you invite Hazel Scott?" She was as conservative as they came. A church lady who barely tolerated vampires but stood in that line in the alley every weekend to get her medicine.

"Yep."

"How did you convince Hazel Scott to drink from a vampire?"

He shrugged. "I told her it was her only option. And it didn't hurt that I set her up with a fine-looking vamp. I'd like to take a bite out of that man myself."

Wait until her husband found out about it.

"Once she got a taste of that freshly squeezed blood, she was more than happy to let him have his turn. They're all willing to give it a shot." He finished his drink and set the glass down. "I was thinking this might be permanent, Charley."

"Yeah, I've been playing with that idea too, but I never expected everyone would agree to it." Patrick had proven me wrong about that. It was the perfect reciprocal relationship. And with so many people around here undergoing treatment for hepatitis, who knew how long it would take to clean up the blood supply. And it was free. That took a huge financial burden off the members. "Our existing donors aren't going to be happy about it."

"Then they better pivot fast. Besides, those vampires aren't our concern. I took an oath to the members."

I scoffed. "You didn't take an oath to anyone."

"I didn't? Then what the hell am I doing this for?"

"This isn't funny, Patrick."

"Do you see me laughing? Besides, those fools are the ones who got themselves infected. The only people we need to worry about are the members."

I patted his chest. "You really do have a heart in there, don't you?"

"Tell anyone and I'll deny it." He stood up to leave. "Seriously, we need to think about it. If it works it works."

I let out a long breath. "It certainly would make things easier for everyone." I was committed to the co-op, but I'd be lying if I said it hadn't been a headache lately. My life was complicated enough.

He lowered his sunglasses back to his eyes. "We'll talk about it later. I have an appointment."

In other words, he had a date.

I walked Patrick out and glanced across the street at the crime scene tape as he climbed into his car. Then I pulled out my phone to call Dog. I could picture Murphy and Carter driving out to the compound and foolishly trying to get past the wolves to question him about that explosion. They wouldn't get very far, but my bigger fear was Crimson PD using a rare show of force. They could put a bullet in one of the wolves and call it self-defense. I doubted Murphy was stupid enough to do something that extreme, but Carter was.

"Pick up your damn phone," I said when it went straight to voicemail.

It was Monday night and the bar was slow, so I decided to run out there and give Dog a heads-up. That text message about needing another night off didn't sit right with me either. Something was up.

I called Beau down to the end of the bar. "Dog's not answering his phone, and I need to let him know Murphy's on the warpath. You're in charge while I run out to the compound."

He looked around the half-empty bar. "Yeah, sure. Is Dog in trouble?"

Not if I could help it. "Murphy's got it in his head that the pack blew up that restaurant."

Beau snorted a laugh but quickly got serious. "Did they?"

"Of course not, but I need to warn Dog before Murphy or Carter find him. I'll be back as soon as possible."

I got in my truck and drove out of town, keeping my eyes open for a Crimson PD patrol car in my rearview mirror. I wouldn't have put it past Murphy to follow me and hope that I was meeting Dog somewhere. After a mile or two of not seeing another car, I relaxed.

As I entered the woods and drove toward the clearing, Lux appeared in my headlights. She was standing in the middle of the road, blocking me from going any farther. At least it wasn't those two pups from the other night.

I turned the engine off and got out. "I need to talk to Dog," I said to her.

Loki stepped out of the woods and joined her in the road. "Go home, Charley."

"Why are you acting like this? I'm not leaving until I talk to Dog." Something was very wrong. I was getting a sick feeling and wondering if Dog had sent that text himself. "Did something happen to him?" Now I was really starting to panic.

When they glanced at each other and then just stared back at me without another word, I tried to walk around them. When Loki grabbed my arm, I looked down at his hand. "You might want to take that off me." The energy was already building in my palm, and I intended to get past both of them one way or another.

He loosened his grip. "I mean it, Charley. You need to go home."

"Fuck it," Lux said. "Let her through."

Finally.

When Loki let go of me, I continued toward the clearing. As I crossed it and headed for Dog's cabin, my chest started to feel heavy. Like a bag of rocks had settled in it. The wolves who were going about their business around the compound kept shooting me strange looks that I couldn't decipher. It was like they knew something awful was about to happen.

I stepped onto the porch and braced myself before knocking. When I didn't hear anything on the other side, I knocked louder. "I'm not leaving, Dog," I yelled through the door.

A minute later, I heard footsteps approaching. The door opened and Dog was standing on the other side. His hair was disheveled, and he looked exhausted. There was also aggression in his eyes. Something wild.

"I wondered when you were going to show up." He pushed the door all the way open and stepped aside. "Might as well come in."

When I walked into the living room, my eyes immediately landed on the problem. Tempest was sitting on the couch. "What is she still doing here?"

Lux walked up and leaned against the doorframe. "Yeah, Dog. Why don't you tell Charley why she's still here?"

My head snapped back to Dog. "What happened to driving her south?"

His jaw clenched. "I changed my mind."

"Jesus, Dog, we're screwed. If you're not going to get her out of town, you need to hand her over to Zane."

He was in my face a second later, his eyes even wilder and filled with rage. "Like fucking hell I will! She's mine!"

I stepped back, shaken by his tone and the anger in his eyes. Dog had never growled at me like that. Ever. And I never wanted to be on the receiving end of that growl again. "What's wrong with you, Dog?"

Lux shook her head and snickered. "Isn't it obvious? Dog got himself a mate. He claimed her."

Her words shocked me. Mated wolves were volatile creatures. The bond primal. Instinctual.

Tempest stood up and walked over to Dog, wrapping her arms around him from behind as she brushed her lips against his shoulder. "I'm not going back, Charley. Dog is mine now, and I'm his." She shook her head. "I'll kill myself before going back to Zane."

"Then this town is about to be caught in the middle of a pack war," I said, remembering the last time Crimson suffered through one. "If they can't get into the compound, they'll start destroying the town to get you to cooperate, and they'll start with my bar."

There was a flash in Dog's eyes. Maybe remorse. But then dark rage filled them again as another growl snaked up his throat. He pulled Tempest's arms tighter around his waist and looked me dead in the eye. "Then let them come. If it's war Zane and his wolves want, then it's war they'll get."

A LETTER FROM LUANNE

Thank you for reading *Bloodlust Shadows* and the rest of the series. It's been a blast to write! I hope you'll continue because there's so much more to come!

Stay up to date with my latest releases by signing up at the link below. Your email address will never be shared, and you can unsubscribe at any time.

www.secondskybooks.com/luanne_bennett

If you enjoyed *Bloodlust Shadows*, please consider leaving a brief review. It's one of the best ways to support an author. It really does make a difference, and I appreciate every one of them.

Just a reminder that I love to hear from readers. Get in touch on my social media or website. And don't forget to follow me!

www.luannebennett.com

facebook.com/LuanneBennettBooks

x.com/Luanne_Bennett

instagram.com/luannebennettbooks

bookbub.com/authors/luanne-bennett

goodreads.com/lbennett14

ACKNOWLEDGMENTS

Thank you to the team at Second Sky and Bookouture for all your support. A huge thank you to my editor, Jack Renninson, for pushing me for more. And more and more. Seriously, though, it really did make the story so much better.

Family and friends, you're the best. Let's do it all over again!

And no acknowledgment would be complete without a nod to Bear and the rest of the best writing buddies a person could ever have. Tails off the keyboard, please.

PUBLISHING TEAM

Turning a manuscript into a book requires the efforts of many people. The publishing team at Bookouture would like to acknowledge everyone who contributed to this publication.

Audio
Alba Proko
Melissa Tran
Sinead O'Connor

Commercial
Lauren Morrissette
Hannah Richmond
Imogen Allport

Cover design
Damonza.com

Data and analysis
Mark Alder
Mohamed Bussuri

Editorial
Jack Renninson
Melissa Tran

Copyeditor
Rhian McKay

Proofreader
Jon Appleton

Marketing
Alex Crow
Melanie Price
Occy Carr
Cíara Rosney
Martyna Młynarska

Operations and distribution
Marina Valles
Stephanie Straub
Joe Morris

Production
Hannah Snetsinger
Mandy Kullar
Ria Clare
Nadia Michael

Publicity
Kim Nash
Noelle Holten
Jess Readett
Sarah Hardy

Rights and contracts
Peta Nightingale
Richard King
Saidah Graham

Dear Reader,

We'd love your attention for one more page to tell you about the crisis in children's reading, and what we can all do.

Studies have shown that reading for fun is the **single biggest predictor of a child's future life chances** – more than family circumstance, parents' educational background or income. It improves academic results, mental health, wealth, communication skills, ambition and happiness.

The number of children reading for fun is in rapid decline. Young people have a lot of competition for their time, and a worryingly high number do not have a single book at home.

Hachette works extensively with schools, libraries and literacy charities, but here are some ways we can all raise more readers:

- Reading to children for just 10 minutes a day makes a difference
- Don't give up if children aren't regular readers – there will be books for them!

- Visit bookshops and libraries to get recommendations
- Encourage them to listen to audiobooks
- Support school libraries
- Give books as gifts

There's a lot more information about how to encourage children to read on our websites: **www.RaisingReaders.co.uk** and **www.JoinRaisingReaders.com**.

Thank you for reading.